# Banished Mates

## Omega Heat

### Allie Santos

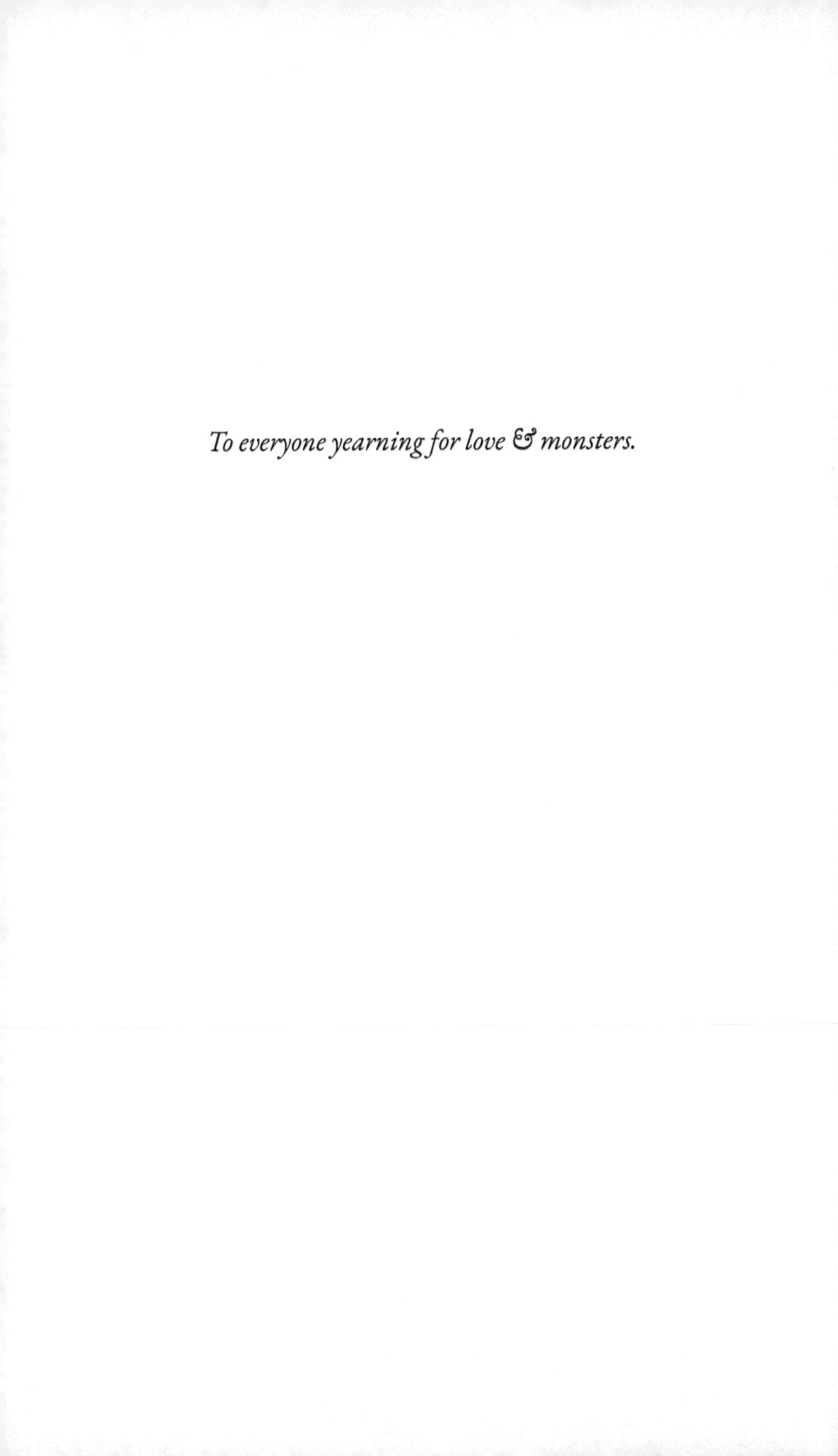

*To everyone yearning for love & monsters.*

# A Note from Allie

I'm about to bare my soul a bit here, but I've always had this obsession with the endearment 'lass', which I'm positive stemmed from the copious historical romance novels I devoured growing up. There's just something so . . . mouthwatering about it. That was a roundabout way to say that I really wanted to write a Hero that used the term and so, I introduce *Banished Mates*. I hope you enjoy this novel of monsters, love, and smut as much as I loved writing it.

All right then, I'm off to watch Outlander or Made of Honor lol.

# Content Warnings

Murder (on page), Descriptive Sex, Foul Language, Descriptive Violence, Physical Abuse, Kidnapping, Attempted rape of the heroine (not by MMCs)

Please be advised that the following trigger and content warnings contain spoilers for the story and plot of the novel.

BANISHED MATES is a Why-Choose Paranormal Romance. There is primal play, heats, nesting, ruts, purring, and knotting. There is shifted sex, *cough* she bangs the monster on the cover. There is no cheating and a happily ever after is guaranteed.
The heroine was in a situation when she was younger, and it caused vocal cord damage to the point where she cannot speak. She uses American Sign Language and writing to communicate.

Some of the novel is set in Scotland. I utilize words that are not the proper spelling but are written how they sound.

Words used: Tae = to, nae = not, Aye = yes
The term "lass" is used.

BANISHED MATES is set in a mythical world and all contents
are purely fiction.

Epilogue Spoiler: See below
*

*

*

*

*

*

*

*

*

*

*

*

*

*

*

*

MFC finds out she is pregnant.

# WILLOW



It took me about two-point-five minutes to track Camden down, much longer than usual. He was in the spot I'd never thought he'd be without me.

*Especially* with a she-wolf.

My heart pounded in my ears, and unfortunately, it wasn't loud enough to drown out Meridith's voice.

I wet my lower lip with my tongue. I was well into my mid-twenties and was still behaving like a skulking pup, padding after my best friend.

But . . . I would do anything for Camden. If I had to save him from her, then so be it—it wasn't like I hadn't gotten into fights over him before.

I just never thought he'd take her to *our* spot. Peeking around the large pine tree, I made sure to keep him from seeing me. If he did, we'd argue . . . just as we'd increasingly argued this past month. I didn't know what was with him, but his short temper was frustrating the shit out of me.

Even so, as soon as I'd heard he was on a potential mating date, I'd come running. He'd be angry if he caught me skulking, but I couldn't sit and twiddle my thumbs while Camden was snatched right from under my nose. Yeah, maybe it was selfish, but not just anyone could have Camden. He was special. He deserved the best possible.

Meridith inched closer, bringing my attention back to the pair as she invaded his space. I narrowed my eyes, my stomach coiling in knots.

"Let's go elsewhere," Camden said, an aggression in his tone.

Meridith's eyes lowered and a slight frown formed on her face. By the dent between her eyebrows, the lowered shoulders and gaze, Camden must have used the full force of his Alpha wolf behind his order.

He shouldn't even be wasting his time on her. I scowled, molars grinding.

Camden rubbed the back of his neck and then stretched his head to the side. My attention stuck on the vein throbbing near the base of his throat.

"Why do we have to—"

"Now," he said, patience running thin. Meridith flinched and sucked in a breath.

Good. He must know I'd go nuts on him for being here with her. Why was he here in the first place, anyway? It was ridiculous, traitorous, and a slew of other words I couldn't come up with right now.

At least he was making her leave. *At least he was making her leave.*

My shoulders relaxed. I was overreacting. Of course Camden wouldn't cross the line, right?

The next moment slowed as Meridith's lips pressed together into a tight line. As Camden turned, she lurched forward. She was a relatively tall person, taller than me, so she simply had to invade his space to meet his plump lips.

My stomach dropped, knees weakened, and my throat . . .

It was like when I got my injury when I was fifteen; the blunt force to my neck crushed my throat, ruining my voice box. The memory of the agony accompanied me to this day. With therapy and much, *much* care, the ache had abated. It no longer hurt to swallow, breathe, or eat. I also no longer choked on my spit randomly.

The hair on my arms lifted as if the aching in my throat had never gone away.

I blinked slowly, struggling to process as Meridith's lips landed at the corner of his mouth. Still too close for comfort.

With my palm pressed into the rough bark, I steadied myself, but it didn't help in calming my racing heart. Camden's lips near hers . . . hurt.

It couldn't have been longer than a beat, but time seemed to slow as Camden lifted his hand to her shoulder and shoved Meridith off so hard that she staggered and fell to the uneven ground. The back of his hand scrubbed across the corner of his mouth. Relief slackened my jaw that he hadn't continued, and my nose burned. Yes, he'd pushed her off, but the visual was ingrained in my mind.

And it wasn't only this, it was the potential of him taking a mate. I knew it would one day come. It was impossible for it not to with him being the next pack leader. He was prepared to take over but he'd been putting off the ceremony.

"Why?" Camden snarled, head lowering. His russet locks fell over his forehead, a chunk of the messy mop slipping across his left eye.

Meridith's chest moved up and down and she gawked, as if

she couldn't believe his reaction. At his aggressive move forward, she scrambled backward in the dirt.

Camden was quiet. He usually stood behind the Alpha, intimidatingly stoic. To the pack, everything rolled off his shoulders and he never seemed bothered by anything . . . that wasn't what he showed me.

When we were alone, I received the full force of his personality, and he was a prickly son of a bitch—with all due respect to his mother.

There were only a handful of times I'd seen him snap on someone with anything resembling irritation.

"Camden, I-I'm sorry—"

I couldn't just stand here and listen to her. My knuckles were white as I clenched my hands into fists. I stepped out from behind the tree and marched directly over to them. Their heads whipped in my direction as the leaves crunched under my heels. Meridith swiftly got to her feet.

I narrowed my eyes at them as I took in their expressions. Camden's brows lowered and knitted together; the corners of his eyes pinched. His lips parted.

Good, if he was stunned, it meant he hadn't heard me skulking after them.

I stepped in front of him and craned my neck to look him in his light brown eyes. The yellow in his irises popped with the autumn colors of the trees surrounding us. The sun reflected off the foliage and bounced off his pale skin—giving it a golden glow.

Camden blinked down at me as his face relaxed.

"What are you doing here, Willow?"

Me? What was *I* doing here? He had to be joking, right?

I scoffed and signed the same question back at him.

"Why are you asking me why I'm here? It's pretty obvious why I'm here," he snapped. I narrowed my eyes into slits.

*"You're young, Den. You have a century and a half at minimum left in your life and you want to mate yourself with someone you know you'll not get along with?"*

I was grasping at straws. I didn't know if he'd eventually get along with her, but I didn't have the guts to stand by and watch it. I was a coward, and I didn't want to give him up even though a *normal* werewolf mate would be good for him. She could rule next to him better than me, who would never shift because it would put me, and the life of everyone I cared about, in danger.

Omegas were not supposed to exist after they'd been hunted into extinction. If any werewolves found out I was one . . . Only horrors could come from it, especially because of what I'd be able to do. I didn't even feel safe or comfortable with my pack finding out. Alpha Torrin couldn't control everyone, and he would undoubtedly use me for his own gain.

There were many willing to destroy entire packs to dominate an Omega. *Me,* causing my loved ones to die? Nausea soured my stomach. If werewolves found out, they'd kill Hector and Camden, and anyone else that got in their way, simply to take me . . . to use me as history stated packs and werewolves used Omegas.

It was the complete opposite of how we were supposed to be treated. Omegas were to be cherished and taken care of— treated as the gifts we were, but instead, we were hunted for various reasons. Jealousy, breeding, sex—you name it. I was born with the target on my back, and if I ever shifted, everything I cared about would be gone, like my mother warned.

*I would cause the death of anyone I loved . . .*

"I have to get mated, Willow," he snapped. "I'm doing what I must. What are you going to do about it?"

The last sentence took me off guard. It seemed like he was daring me, or at the very least trying to set me off. I forced away what I wanted to say.

*"And I mean so little that I can't know?"* My wrist twinged with my exaggerated motion.

His jaw bunched.

"You know that's not it."

I tipped my chin up, grinding my teeth so hard that my jaw popped.

He cupped my chin and his fingers dug into my cheeks, forcing my teeth apart.

"Don't grind your damn teeth." He sighed and his free hand lifted to his hair, brushing back the messy strands so his face was on full display. I devoured his expression, tracing my gaze over the tense muscles around his mouth. I'd always hated his godly good looks. His high cheekbones, sultry eyes, and expressive thick brows all came together to create an unmatched specimen. He received too much attention for my liking. I wanted to be the only one to admire him, but with a face like that, everyone turned to look.

Even with all that, his smile was what did me in. A smile reserved for me. I'd never seen it angled anywhere else, and I ached to keep it that way. Even if it *had* become a rarer occurrence.

Meridith cleared her throat. "We're on a date—"

I whirled so fast the earth spun, but I masked my dizziness with a glower. I hadn't looked at her for a reason. Setting my gaze on her made my blood boil. Meridith frowned as she looked down at me. I was tall too, but she had me beat by a few inches and it was instances like this that I rued that. Her gaze held no real antagonism, as if she didn't see me as any sort of threat.

Who did she think she was, forcing a kiss on someone?

She glared at me before looking over my head to meet Camden's eyes.

My teeth clicked together and I fisted my hand. There were few things that wrought aggression from me, but messing with Camden was one of them.

"Don't," Camden snapped, dragging me behind him with ease. "You can't win against someone that can shift."

I deflated at his lack of belief in me. He had a point, but I refused to admit it. It was no secret that I was a werewolf without the ability to shift, but it wasn't something I liked to randomly throw out when I was in the middle of a stare down with someone. I glared up at his wide, muscled back as he stepped in front of me, blocking me from Meridith's view.

"I think it's best we reschedule," she said, strained.

I huffed. *No shit.* Camden's shoulders twitched at my noisy exhale. It was *best* if they never saw each other again.

Meridith wasn't necessarily a bad person, but she had eyes on my best friend, and I wasn't having it.

We'd made a pact to always have each other's back.

We were only eleven then—with me only a month younger than him—but I'd kept my word. I expected the same.

I poked my head out from around Camden and sneered at her. Immature, yes, but without much of a way to communicate, I had to be dramatic about the way I expressed my emotions.

Her attention dropped to me and the severe line of her lips tightened.

"He can't always tailor to you, Willow," Meridith said, her voice curt. "You're holding on to someone that can't belong to you. You know this. Otherwise, you would already be together." Her words hit me like a sledgehammer. I sucked in a pained breath as a rush filled my ears. I was trying my best to show that her words didn't affect me, but they hurt.

"Meridith. Go."

Her eyes dropped at Camden's sharp order and her shoulders jerked. She bowed her head low, not meeting his eyes as she strode away. I didn't take my attention off her until she disappeared around the tree.

With her gone, my shoulders relaxed, my fingers flexed, and it wasn't until then that I realized I'd grabbed onto Camden's arm when she'd said that. Her words rang true. Why did she have to throw that in my face?

I loosened my grip and let my arms drop to my sides. After a beat of staring at each other, I lifted my hands to sign.

*"I thought I was helping you."*

"You're not making it any easier on me, Willow," Camden said harshly. Each syllable struck me as if they were physical blows. *I* was making it difficult for *him* . . .

Hearing this from him burned my chest and I felt at a loss. The ache in his voice made my body throb. I couldn't have him, and he couldn't have me.

Soon after he turned eighteen and shifted, he'd ended up at my doorstep, smelling of tequila. That night he'd been my first and last lover. An unforgettable night.

His gentle touches, moans, and gasps all replayed in my memory when I needed relief. It was what I lived off of. Those memories and his constant presence in my life. After our tryst, I'd run out of my house while he was still sleeping and avoided him, which was easier to do since he'd left for some training with a different pack. It gave me time to muster the courage to distance myself and to come up with what to text him.

The message I'd sent still burned my heart. I told him it was a mistake, and I didn't want to ruin our relationship—and he'd easily acquiesced. Did some small part of me want him to fight me on it? Of course, but nothing came of fruitless hopes, so I did what I knew he would eventually have to—and broke it off.

My hand trembled and I clenched it into a fist.

It was years later, and I was still haunted. Not even having him by my side abated my hunger for him, but it was pointless. I couldn't shift because it would mean his death, and he couldn't mate me as a shiftless werewolf.

We couldn't be together.

My heart ached at the thought.

I couldn't put his life in danger. Not him. Never. I needed to protect him and for him to be safe and live an uneventful life. For that, I had to be out of the picture.

*"Fine. I'll give you your space to find yourself a mate. Sorry I've been a bother."* I turned on my heel to walk away. I'd been selfish and let my rashness and possessiveness get in the way.

"Dammit, Willow!"

My shoulders hiked to my ears. He could have easily stopped me . . . but he didn't.

The farther I got from him, the more energy left my body, until I was dragging my feet.

It was a no-brainer. He never mentioned that passionate night, and my attachment to him was one-sided. Maybe he'd fucked me out of pity or regretted it. When he'd returned from that training, he'd acted like nothing happened, and it stayed at that. I was eighteen by that time, and he knew I couldn't shift, so he must have been relieved I hadn't brought that night up again.

My nose burned and I let out a shaky breath. I never considered it until now, but he must have seen me as some sad, pitiful girl following him everywhere he went. He must have been tired of me.

Everyone in the pack knew I was attached to his hip, but until now, I never stopped to think I bothered him.

He was my haven. And I was . . . useless.

It was ingrained in us since we were children that pack Alphas must have strong mates, and to be a solid mated couple, they both must have strong wolves. Especially since he would become the pack Alpha very soon.

Everyone, including Camden, thought I was a defective werewolf. Someone with a wolf so weak it couldn't come to the forefront. If only he knew I was an Omega and could call my wolf forward whenever I wanted.

But that wasn't our only hurdle, there were some ignorant pack members that considered me deficient. Being mute didn't make me less, but to some werewolves, I was ruined goods.

*Idiots.*

The steps leading to the porch creaked and I shoved the screen door open. My dad, Hector, lifted his head off the couch pillow, and grunted at me.

"Heading to bed, Willow?"

I nodded and forced the corners of my lips up. He seemed satisfied with that response, so his attention returned to the television. I needed to get some rest so I was prepared for work tomorrow.

# Willow

I lay on my bedroom mattress and gazed at the popcorn ceiling, valiantly trying to stifle my tears. If I wasn't near Hector, I wouldn't worry about it, but my eyes became scarily red when I cried and stayed that way for a while.

Once my hands lifted to my face, I scrubbed my eyes with my palms. Living with your family was normal in a werewolf community, even at my age. Many got their own home only once they settled down with someone.

Plus, I didn't want to leave Hector after what my mother, Nola, put him through. He'd been through enough. We'd been happy the earlier years of my life while living in a small pack in Washington, but even back then I recalled her skittishness—she never relaxed. The day after my tenth birthday, she asked to separate from him. Her desire for not being discovered as an Omega overpowered her love for Hector . . . and me.

It was one thing after another once that happened. She packed me up in her car along with her stuff, and spent the entire drive across the country telling me how dangerous we were and what happened to her family when she was a little girl.

Throats ripped out, blood coating the ground . . . the description of the slaughter was horrifying.

Instead of joining a new pack as she promised, she left me at a gas station. One moment she was kissing my forehead before I went into the restroom and the next, child protective services had me in their custody. It was close to a year before they tracked down my dad.

Although it was traumatizing, it drove in the seriousness of what I was and the risks I posed. Being close to werewolves was dangerous, and being surrounded by loved ones would only bring them harm. The sour taste spread on my tongue.

At first, I'd refused to go with Hector, but he had insisted. As an eleven-year-old, I'd had little choice, so he'd brought me back to the pack he'd grown up in—Redwood Pack.

My father had been distraught, and I couldn't bring myself to run away, so I resolved never to shift. It'd been fifteen years since I arrived here and at twenty-six, I still lived with him. He wasn't home often since he patrolled as a pack enforcer, which consisted of the most dominant pack members. There were few instances where there were Alphas who had no desire to lead a pack, like Hector, but still wanted to be a part of one. Because of his dominance, Torrin allowed him say as his Beta, but only because Hector never attempted or hinted at desiring more.

I could have asked Hector to petition to get me an individual home, but even with his influence and clout, I doubted he'd succeed.

Especially with Alpha Torrin in charge. If you were male, it was easier to get Alpha approval to build a home, but females? *Forget about it.*

It was extremely biased and sexist, but there was only so much I could do to go against that since I held absolutely no power here. Actually, according to many females here, the shred of protection I held was due to Camden. No one messed with me because of him, which they irritatingly made clear.

After Camden took over, he'd approve me for my own place, because he always took care of me . . . My unwavering shadow. There to argue with and get into trouble with since we were kids.

The first day I'd stepped onto these pack lands after Hector and I came here, Camden and I had been at each other's throats. It was only after I helped him escape one of the traps the other pack kids had set on him that he'd let me past the wall he barricaded himself behind. Camden's growth was slower than other pups', so he'd been picked on even though he was the Alpha's kid.

And since Torrin expected him to handle himself, he'd done and said nothing.

The day I got him out of the trap, he promised me he'd never leave my side and he'd protect me. My chest constricted, a knot forming in my throat. We'd had each other's backs since then and he'd outgrown me by a ton, but instead of leaving me in his dust, he'd been my fierce protector.

He'd gone nuts the day I'd taken the hit that ruined my voice box. He never left my side, and it'd been his idea to learn ASL.

A small smile tugged at my lips.

But . . . but now he was going on mating dates. My stomach churned, and I lifted my legs to my chest as I turned onto my side. I didn't want to be around for that. No fucking way. Someone would take him from me.

My heart pounded against my rib cage. Each thud racked through my body in painful strikes.

Everything was changing because Camden's father was stepping down as Alpha very soon.

Camden would be busy with pack disputes, dates, and who knew what else. There would be no room for me.

My lower lip trembled as I sucked in a shaky breath.

Living elsewhere was always an option, but I didn't want to be away from Camden or Hector. There was also the fact that if I wanted to leave, I'd have to petition the Alpha, and he wasn't the fondest of me, which should work in my favor, but . . . it wouldn't always be Torrin. It would be Camden. Would Camden release me? It could be my opportunity to discover if I was truly a bother to him . . .

The strain behind my eyes worsened and I stifled a yawn as I weighed all my options.

My income wasn't enough for me to survive off of, so that meant having roommates, and that was a different can of worms.

Pale sunlight filtered through the blinds, and I squeezed my fisted hands to my closed eyes.

I'd agonized for an entire night. No wonder they felt like sawdust.

I snatched my cell phone from the nightstand.

Crap. I had to be at work in a few hours. I needed to shower and get ready to head out.

I placed my arms over my face with a groan, but it sounded more like a vibrating hum coming from my throat.

As I was about to force myself up, the door creaked open and then clicked shut before the corner of my bed dipped. A familiar floral scent wafted to my nose.

I propped up on my elbows and my mass of wavy hair

tickled my arms. I set my widened eyes on Britt, the pack's Luna and Camden's mother.

As I blinked at her, I struggled to understand why she was here.

She'd always been pleasant to me. Kind and welcoming, unlike her harder mate—the Alpha. Embarrassment flooded me at the state of my bedroom. The bra hanging over my desk. I scooted upright on the bed and combed my fingers through my hair.

Britt pressed her lips together before exhaling, as if she had the weight of the world on her shoulders.

A heaviness settled in my stomach. I had such a bad feeling about what was about to exit her mouth.

"Alpha ordered Camden to claim Meridith."

My entire world shifted on its axis. That was why he was talking to her when he'd never angled his attention toward women. How long had he known he would mate Meridith?

My fingers dug into the mattress, bunching my blankets. I scooted to the edge of the bed until I sat beside Brit.

"He's about to be Alpha and there's already unease because of his loyalty to you." She cleared her throat, and I fixed my gaze on her profile. "As you know, Alphas need to put their packs at the forefront. The priority should always be the well-being of the whole. Torrin believes Camden will prove his loyalty by taking a mate that will lead appropriately."

My sight blurred and my lips parted. This was coming. I *saw* it coming a mile away, but it stung like hell. The bed creaked as she turned to look at me, but her features were hazy.

"I'm sorry, Willow." Her voice was low and urgent. "I hate to ask this of you, but can you convince Camden that it's in his best interest? He's refusing and it's holding up the ceremony."

I struggled to swallow, and forced myself to nod.

In such a short amount of time, I'd never experienced the array of emotions that worked through me. Pain and betrayal that he'd met with Meridith. Agony at the thought of him mated. Glee at the fact he'd refused.

"If he feels like you'll be okay without him . . . that's what's holding him back. After your accident, his guilt . . ."

The words were a slap to the face and I recoiled. It only drove in my earlier thoughts. I was a burden.

The tears rushed forward. I ground my teeth, valiantly trying to hold back my waterworks.

Camden's mom had taken me under her wing when I arrived. It was heartbreaking hearing these words from her. Like a fucking betrayal, and each syllable uttered was a slash across my heart. I thought she was on my side. I thought she loved me and accepted me for Camden. It was as if I were bleeding out before her, yet she stared at me beseechingly as if what she requested was nothing.

I suppose I shouldn't be surprised; we would have already gotten together if we were going to, right?

My heart constricted in my chest.

I licked my dry lips, mustering the energy to get it together. I dipped my chin in a tight nod.

She exhaled. I was sure there was a smile on her face, but I didn't bother looking up. I didn't want her to see the agony etched in my expression.

When Camden was mated, I would lose him and his mother. Except, it seemed like their care for me stemmed from pity.

*That wasn't fair.* Camden had been by my side for years.

This day was bound to come. As pack Alpha, Camden

needed a strong mate at his side. I'd always known this. But fuck, I never thought it would hurt this much. I never expected his mother would ask me to encourage him to do it. Like she was ready to give another girl the affection she'd always given me. And then Camden would . . .

No. I couldn't endure it. I couldn't do it. Unless . . .

Would the pack accept me as Camden's mate if I shifted?

Would Camden finally take the steps to be with me if I did?

None of it mattered.

Even if I shifted, I didn't want him to only choose me because I had a wolf, or out of some sense of guilt. That was unfair to me. I deserved to be loved unconditionally. And he deserved to have a mate that wouldn't put him in danger by being an Omega.

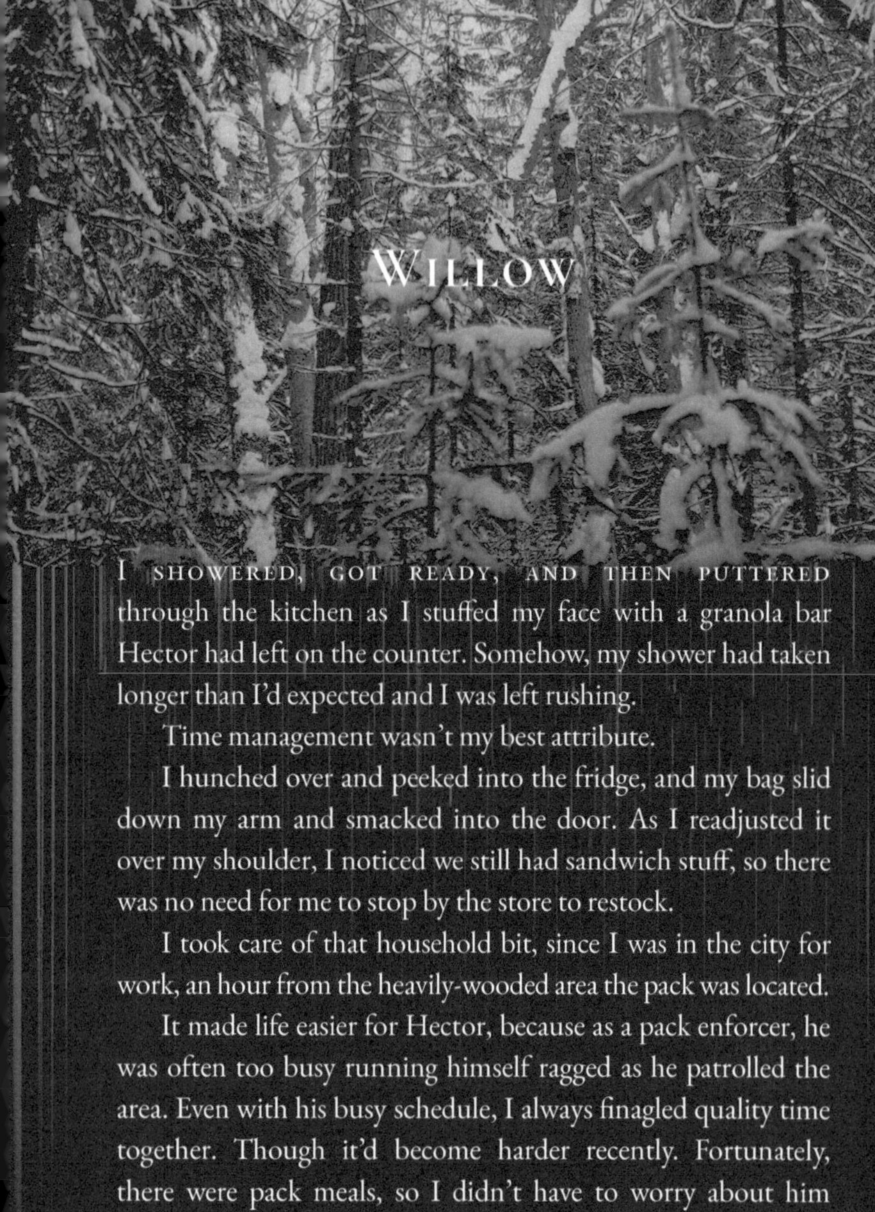

# Willow



I SHOWERED, GOT READY, AND THEN PUTTERED through the kitchen as I stuffed my face with a granola bar Hector had left on the counter. Somehow, my shower had taken longer than I'd expected and I was left rushing.

Time management wasn't my best attribute.

I hunched over and peeked into the fridge, and my bag slid down my arm and smacked into the door. As I readjusted it over my shoulder, I noticed we still had sandwich stuff, so there was no need for me to stop by the store to restock.

I took care of that household bit, since I was in the city for work, an hour from the heavily-wooded area the pack was located.

It made life easier for Hector, because as a pack enforcer, he was often too busy running himself ragged as he patrolled the area. Even with his busy schedule, I always finagled quality time together. Though it'd become harder recently. Fortunately, there were pack meals, so I didn't have to worry about him starving. Werewolves were notorious for eating constantly.

Nearing the door, I smoothed the carpet that folded under

Hector's heavy boots and exited, the door clicking shut behind me. It was nice not having to worry about locking the doors on pack land.

The cool air hit my face and a chill crawled up my neck, racking a shiver from my limbs. My wet hair wasn't making it any better, but I was on a mission: talk to Camden before I rushed out of here in Hector's spare beat up old car.

Rounding my house toward the heavier wooded area, I stepped over one of the fallen redwoods. It was fortunately a small one. Some of these trees were absolute monsters.

A few minutes later, I was pushing away some of the foliage to see his home. The one he'd built after the Alpha informed him that he wouldn't allow him to move out of the pack house. It was a one bedroom, one bath, with a living room and entertainment room, but each space was huge.

What I loved most about it was that it was well into the woods, away from the tons of pack members.

A thump accompanied by a grunt echoed through the trees, disturbing the peaceful silence. I followed the sound, rounding the house to the back side.

I skidded to a stop as a shirtless Camden lifted an axe over his head, eyes narrowed in on the stump in front of him. The muscles beneath his firm, taut flesh twitched as he brought the axe down to its target.

The thud vibrated up my spine, and my body clenched. Heat spawned near my belly and spread downward. As if molasses had been slathered there and dripped down, coating my throbbing pussy.

*Sweet baby werewolf*, he was hot.

My knuckles popped as I fisted my hands. His attractiveness

was nothing new, but the blatant sexual appeal in front of me was a damn menace.

I clenched my thighs together, forced my hands to relax and cleared my throat. Camden looked over at me, no surprise in his expression at my presence.

My eyes tracked a bead of sweat making its way down his defined chest. It twisted with each hollow and dip of his muscles.

Licking my lips, I mentally shook myself and ripped my attention from his abs to find him frowning at me.

"Why are your eyes puffy and red?" he asked, although it sounded more like an order. Most of his phrases sounded aggressive like that recently. Camden walked over to me in a few long strides. He clasped my chin and tilted my face up. The ease in which he handled me made my blood boil. He touched me with such calmness—as if his heart didn't skip out of rhythm when our skin met.

So unaffected. Unlike me.

I clenched my hands into fists, squeezing until my nails dug into my palms. I needed to get a handle on my heart, or it would pound out of my body. After all, us not being together was my fault, I always pushed him away. Exhaling slowly, I lifted my hands to sign.

*"Are you interested in her?"* I'd had time to think about the question and still asked it—the undeniable ache of the query making it difficult to complete the gestures. *"Do you feel guilty? Because I took the hit instead of you?"* Camden's eyebrows furrowed.

"What kind of questions are those, Willow?" His jaw tightened and nostrils flared.

I sucked in a harsh breath. The insecurities rushed forward.

This was unfair of me, but the desperate jealousy wanted out. I swiped my face with my hands.

Though we couldn't be together, I never thought we wouldn't be number one to each other. We never let anything or anyone get between us. Even as the years passed and he was increasingly sent away for physical and strategy trainings his father put him through. Part of me was sure the Alpha sent him away so much so he wouldn't be near me. But the distance didn't cause a rift either, nor when I started working while he was gone for a couple of months.

That was how it used to be; I would sit around, twiddling my thumbs, waiting weeks on end as he went on business trips with his father. Visiting packs and making connections, but never did it occur to me that he wasn't happy to see me when he returned.

And maybe he was. Maybe it was all just happiness at seeing someone he regarded with fondness. Maybe when I pushed him away, he'd gotten over me . . . which he had every right to.

I was the only one left pining, but I'd held onto hope when I never saw him with another woman. Not even a hint of it, and his cell phone? Dry as fuck. No messages—nothing.

Last night, our time together had flashed through my mind. It was me always following him around while he'd become reserved. I was the one always looking for him. Though he never turned away or gave me any indication he was annoyed, he'd changed. And in the last few months, he'd become more detached than he ever had before.

The curt responses and avoidance . . . now that he was about to be Alpha, he understood where to draw the line.

This was my fault and my misunderstanding of what was between us. I was foolish. Even if *I* stayed away from other men, even though he could never be mine, it didn't mean he felt or did the same.

"Will," he snapped. I shook my head and swallowed hard. Yanking my chin out of his grip, I took a staggering step back, yet kept my back straight as an arrow.

*"I release you from the guilt, Camden. Stop looking after me. You don't need to repay me for anything."*

"What?" he snapped, the word rough and violent. I bit my lip. His tone was the same as it'd been with me the last few months—harsh. Frustration boiled in my blood, spilling over the metaphorical pot that simmered inside my body. My teeth clicked together.

I narrowed my eyes at him and pressed my palms into his chest and gave a hefty shove. He didn't even budge.

My nostrils flared and I lifted my hands to sign.

*"You should just get your stupid mating over with."*

Camden's shoulders tightened as he straightened, towering above me, his lips flattening into a grim line.

I pushed myself to meet his gaze head-on, forcing deep breaths to regulate my heart rate. With each inhalation, my heart chipped away.

Camden's eyebrow twitched. He got that look on his face. The one he got whenever he was mad at me . . . which was pretty often.

"Thank you for your input on my mating," he hissed. His words weighed on my stomach.

Gritting my teeth, I dropped my chin, and I whirled, storming away.

I needed to make a hasty exit because the tears were slipping, and I didn't want to look more of a fool than I already did.

It was enough. This was for the best. I couldn't be selfish any longer, and he didn't deserve it. These last months, he'd been stretched thin, and I didn't want to be a negative factor in his life.

I didn't want to hold him back any longer.

I BLINKED the well of tears out of my eyes so the road would clear up. Since I was driving, I had to stifle my emotions.

With my palm flat against my chest, I rubbed the section that ached. Each heartbeat sent a pang through my chest. It hurt like a bitch and the burgeoning headache wasn't helping.

The trees lining the road became thinner and soon were replaced by buildings as I drove into the town closest to pack lands. It was decently sized with all the necessary shopping marts, stores, etcetera.

The blinker sound filled the car and I took the left up the driveway of the coffee shop. Morning coffee sounded lifesaving about now since the lack of caffeine strained my already scrambled brain.

Once I put the car into park, I turned the key, and the radio went silent. I curled my fingers into fists on my lap and squeezed my eyes shut.

*Get it together.*

I couldn't afford to let myself fall apart and arrive at work with my face swollen and puffy. Although, the casino lighting was dim, and it was doubtful anyone could see me as I processed and counted money.

Sighing, I slipped my keys into my bag, grabbed the straps, and opened the car door. A few yards away, I strode into the shop. It was relatively vacant this early in the morning, or at least it was inside. The door dinged as it closed, and I went directly to the counter to place my order.

The barista looked up at me and smiled wide. I matched it and wiggled my fingers. Lee had that bad-boy look to him, complete with a pierced brow. If I didn't have Camden in my life, I would have been drooling all over him. He was nice to look at, but he had nothing on my—

Whoa.

Yeah, I needed to step away from the Camden thoughts.

"Willow, the usual?"

Lee's head tilted to the side and his thick brows furrowed over his black-brown irises. The lighter part of his eyes reminded me of his wolf pelt.

I nodded, forcing a smile. Inhaling deeply, I sucked in the scents of coffee bean and sugar, but even that didn't lighten my mood. I sighed, rubbing the back of my neck as I fished out my debit card.

The cool counter dug into my hip as I slipped the card into the chip reader. Once the payment was complete, I dropped it back into the side pocket and zipped it up.

"You okay? You seem a little off today?"

I blinked up at Lee and pursed my lips. His question didn't go far in helping me keep control of my emotions. I was going to lose it. His eyebrows lowered further, but I sucked in a breath. Bursting into tears in a coffee shop would be embarrassing.

Lee was from my pack. Nice guy. I saw him around, but he never approached me on pack lands. I didn't know if it was simply the job that made him talk to me, but I didn't care much.

"Willow?"

I swept my gaze up to meet his and shook my head, forcing a smile. He frowned, but before he could say anymore, I turned my back on him and inched over to wait for my coffee.

I could feel his attention on me and luckily someone else walked up to the register, so he had to take care of them. Soon I had my drink in hand and was out the door.

I'd decided to work so I could distract myself from always missing him, and all it did was put a bandage over the ache. Looked like I would be in a shit mood during my shift.

I plopped into the seat and slammed the car door. It was as if the act sliced through the faux string of happiness and I deflated, thumping my head back against the headrest. I never hated what I was more than in that moment. It was the very reason I couldn't be with Den.

The car door suddenly clicked open, and my shoulders hiked.

I didn't lock it.

I was so distracted, I didn't do my customary locking of the door as soon as I was in my car. My eyes popped open in time for a rag to be slapped over my nose and mouth.

A hand gripped my neck and squeezed so hard my eyes watered at the pinch. I sucked in a breath as my thoughts rushed to process what was happening.

Light filtered through my blurred vision. The edges darkened and expanded. Undulating like a wave toward the middle. Then, everything was black.

# CAMDEN



My ass was numb from sitting on Willow's front steps. *Where the hell was she?* I raked my fingers through my hair for the hundredth time and then rested my arms over my bent knees. Was she avoiding me? Working late?

Dammit.

I pulled my cell out of my pocket to check the time again. She should have been home about an hour ago, but she was probably taking longer to spite me.

With a sigh, I pushed to my feet and slipped into her house. Hector would know I was here, which he wasn't a fan of, but I wanted to wait for her in the house now that it was getting darker. That way she couldn't avoid me.

I huffed when I opened the door to a messy bedroom. Shaking my head, I collected her clothes and placed them in the hamper. A shirt lay on the ground a few feet to the left from the hamper, as if she'd tossed it in the direction of the basket but hadn't made it. I couldn't help the way my lips tipped up at the corners. Will was the definition of messy.

Once I lifted the shirt to my nostrils, I breathed in a lungful of her sweet berry scent. It filled my body, warming me. A nervous restlessness prompted my wolf's attention, and he tried pushing to the forefront. I flattened the shirt on my cheek and rubbed her smell on my face. My cock twitched to life, hardening.

With the shirt hooked around my neck, I reclined on her mattress, my feet hanging off the end of the bed, and folded my arms behind my head. I sighed, looking up at the plastic stars I'd pasted to her ceiling. It'd been a bitch to stick them to the uneven surface.

She'd had a rough year after the incident that should have only affected me.

As it always did, the memory of the piece of plywood slamming into her throat caused mine to constrict. I shuddered, exhaling. If she hadn't thrown herself in front of me to take the hit, then she wouldn't have struggled as much as she had. It was the day my world shattered. If I hadn't purposefully set Torrin off . . .

I shook my head and placed my palm on my rapidly heaving chest. Recalling the event always left me twisted inside, even though Willow didn't blame me. It hadn't taken her long to get back to herself, and I had no doubt that was due to her concern for me.

And now she was pissed off at me, which was my intention. It would have worked well if Meridith hadn't chosen *that* spot. Jealousy had worked in my favor when we were kids—but going *there* took it too far. Meridith was supposed to meet me near the Alpha's house, but she texted last minute and, when I saw the location, my stomach dropped.

This fucking pressure in my chest wouldn't let up and it was my fault. Just because I'd wanted a reaction from her. I *had never* and *would never* have any intentions toward anyone else. Even before I could name this emotion rushing through me from the moment I saw her. She'd always been it for me.

I should have set her straight, but I wanted a reaction from her. She wouldn't fucking *open* up and it was driving me wild.

Every little expression she made had me on edge and it only worsened. I was perilously close to losing control and fucking her, of finally ripping through the wall she'd built between us. I'd waited long enough. Then she'd thrown those accusations at me. She'd been jealous. Elation had been riding me hard and I'd fucked up trying to get her to admit I was hers and she was mine. To order me not to be with anyone.

I was strong enough to protect and support her now.

Which wasn't always the case. I'd known for a long time that she was my forever, but it wasn't until I was seventeen that I was able to put it into words. Back then, Torrin said if I wanted him to accept the mating, then I'd have to wait until she turned eighteen, which was only a month after me. It should have all gone as planned.

The last and first time we fucked was the primary material for my fantasies. I needed to fuck her and bury myself so deep inside her that my cock was imprinted on her tight pussy . . . I groaned.

But what led to that still curdled my blood. I sneered.

That weak wolf, Riley, had kissed her. I knew why she'd allowed it. Since going through my growth spurt, she-wolves surrounded me at all times. I'd done my best to politely force them away, but she'd seen one toss herself at me. She'd left before seeing that the bitch hadn't pressed her lips on mine.

I'd given her time to cool her temper because she was bound

to kick the shit out of my shin, but I'd given her too much time and found her with the mutt.

My body tightened painfully, and my lip lifted in a snarl at the memory.

As soon as she'd walked away, I'd beaten the fuck out of him, his face a mass of blood.

That night, I'd been drinking and ended up at her door. I wasn't drunk enough to *not* know what I was doing. Seeing her near another werewolf set me off. Adrenaline had coursed through me as did the extreme need to rub my scent and cum all over her.

I pressed my forearm over my eyes in memory of her silky tanned skin sliding across mine . . .

My body and wolf instinct guided me in claiming her. I'd licked her pussy until she was sopping wet, making her come repeatedly.

Only when she was clawing at my shoulders, desperately tugging at me, had I slid my cock into her silky depths. Her tight pussy squeezed me, inviting me home . . . and we'd fucked and fucked.

Her breathy exhales replayed in mind and my spine tightened.

I grasped my hard cock through my pants and groaned. The zipper dug into my dick before I slid it down. My erection sprung free and I gripped it in my palm. The engorged head throbbed, a bead of pre-cum rolling down the side and sliding onto my hand.

Stroking down, a tingle crawled up my spine and I sucked in a breath as I squeezed my eyes shut. Willow touching me like this . . . that was what I wanted. I tugged my dick again and more cum leaked from the tip. Her small fingers wrapped around me as she worked to milk me . . . I groaned.

Her beautiful face flashed in my mind's eye. The only face ingrained in my memory. From the sly smile on her lips that curled up higher on one side than the other, to the tip of her pert, pointed nose, to the sleepy half-lidded look she always had. Sexy.

A moan wrenched from my throat as my balls drew tight.

"Fuck," I hissed and dragged the pillow laying to the side over my cock before thrusting into the cotton. My release was swift and hard as I tugged my cock and coated the pillow in my cum.

My hips dropped and I placed the pillow to the side, the glint of my release shining in the minimal light coming through the shades of the room.

I liked the idea of her smeared in my cum—sleeping in it.

My cock throbbed at the thought, and I gritted my teeth, shoving it into my jeans and zipping up. Fuck. I needed to dispose of the pillowcase.

I groaned and tipped my head back. I'd reached a new low, but I couldn't help it. She enthralled me in every way.

After that altering night, she pushed me away. She was lucky Torrin took me with him on a month-long visit with an allied pack because it was the only way she got away with ignoring me. We were gone for her birthday, and I wasn't here for her when we discovered she wouldn't be able to shift. I expected tears, *something*, but she hadn't seemed affected, which I was thankful for. As long as she was okay, that was all that mattered.

Yet, Torrin gripped onto that with two hands, claiming it was impossible for him to permit *his* son to mate a defective. I sneered. He didn't permit it and his word was law. At the time, I had no choice but to acquiesce to his dominance. Taking her away from here was the only option, but when I'd prodded her about leaving the pack, she said she couldn't leave her father alone . . . which meant I was stuck. That, combined with Torrin's order, left me with little choice but to wait. He took advantage and sent me all over the world, visiting various packs on his behalf.

I was at my breaking point two years after I shifted, then my wolf rebelled against one of Torrin's orders. That day I knew—I would be an Alpha dominant enough to take Torrin's place, and as soon as he saw, he began training me in earnest to take over for the time I would be stronger than him. Stepping down was a tactic many pack Alphas did to keep the peace within the pack. Especially when it was within the family line.

But after the discovery, my already extensive training worsened and took me away from Redwood Pack.

I didn't see Will nearly as much as I needed to, but each time I counted the days until I returned.

Soon. She would be mine soon.

I needed to remain steady. If I gave in slightly, I wouldn't be able to stop from claiming her. Our joining was inevitable, and I'd been patient until now, but if Torrin attempted to deny me, I'd challenge him and take the pack by force—even if it meant killing him.

I would make her mine and offer her every protection under the moon.

I'd waited long enough and having her close, yet not making her mine was harder by the second.

Earlier today, we'd blown the situation out of proportion. I'd spurred it on, but her retreat pissed me the fuck off; she should have known better. I'd not looked at another woman in the years we'd known each other, and I would never.

I'd only gone to meet Meridith to get a reaction from Will. Then Meridith texted me the new location she wanted to meet, and I'd replied to meet me elsewhere, but she hadn't responded. Without another option, I went, prepared to tell her that Torrin's promises were baseless. But before I could get the words out, Willow had stormed up and my plan backfired. I wanted Willow angry enough to claim I was hers, not to use it to push me away.

*"I release you from the burden . . ."* The phrase had bounced around my head since she'd said it. What had Willow meant by that? Just like when she first signed the words at me, it infuriated me.

That was another thing I wanted to ask her about when she got home.

I frowned and fished my cell phone out. It was already well past the time she usually arrived. And there was no text from her informing me she'd be late. She was usually stubborn, but this was pushing it.

Our fights never stuck for long, which meant she should have already contacted me.

My chest constricted.

The device vibrated in my hand, and it was at my ear within the next beat.

"Willow," I barked.

Silence and then, "No, it's me, son."

"Have you spoken to Willow?"

Britt went quiet and cleared her throat. Her nervousness practically seeped through. I shot into a sitting position.

"Did she tell you about our conversation, then?" Her strained voice put me on edge.

"What did you say to her?" I snapped. She may have birthed me, but hurting Willow crossed the line.

"I-I didn't want to hurt her feelings. I just wanted to look out for you—"

"I'm coming over." I pocketed my phone.

With my teeth gritted, I balled the sullied pillowcase as I left Willow's bedroom and then out the front door. A throb started in my chest. Hurt feelings? She'd been hurt by what Britt had said . . . and after my petty comment to her? I rubbed the back of my neck, my pulse picking up. It was the last thing my Willow deserved.

My stride ate up the space as I made my way to the pack house. Various scenarios filled my head, but I tried to calm my raging wolf. There was something off and his frustration bled into mine, heightening my overall emotions.

On my way to the front door, I tossed the pillowcase into the large can outside of the pack house.

The front door slammed into the wall and a crack snapped through the silence.

I exhaled through my mouth, attempting to rein in my aggression, but it was fucking difficult. Her sad eyes kept flashing through my thoughts.

I shouldn't have allowed my temper to guide my words, but frustration had gotten the best of me. The stubborn girl needed to choose me.

My wolf pushed against my skin, and I popped my neck, a growl building in my throat. I turned sharply, following my mother's scent to the living room where she wrung her hands.

Her widened eyes met mine.

What had she done? Her iris's expanded, the blue rings thickening.

My nostrils flared and my wolf puffed up so much he pushed at my insides for release. He felt the wrongness—something happened, and it all started with Britt.

"Tell me," I ordered quietly, my body becoming eerily still. Her hands trembled as she swept her hair over her shoulder.

"I simply asked her to convince you to accept your mating." She almost whispered the words, but they punched me straight in the gut. I hated the thought of the woman I loved being asked to do such a thing, but she didn't feel for me what I felt for her, so it shouldn't have bothered her. "She seemed upset . . ."

My stomach tightened and anger surfaced. Upset? My wolf's anxiety bled into me, mixing with my irritation at hearing this. In a few swift steps, I was next to Britt, eyes narrowed on her. She cowered.

Some part of my brain acknowledged I shouldn't be this way toward the woman, but I couldn't help it. As soon as Willow walked into my life, she took forefront in the short list of people I cared about.

A growl ripped through the room and I was shoved back. The Alpha stepped in front of me, gaze set on mine. I ground my teeth and forced my eyes to the side, fighting my wolf who wanted to challenge him. My knuckles popped.

We shared many features, but he had thirty years on me.

"Are you going on about that bitch again?"

All I had to hear was the derogatory tone and I was in his face, gripping the collar of his shirt. There was only one trigger between us and that was Willow. After he'd caused her to lose her voice, I'd been unable to forgive him. My wolf less so—to him, Torrin was the enemy.

I met his gaze head-on, top lip curled in a snarl. Torrin growled, but the threat seemed to inflame my wolf's anger further. I was already more dominant than him and each time he looked at me, my wolf clawed to show him.

Britt's small hands shoved at my arm, but it was as effective as a fly landing on my shoulder. I pushed forward and Torrin stumbled back.

"Your obsession with this girl needs to end. I've already pushed out the date you take over the pack because of your stupid notions. She's nothing but a defective wolf, Camden." His face was ruddy, and a vein popped at his forehead. "You need someone worthy to be Luna."

*Enough.*

I snarled and slammed my fist into his cheek. Blood spurt from his mouth. He laughed, his blood-coated teeth flashing. My shoulders tensed and my wolf remained still within me, prepared to shift and sink his teeth into Torrin.

A ringing ripped through the eerie silence.

Britt lifted the cell phone to her ear and said, "Hector?"

Hearing Willow's father's name snapped my attention to her.

"Torrin, Willow's not back, and she was supposed to return three hours ago. He said he can't get a hold of her." Britt's voice shook. A roar in my ears deafened me, and my mind raced.

Three hours ago? My lungs deflated. So she wasn't avoiding me?

Torrin met my gaze.

"Hopefully she stays gone."

My knuckles popped as I clenched my hand. I shook my

head and scoffed. I couldn't let my temper get to me, so I slowly turned and walked away. She better be okay. She had to be. Willow was surely punishing me for making her worry and for my stupid, rash words.

"Hector's going to look for her. Stay out of it. Think of how it'll look to Meridith if you leave at a whiff of her absence."

My steps didn't falter.

"Camden. This is a direct order from the Alpha. Do. Not. Leave. Pack. Lands."

I shoved open the front door and the werewolf about to enter scuttled back to avoid my aggressive stride.

"If you leave, don't return."

I didn't bother turning around. I was heading in that direction either way. Fuck him and this pack. I wanted to make sure Willow was okay and there was this sick feeling in the pit of my stomach that said she wasn't. I refused to ignore it.

A growl turned into a snarl and a furry body slammed into my back, throwing me to the ground. Teeth sliced into my shoulder. I caught myself and rolled to the side, letting my shift take over. My skin stretched and popped as fur covered my shifting body.

Torrin charged at me again and I feigned to the left. His burnished red fur was a few shades lighter than mine and the hair on the back of his neck stood up. His yellow-brown glinting eyes, so similar to mine, rounded toward me.

I snarled and lowered my head, my wolf shoving forward. He only saw Torrin as the roadblock to Willow and nothing more.

The threats of kicking her out of the pack, his part in hurting her throat . . . echoed in my head and I didn't hold back. I lunged and sank my teeth into his shoulder, biting down until blood coated my tongue. The bitter taste filled my mouth. My wolf wanted more, so I ceded control.

With my jaw locked, I shook my head without releasing, burying my fangs and teeth so deep they hit bone. The half whimper he released faded into the background, and I used my hold to yank to the side, flinging him a few feet away.

He fell into a boneless heap and his paws scratched at the ground as he struggled to stand.

"Stop, Camden," Britt sobbed, dropping to her knees and tossing her torso over Torrin's heaving, bloody body.

I shook out my fur and blood sprayed across Britt's face, splattering little dots across her cheek. She flinched, but she wasn't my concern. Willow wasn't back when she was supposed to be. If the Moon Goddess existed, I prayed that she kept my female safe.

I bared my teeth at the pack Alpha once more. Forcing my instincts back, I regained a semblance of my human thinking and logic. Willow was what was important.

Burying my claws into the ground, I kicked up dirt as I dashed away.

# Willow

I sucked in a breath and attempted to sit up, only to bang my head into something cold. A sting burned my forehead and I clasped the spot. Faint beams of lights speared through the small holes littering the top surface allowing me to see my fingertips come away dotted with dark moisture, which I could only assume was blood in the dim lighting.

Feeling around, my hands connected with a flat metal surface. I slid upright slowly, making sure not to bang my head again. A pinch assaulted my side and I hunched forward, hugging my knees.

Maybe there was a latch or something I could pull. I put out my hands and slid my palms across metal. Reaching overhead, little divots littered the metal above me. I tipped my head back, squinting, but I couldn't see anything through them.

I groaned, rubbing my nose. This would be a great time for me to be able to shout and yell. My knee banged against the side with a loud thump. I *could* make noise.

I pounded both fists into the metal, and thuds reverberated

through the small metal box. Again and again, until my hands became numb. This couldn't be it, someone had to hear me.

Rearing my leg back, I kicked the shit out of the surface, and with each strike, the thud echoed louder.

I kicked again and it bent the front of my shoe, wrenching my toes. I winced, palming the injury. What a fucking failure.

A thump overhead vibrated the enclosure and I sucked in a breath, stilling. *Thunk*. It was being opened.

The top swung open to a man with a blue surgical mask covering half his face.

"Shut up," the man hissed. A sound of an engine whirred, loud and large. It sounded like an airplane. My head popped out of the square enclosure and my gaze swept over the box-littered storage-looking space. The ceiling was low and metal while the walls to the sides were slightly rounded. Exactly what I'd imagined a storage area of a plane to look like.

He grabbed the back of my neck, pulling my hair with the grip, and dragged my attention back to him.

His eyes glinted; all sorts of malicious intent reflected in their depths. His gaze dragged down my body and stopped at my breasts.

My stomach dropped and I hugged myself, mind racing.

If he touched me, I was going crazy on him. He just needed to get close enough so I could kick him in the dick.

But it didn't go my way, of course it didn't. Before I could even think to do anything, a syringe sank into my arm.

Oh, fuck no. Time to move. I threw myself over the lip of the container and bolted forward, but my legs weren't cooperating . . . and I wasn't moving fast enough.

The man barreled into my back, sending me down, face

forward. I sprawled and quickly rolled onto my back to get myself out of the vulnerable position.

He yanked my wrists over my head with one hand and pushed his knee into my thigh. My mouth opened on a silent scream and his other hand raked up my shirt, baring my bra-covered breasts.

Nausea crawled up my throat.

I didn't want this. *Camden! I needed Camden.* Tears sprang to my eyes as I tugged my wrists, but every move was sluggish.

He ripped my bra off, exposing my breasts. Vomit exploded from my mouth, dripping down my chest and tangled into the tips of my hair. The man cringed back, releasing me.

"You disgusting Omega bitch!"

He brought his boot down on my cheek and my head thumped into the metal floor of the plane. My hand trembled as I weakly tugged my shirt down to cover myself. *Don't think about the vomit.*

There was rustling and then he had the back of my shirt in a tight grip and was dragging me into an upward position. The plane tipped and my shoes slipped across the uneven surface. The collar of my shirt constricted around my throat. I sputtered as he easily toted me upright.

He released the material and yanked me by my hair. Blue latex flashed in my sight. He'd put on gloves after he'd smacked me—that was what his shuffling was about.

The *shink* sound of shears slicing through my locks of hair echoed to my ears. My *hair.* My stomach clenched as strands floated to the ground.

He cut my hair!? My teeth clicked together, and I sneered up at him. It was all I could do since my movements were sluggish.

I slumped, my limbs turning to noodles. He still stared at me with those hate-filled eyes as he tossed the vomited-on strands aside. My fingers went numb and I shuddered.

I couldn't fall apart.

Exhaling slowly, I tried scrambling back, breathing harshly, but it was no use. My limbs refused to cooperate. The short strands kissed my cheeks and I flinched.

My toes curled in my shoes and numbness spread up my calves. Someone must have discovered I was an Omega.

A knot formed in my gut, thickening with each second.

Where was I?

What would he do to me?

My stomach swam and I gagged. Would he force me to shift?

He lifted me, bringing me close to his crazed gaze as he hooked his arm under the back of my knees. He dumped me into the steel box and sealed me back into the darkness.

I curled into a ball on my side and hugged my knees.

Was anyone looking for me?

I swallowed audibly. I didn't want anyone to be in danger, but that wasn't something to worry over. No one would know how I disappeared. There would be no way to track me down, and if someone knew I was an Omega . . . I didn't want them to even find me.

I hugged myself tighter, rubbing my arms. Fear . . . I'd had a comparable experience after Nola left me at the gas station. The not knowing what would happen next was the worst part.

# Willow

When I finally pried my eyes open again, it was dark and my lashes were crusty and stuck together. The cotton feeling in my mouth combined with the aches in my body told me I'd been unconscious for a while.

My hand scraped against the cold cement ground. I pushed off my side, and my foot smacked into something. A loud clash and clang resonated through the room, and I sucked in a breath, inhaling the nastiest scent I'd ever had the displeasure of smelling. I gagged and quickly swallowed to force the nausea down, but my spinning head wasn't helping.

Where was I? Obviously, we had arrived somewhere since I was out of the metal crate, but I could be anywhere in the world at this point. As I inhaled, the pressure in my ears expanded and popped.

I couldn't see anything but it was incredibly cold. The chill of the stone beneath my hands seeped into my skin.

I groaned from the soreness radiated up my spine. Once I forced myself to my feet, I stumbled forward, catching myself on some rough-feeling vertical bars. The gritty rust scraped my palm, flaking off.

The guy had dragged me onto a plane, drugged me, and now this? I stepped back from and massaged the tips of my fingers into my aching temples. The metal aroma of the bars clung to my hands and I grimaced.

Where the hell was I? My shoe prodded something soft, and I crouched with my hand out. My fingers bumped into a pillowy thing. Wait a second . . .

Was it a forearm? I dragged my hand up and pressed it into the lean bicep.

I shook the limb, but there was no reaction, so I inched my hand higher. The cheek was full, and hair tangled with my fingers as the tip of my index finger collided with something wet.

My stomach heaved and I tensed. Shit. I slowly withdrew my hand and swallowed hard. Unresponsive body, bloody temple . . . it wasn't much of a stretch to imagine what was wrong.

Slowly backing into the rusted bars, I dropped to my ass and shivered as I tucked my knees tighter to my chest.

Nausea churned in my stomach.

I missed Camden so much. Tears spilled down my cheeks.

My body was limp and I was dehydrated. I couldn't tell how long it had been since I'd seen the sun, and the only other interaction I got was when the nasty asshole keeping me here came to torment me.

My cheek still throbbed from the time he'd smacked me with the bowl of food and beaten me until I'd lost consciousness. He hated that I couldn't speak, and he was taking my silence as some sort of game, as if he could force a nonexistent voice from me.

He was fucking sick.

As if that wasn't enough, there wasn't a doubt in my mind that I was on the verge of freezing to death.

I sucked in a shallow breath since I couldn't breathe in the icy air too deeply or I'd vomit from the smell coating the room. I'd had to resort to a bathroom bucket, which he didn't clean out often. How long had it been since I'd had access to a shower? Despite how many air fresheners the freak hung in the cell, it did nothing to block the stench.

The scent of rotting flesh was easily discernible to me now. Putrid, sickening, and rancid. And combined with the state I was in? I shivered. It was not good.

A slam vibrated from a distance, causing the lavender scent to permeate the small cell. Here he came. A light flickered on, blinding me. He only turned it on when he visited me, which wasn't often. It was both unfortunate and fortunate. On the one hand, it meant I didn't eat often, but on the other hand, I didn't have to see his creeper ass.

Bars lined the entire half of the bricked-up room and led to ascending stairs. My only method of escape, blocked by bars. I'd tried busting through them, but it was no use.

His gaze peeked over the mask that covered everything except his eyes, and a plastic barrier shielded bright blues.

The ugly fuck jerked at the lock on the first slat of bars with gloved hands and shoved it open. Honestly, by attractive standards, he could be considered handsome, at least from what I saw when we were on the plane and he first tried to touch me, but a pretty face could never compensate for a dirty soul.

He kept walking toward me, and with every one of his steps closer, I tensed. A clear plastic coat hugged his tall form. Shit. Shit. Another beating so soon?

His obsession with cleanliness was both my curse and savior. This guy was a double-edged sword. Despite how I handled him, I got cut.

My hands trembled as the memories of his groping touch seared my brain. It couldn't have been longer than a few weeks since he attempted to rape me on the plane. Vomiting all over myself had saved me.

It was gross, but I'd do it a million times over because he'd left me alone since then.

I preferred that to the hypersexual threats he tossed my way. The only part holding him back from sodomizing me was my disgusting state. He'd made it clear.

Did the smell seeping from me make my eyes water? Definitely, but I wouldn't change it for anything.

He swung open the cage and stepped inside. That stupid checkered button-down was tucked into his khaki slacks.

Ugly grabbed my arm and yanked me to my numb feet, the clear plastic covering him crackling. For the first time in forever, I was outside the boundaries of the cage and I couldn't even enjoy it because I struggled to stay conscious.

"The time has come, precious girl."

Gag me.

I swallowed back the nausea and remained still. I wished I didn't know what that meant, but I regrettably did. The sick man was obsessed with *talking* about all the ways he would defile me. His soul was one of the ugliest I'd encountered.

"I'm finally going to be able to sink my cock into your body."

The knot in my throat grew. He must have gotten that room ready. According to one of his monologues, he was preparing a space for me. The thickness in my throat tightened further.

He stretched the wrapping around himself, the material crinkling as he unwound the chain that hadn't been touched since those initial days. The barrel of a gun slammed into my temple and he wrapped his gloved fingers in my short hair. I shivered, stumbling after him unsteadily.

He pulled me up the first step and my shin hit the stair. My leg gave out, causing my knee to slam into another stair. I gasped in pain, but he didn't stop as my body collapsed on the uneven steps. He just continued dragging me with a disgruntled snarl.

Each slam added another ache to my body, and I mentally detached. Ugly—Uggo as I preferred to think of him—shoved open the door at the top of the stairs and lights seared my eyes. I hadn't been in some basement of a house; I'd been in a fucking hole. The door opened to a tiny shack and then foliage crunched beneath our feet.

"I can finally have you to myself." My stomach soured. "I'll clean you all up." The slight growl in his voice made me want to shrink into myself but he continued to manhandle me.

My sight blurred from the light beams aimed in our direction. He took about five more steps, and I was no longer blinded. It was headlights. I craned my neck to look up into the starry night. How long had I been captive? He grabbed me and shoved me into the front seat of a beaten-up vehicle, forcing me to scoot over to the furthest plastic-covered seat.

"You reek."

*Which is your fucking fault.* I glowered at him.

Fucking asshole. Disgusting excuse of a werewolf. The rise and fall of my chest was rapid and mimicked the pace of my thudding heart. I studied him with narrowed eyes, focusing on his throat. Clenching my hands, I reminded myself I wasn't strong enough to go against anyone. Even now, weakness pulsed through my veins.

The slam of the car door snapped me out of my bloodthirsty thoughts, and I wrapped my arms around my torso, making myself seem vulnerable. By the quick look Uggo sent me, it was successful. He put the car into drive, and the tires squealed as he slammed his foot down on the accelerator.

I jerked and slid with his erratic driving as he sped down a dark road.

# Willow

My mind raced. Five minutes had passed on the dashboard clock but the seconds stretched excruciatingly. The vehicle wobbled as he took a swift turn. Time was wasting. Soon he would have me where he wanted me and then it would be over. I had to give escaping a shot now.

Another turn was coming up. This was my chance. I twisted my torso and put everything behind it before I brought my fist down on his junk. He screamed, and I threw myself to the side, popping the lock, and flinging myself out of the moving truck.

I smacked into the ground and rolled with the downhill momentum. A snap resonated to my ears and my mouth opened on a silent shout at the sound of my arm. It hurt like a bitch.

A throb radiated up my side and seeped into the rest of my body as leaves crunched beneath me. I finally rolled to a stop with tears streaming down my face. My arm laid limp beside me. I couldn't be a sitting duck. For all I knew, he could have shifted and was after me.

I bit my lip as I sat up and cradled my arm to my chest with my other hand. Fortunately, my legs were okay. As much as I wanted to scream, all the noise my throat could make was a little airy whimper. I struggled to my feet, my knees buckling with my first step.

I fell face-first onto the ground. Moist dirt flaked my lips and I sputtered from the taste.

I struggled to right myself as my lungs worked overtime to drag in puffs of oxygen.

Moss covered the trees and surrounding rocks. And a heavy fog coated the ground, but fortunately the moonlight speared through for me to semi-see. I shivered, the thin shirt and jeans doing nothing to protect me from the elements. I was already frozen to the bone.

Fur . . . fur would protect me.

But if I shifted and he caught me . . . it would be over for me. I'd have heats and the uncontrollable need that came from that would shred any self-control I had.

I flattened my foot on the ground and pushed up, my legs unsteady.

Limping forward, I hugged my arm to my chest. Each step worsened the throb of my broken arm. This sucked so fucking much—I didn't ask to be born an Omega. Tears filled my eyes.

A rustle through the leaves forced me to duck, and I stilled, holding my breath. Shit. Shit. A closer crunch and I was pushing my legs forward, my chest pumping with strain. It sounded like he was nearby.

My heart thundered in my ears. He would catch me and do all that shit he'd crowed about. A snarl echoed and foliage crunched.

I had no other choice. He was going to catch me. At least if I shifted, I would have a sliver of a shot at escaping.

*There was no other choice.*

I exhaled raggedly, my lungs burning as I pushed ahead. According to Camden, shifting was something you pulled forward; or often your wolf, who had their own mind, would burst forward and your human mind had to allow it. But that was only when you already had your wolf.

Once I did this, there was no turning back.

I licked my lips and took a deep breath. I didn't know what exactly I was supposed to do . . . I let my emotions take over, feeling for *something* inside. The tug in my gut wrenched a gasp from my throat. The sudden feeling shocked me so much I doubled over, my palms catching me. The fact that I was severely exhausted and malnourished wouldn't make this any easier.

My bones snapped and popped, lengthening as agony overtook my body. Heat spread through me, and I shook my head as I jerked and fell to my side.

Brown fur erupted from my arm. My vision blurred, and I sucked in a breath as my jaw popped and stretched.

I lay on my side, panting as I struggled to suck air into my lungs. My sides heaved, the dirt and pebbles I lay on dug into me, but on the upside, I was no longer freezing with the layers of fur covering my body.

She was inside me. Now a part of me, so close to the surface. She wanted to run and run. Energy coursed through my body.

I pushed to my paws, and my front limb buckled, but I caught myself. My arm was no longer broken.

Elders told stories of Omegas. General information was

passed down in some packs, and for a while . . . I had Mom to answer my questions.

My voice would have returned if I'd shifted after the attack happened, since any recent wounds, deadly or not, were healed when an Omega first shifted. It was a gift from the Moon Goddess.

Far off to the left was the drop of a cliff. Between the breaks of the trees, mountains rolled over the expansive space—large and ominous and covered with rolling grass that spanned the vastness.

My wolf pushed to the surface again, insistent on taking control of my body. She took off in a sprint, forcing us to run.

I wasn't sure how long I sprinted, but my legs screamed with exhaustion.

Sides heaving, my tongue lolled out. Relentlessly running zapped my energy. I bared my teeth and my ears twitched. The air felt different. Foggier and thicker. The hair on the nape of my neck lifted as my head lowered—I was no longer alone. I quickened my speed.

A sudden snap to the left spurred me on but something smashed into my side, and I went flying until my head smacked into a mossy rock, blurring my vision. I didn't have time to wallow in the pain.

Once I rolled to my paws, I bared my teeth as another attack came at me full force.

I rocked back as teeth pressed into my throat and I struggled to keep my balance, but it was no use. I had no energy left.

My wolf itched for control and I released some to her as she twisted in a quick move that caused fur to pull from my skin.

It would hurt like a bitch later, but adrenaline was rushing through my body, not allowing me to feel it.

I backed up, lifting my snout toward my attacker. The wolf was much larger than me. I sucked in a hard breath and every muscle in my body locked up as the pine scent enveloped me.

It was as if a fist had been driven directly into my chest. His giant size wasn't what had taken me off guard. My heart thundered painfully as a sensation of rightness fell over me.

Since my wolf was at the front, controlling things, she lowered her head, studying him.

His thick fur was perfect to rub against . . .

I crouched lowered to the ground and whined, inching closer.

He threw his head back and released a deep, terrifying howl. I whined, tail swishing as I inched another step forward. *She* wanted him, but all I saw was a predator. Those wild eyes . . . the flash of fangs . . .

My wolf forced me to crawl another inch closer and rushed to the forefront, trying to push my smidge of control to the back. Oh, hells no.

I grappled with her, forcing her excitement to a standstill. She was ready to rub herself all over him and I couldn't have that. No way.

No. No. He couldn't be my mate.

Yes, Omegas had multiple mates, but there was never a sure number, it could be anywhere between two to five, or was it six? I couldn't remember, but all I could think about was Camden's position being at a disadvantage, and if he wasn't my mate, that meant he was someone else's.

My heart throbbed and ached at the thought of him belonging to another.

The gray wolf snapped his teeth in my face, dragging my attention back to him. As if he'd sensed I was thinking of someone else. He tensed, and apprehension blanketed his gaze. My stomach trembled.

Guilt burrowed beneath the onslaught of aching need. My hind legs twitched and I sniffed deeply, wanting to inhale more of his divine scent.

His gray pelt shimmered, and his ears flicked toward me as his head dipped.

That didn't look good. He snuffled and a deep whining grunt rolled through the air.

His teeth flashed and he pounced, coming at me full force, his eyes glinting in the moonlight.

# KIT

What the fuck was Rowan howling about now? I sighed and rubbed my forehead with my thumb and forefinger. He knew better than to be making all that noise. We weren't to howl—ever.

With wolves having been hunted from existence in Scotland, it was vital we didn't bring attention to ourselves. Even if we were in the Highlands, far from civilization, we couldn't risk it.

I'd waited for him to come back for hours and nothing. Looked like it was another night of me tracking him down to bring him back to the house.

Twigs crunched beneath my boots, and moss blanketed the rocks littering the ground. My breath puffed out in a cloud. It would be an icy season.

The only thing I'd ever seen bring Rowan any excitement was hunting rabbits, but they had to be going under for the winter. The fucker loved chasing and playing around with the fluffy things.

He was feral, which was a . . . condition some wolves were

born with, where they didn't have a human mindset. Instead, he was all wolf, even when he was in human form. When we were young, it was easy for him to be controlled, but as the years passed, he became dominant and unruly.

As an Alpha, it meant he didn't listen to anyone that wasn't more dominant than him—which meant he didn't listen to anyone. The only one he semi-listened to was me and that was because he was my twin.

Hence our banishment from the pack.

I'd had a choice back then, but I'd refused to put him down after he killed three pack mates. I could have brushed it off if it weren't for his past mistakes. He really detested others invading his space.

I resented him for it. My position—being pack Alpha—down the drain.

A shuffle behind me stopped me in my tracks and I narrowed my eyes, letting my wolf simmer at the surface. He easily blended with my human mentality. I accessed his heightened senses while also maintaining control.

Heavy breathing accompanied by dragging infiltrated my ears, and I rounded back toward the house.

Our moss-covered home stretched into the night sky. I hadn't realized how far I'd walked from it. Clouds overhead indicated the downturn of the weather. Soon, snow would cover the landscape.

The front door was agape, and I crossed the threshold. The lamp shined light over the wolves huddled at the entrance.

One as recognizable as my own.

The gray of Rowan's shaggy fur almost blocked the bundle beneath him. He was guarding the animal he'd dragged in here, keeping me within sight.

Even so, a head poked out from near his front paw. A female wolf?

The white of her eyes shone, and the brown of her pelt was matted, but I couldn't tear my eyes away. A sweet scent of berries flooded my senses. My body became numb.

I dropped to my knees, sucking in a deep breath, needing more of it. A roar filled my ears and my heart thundered as my wolf lunged to the forefront.

*Claim. Claim.*

My thigh muscles twitched and my cock hardened.

*Mine.* That brown-furred female under him was *mine.*

Fuck.

Baring my teeth at my twin, I struggled to rein in the violence coursing through me. Clenching my jaw, I hissed in a breath as I glared at him.

He snarled, drool dripping from his fangs. He defended the tiny wolf beneath him with a ferocity I'd never seen.

His eyes were glazed and hard—maddened. The way he behaved told me he was under the impression she was his.

I didn't like that. My wolf bristled and I struggled for control. I exhaled with a shudder.

If I shifted, it would be a slaughter.

I wouldn't give into him if it was a fight for my mate and we were evenly matched. Without a doubt, we would take each other out.

The hair on his neck stood straight up and I returned his snarl. Usually that got him back in line, but not this time. He seemed as possessive as me.

A fissure divided us. One caused by a she-wolf, which I never thought possible.

The bundle twitched, and a breathy whine left her throat.

My cock hardened and I battled the urge to shift and fuck her. My chest heaved as I staggered to my feet.

Kicking out, my boot slammed into Rowan's muzzle, and he flinched to the side, allowing the bundle under him to wiggle away. The movement jerked my wolf forward and I was already after her with Rowan at my side. She slunk down the hall to the vacant room at the end.

Her ball-tightening scent filled my nose and I groaned at the pressure.

"Fuck," I growled and shook my head. I could not stop sucking in lungfuls of the sweetness. It was inexplicably mind scrambling.

My dick throbbed.

She backed into the wall, baring her teeth, her eyes glinting in the darker room.

Rowan snapped his teeth toward the light mocha-colored wolf.

In his mind, there was no other way than to claim. He didn't understand that the tremble in her body was fear. That she was cringing back to get away. In his mind, it was all about devouring her and making her his.

"Rowan," I said, the name coming out in a half-growl. He ignored me, inching closer to her. I was about to intervene, even if it meant knocking him out.

Then she snapped her teeth in his face and to my utter astonishment, he jerked back, dipping his head like a scolded pup. He'd listened to her.

She was *our* mate. *She was an Omega.*

She prepared to spring forward, but Rowan stopped her advancement with a swift bark as he lowered his head in warning. The message was clear. Try to leave and she was going down.

If he hadn't, I would have done it.

She sneezed but kept us within her sights. Rowan lowered to the ground, his belly flattening, but he kept his gaze trained on her. The hair down her spine stuck straight up and she trembled. I didn't want to terrify her further, so I backed up until the opposite wall pressed into my shoulder blades. Her attention switched to me and all I could see reflected in her canine expression was wariness. Fear bled from her pores, and it physically pained me not to pull her into my lap to comfort her.

I groaned, inhaling as much of her scent as I could to calm the nervousness spreading to my limbs. Letting my head fall back, it smacked the wall and a dull pain radiated down my neck. It did nothing to assuage the ache in my cock.

My stomach tightened with the urge to bury myself inside her. I needed her more than I needed to breathe, but I didn't dare approach her with how skittish she behaved.

My eyes tracked her blood-matted fur and I sneered at Rowan. He must have hurt her when he was dragging her into the house.

He was lucky he was my brother, or I would have snapped his neck.

# Camden



Blood stained the seedy hotel room walls. I'd done every conceivable thing in the last few weeks to find Willow.

I flicked blood off my fingers, splattering the beaten male on the ground. I was growing careless with who I hurt.

The knowledge that some sick fuck had her, gnawed at my insides. There were only two things I hoped for; her well-being and for her to keep track of every fucking creep that touched even a strand of her hair.

After reviewing the footage provided by the coffee shop, I'd learned the wriggling piece of shit beneath my foot was one of them.

It'd taken me almost a month to track the fucker down. He bared his teeth at me.

I applied more pressure on his throat and he stilled, eyes peeled wide open. I shoved his face into the stain on the carpet.

"I don't know who you're talking about." His voice grated on my ears. I pulled out my cell and flashed him the image of

Willow. He squinted from the bright light and recognition flashed in his eyes.

"You're going to tell me every-fucking-thing."

The whites of his eyes shone and his attention fixed over my shoulder. He couldn't meet my gaze because of my dominance, but this was outright defiance.

I snapped my teeth together and, in a quick move, I slammed my boot down onto his shoulder.

A snap cracked through the air, and he screamed. It cut off when I reapplied pressure to his throat. He gripped my ankle, and I pressed harder in warning.

"I'm just the transport. I-I'll tell you everything I know, just don't kill me," he pleaded. I narrowed my eyes at him.

"Speak, then." I lifted my boot off so he could get words I could understand out and not that muffled shit.

"I was the one that picked her up in the parking lot."

"Why her?"

"No reason. She was a beauty and I could get good money for her. I also heard she was from the Redwood Pack," he blurted. Trafficking women? I sneered down at him, disgust eating my gut. It seemed more sinister than a coincidence. "A woman is a woman."

A snarl slipped free as my wolf lunged forward. I closed my eyes, battling for control. Willow wasn't useless, even as a dormant. She was intelligent, kind, determined, and those were just the few things I could articulate in the moment. The fact that this bastard under my boot would speak of her in such a low manner boiled my fucking blood.

"That's all I know." I forcefully pushed my foot back down. "I swear! I told you everything," he wheezed. "You agreed not to kill me."

I smirked, lifting an eyebrow.

"I never said I was a wolf of my word."

Drawing my boot back, I slammed my foot against his face, and blood erupted from his now broken nose. He yelped and used his heels to scoot back. Couldn't have that, so I smashed his knee until it snapped.

A snarl lifted my lips as I continued beating him. He tried shifting a few times, but I had broken more than a few bones.

This man was sick, and he'd had his hands on my Willow.

Rage. Unmatched rage bubbled over, and I leaned down as he stared at me with terrorized and pained eyes. Wrapping my hands around his throat, I snapped his neck.

Life drained from his gaze and silence fell over the motel room. I remained silent, debating my next move.

I gently lifted her hair band from my pocket and brought it to my nostrils, sucking in her scent, letting it soothe my soul.

I was at a dead end, which meant I needed to find someone to get me information . . . and I knew who I could contact.

He'd cost a pretty penny, but if it got me my Willow back, I was willing to pay it.

# Willow

I eyed the two wolves that hadn't budged since I'd run in here. The one in human form stared at me so intently I couldn't help but feel nervous. The weight of his gaze had caused a constant tension in my gut.

Restlessness nipped at my haunches, but I stayed in my defensive posture.

If he tried to approach me again, I would rake my claws down his face. My heart hadn't stopped thumping erratically, and I didn't miss the way their scent called my wolf forward. Rubbing up on them . . . a Willow sandwich, if you will, was all that was going through my brain, and it irked the shit out of me.

I wanted them. My mates . . . but I wouldn't give into the desire. I clenched my jaw, holding back my wolfish needs with iron will while battling the spreading heat thickening my blood.

The one in his human form sat on the ground across from me, spine painfully straight as he stared at me impassively. Light spilled into the large empty bedroom from the hall. The chill reached through my coat and curled around my bones. I flexed my claws into the hard floor beneath my paws, keeping my head low to dash off when the opportunity presented itself. But damn, they were relentless.

"Shift, lass," he ordered for the umpteenth time in that spine-tingling Scottish brogue. And like all the other times, I ignored him.

For good measure, I lifted my muzzle higher, showing off my teeth.

His large hand scrubbed over his face.

In my mad sprinting across the landscape, I'd absorbed the environment. The moss and the feel in the air was different. I was used to towering, sky-scraping redwood trees, not the lush moss and rolling hills. It wasn't much of a deduction that I wasn't anywhere near home, but the accent drove it in.

A whine brought my attention to the werewolf. His body was close to the ground, but he still dwarfed me in our shifted form. I clicked my teeth and he stopped his forward progress. He wasn't slick, I noticed the inch-by-inch progress to get closer to me.

I fought with the feelings of safety blanketing me. Their scent, their proximity, it all calmed me. The swirling scents of rose and pine coming from the shifted wolf and the orange and bergamot from the one ordering me to shift, complemented each other well. But still, I refused to let my guard down. I didn't know what they would do to me if they got close.

They were my mates. They were *made* for me. Protecting me was in their DNA, but I couldn't erase the trauma weighing on me from the last few weeks . . . Months?

I would have taken off running and damned the consequences, but the shaggy-haired gray wolf watched me from a few feet away. His unblinking eyes were eerily trained on me.

The shaking finally abated and my heart calmed. I was pretty sure my body was shutting down.

My mate across from me straightened and I kept myself at attention as his intimidating height blocked out the light from the hall. He ruffled his short waves to the side and light bounced off the brown of his hair and illuminated his prominent high cheekbones tight with tension. A shiver coursed through my body. Those observant moss-colored eyes swept over me again.

He *was approaching*. My heart rate accelerated and I lowered my head, bunching the muscles in my hind legs to lunge at him.

Within moments, he was in my face and my sluggish reaction didn't allow me to avoid his palm wrapping around my muzzle. His other arm curved over me and he lifted me against his chest with a tight grip on my torso. His heat was encompassing, coaxing me to give in. I grunted and thrashed as much as I could. My legs trembled, movements slowing until there was no strength left in my body.

"Enough," he snapped. "I will nae hurt you." The command urged my wolf to go supple. Damn her.

We liked that commanding tone of his.

Even though his tone was harsh, his hold was gentle. Warmth radiated from his flesh and seeped into mine. I didn't realize how frozen I was. It was cold as shit here.

An aggressive growl vibrated through the room, and I tensed.

"Back the fuck up, Rowan. I have tae get her cleaned up after the mess you made of her."

Rowan bared his teeth as my nameless mate pressed his palm to my back, combing his fingers through the fur.

He hoisted me higher onto his chest, fitting his arm under my belly and up to my chest as his other hand cupped under my hind thighs.

Before I knew it, my head was against his chest and I was snuffing out a pleased breath. He smelled so damn good.

His chest rumbled beneath my ear and I lifted my head. I shoved my wolf back and snapped my teeth up toward his neck.

I remained alert, focusing on any aggressive change in his mannerisms as his steps thudded down the hall. A flash of a bed. My body tensed and he passed it and stepped into a bathroom, opening the glass door and turning the knob so the showerhead sputtered to life. I hadn't bathed in so long I ached to lunge into the water, but held myself back.

He unbuckled his belt and I tensed, kicking a leg out to escape but stilled as soon as he stopped taking off his clothing. My sides heaved. I didn't want a repeat of what Uggo tried to do to me . . . but instead, he stepped inside with me, his clothing getting drenched. Water poured into my fur, thawing my flesh.

"Rowan, get one of my shirts and set out bread and juice in the living room." The scrape of claws retreated and the mate holding me turned his attention back to me. He hoisted me higher into his arms, letting the water soak my fur. Warmth curled around my bones, and I slumped against him. Energy seeped from my limbs as he lowered to his knees and spread his legs to set me between them. He hugged me to his chest, petting my fur in soothing motions.

"Shift," he ordered, his dominance flowing over my wolf. Although Omegas could sense dominance, I could ignore the push, but weakness dragged my wolf down and she pushed for the shift. I cringed from the burning pain stretching my body.

My bones popped, fur receding as flesh took over. Water sprinkled onto my skin, the heat on the verge of burning.

"Who did this to you?" he said, his words accompanied by a growl. His fingertips gently dragged down my side where my ribs poked out. Fury shook his voice and his palm trembled against my skin. I bowed my head forward, hugging myself tighter.

If he was this mad, then he would have been maddened by the bruises that had bloomed across my skin before my first shift healed them.

"I will kill them." The barely contained rage wrenched my breath away, and I lowered my head further, turning away from the sneer on his lips. With a hard exhale, he stopped the questioning and reached for the bottle and squirted soap on his palm. I tensed, but he lathered his hands and rubbed them into my hair.

Bubbles washed over my body, and I licked my lips. He gripped my hand before squirting more product into it. He returned to massaging my scalp.

I blinked quickly at the gentle touches, the tears in my eyes washing away with the water. I rubbed my palms briskly over my body, making sure to get every nook and cranny. Every speck of embarrassment washed away as my flesh pinkened. I was clean.

I shuddered.

"All done, lass."

I shook my head and he paused, frowning at me. Lifting my gaze, I fixed it on the razor behind him. It was part of my routine . . . when I had one, and I needed a semblance of normalcy.

"We have to get you fed."

I shook my head again.

He slicked his damp hair back. With his lips pressed together, he handed over the razor. I scooted back as he watched without moving. I poked my leg out so my foot was between his legs and popped the cap off the razor.

My mate lathered his hands with shaving cream and rubbed them against my calf. I watched, throat knotted and body tense, waiting for his next move. But as soon as my limb was soaped up, he retreated.

He would not hurt me.

I shuddered and poised the razor at my ankle. The damn thing wouldn't stop shaking. He cupped my hand and gently took the handle and dragged it up the length of my leg, stopping near my knee. He repeated the motion.

The muscles in his cheek bunched and I focused on his thick lashes framing green eyes. It didn't take him long to finish and move on to my next leg. I pressed one of my arms over my breasts and the other over my pussy, nerves seeping through now that I felt more myself. Yet, he didn't look at anything but my legs and eyes.

I leaned back so the spray fell over my hair as he finished. He handed the razor back to me.

"I'll retrieve the towel for you, lass."

The glass door rattled as he closed it, and I focused on shaving my armpits and panty line. I did quick work of it and rinsed off in time for him to nudge the door open. He turned the water off.

"Shift, if you'd like." I stared up at him, water dripping from my fingertips. He understood my fear. If I shifted, I could protect myself. I would *feel* safer. Tears pricked my eyes so I pushed my wolf forward, needing to hide the building waterworks. A burn worked through my sore, overexerted body. Fur erupted from my skin and I shrunk into my wolf form.

He wrapped a towel around my midsection and lifted me with ease. With one arm hooked under my belly and the other under my chest, he carried me down the hall. We passed another dark room, then he was rounding the corner into a living room with a fire crackling. As soon as he was past the threshold, heat from the fire seeped into my muscles. They helplessly trembled as my limbs became limp.

My mate dropped to his knees and a wet nose nudged my cheek, and I shrank away from Rowan as he got in my face.

He didn't get the hint; his long, wet tongue licked the fur at my neck.

I yanked my head side to side to get away. Baring my teeth at him, I met his shadowed eyes. Rowan stared back at me, but his tongue hung outside his mouth with his panting.

The nameless mate's grip on me tightened and he lifted one of his hands and shoved at Rowan's chest, which hardly budged him, then rubbed my damp fur in quick calming strokes.

At the contact, my body shook. I weakened with a simple touch, groaning as I went supine against him as he stroked my body with stern swipes.

He reached for the loaf of bread sitting on a tray, tore it, and lifted it to my muzzle.

"Sorry, lass. This will have tae do for now. I do nae want you tae sicken."

I gingerly bit it from his hand and ate the pieces he fed me. I'd torn through most of the loaf when my stomach rebelled. I turned away from the next bite. He set it aside and lifted a bowl of juice. I lapped the liquid to wash down the dry bread.

Rowan invaded my space and swept his tongue over the fur

on my forehead, somehow licking my eye. I jerked back, blinking in quick succession to clear my vision. Clicking my teeth near his face didn't stop him, he just switched to licking my ear. So, I just let it happen.

My eyes fell shut. A moment later, nameless mate burrowed his palm into my fur.

"Skin and bones," he murmured softly and tsked. I huffed. Despite my fervent effort, my body relaxed as heat sank into my fur. "That's a good lass."

The other wolf nudged close, pressing into my free side until I was caged in. I'd never felt so taken care of . . . Camden came to mind. He was the only other one that made me feel this way. Taken care of, loved. If not by being touched, then by his actions. He was always there for me.

I missed him . . . but he couldn't be mine. I could never return to my pack, and now that I'd shifted into my Omega, anyone I cared for would be in danger because of me.

I shouldn't be in anyone's life if all I would be is a liability— if I caused people's deaths.

Swallowing became difficult.

Nameless mate sifted his fingers into my side.

"You're safe now."

His calm words soothed my anxiety. I couldn't rely on it too much. I couldn't let myself want this. *Them.* I refused to put anyone in danger.

# Willow

"Where do you think you're going?" my mate said. The big male hadn't moved an inch this entire time.

I froze, wincing. The gray wolf hadn't budged for the last few hours, in fact, he lay on his back stretched out with his tongue out.

His gaze was fixed on me expectantly. I needed to get him to understand that I was a danger to keep around.

Inhaling deeply, I sought my human form while pushing my wolf back. As much as you tried, while in wolf form, your primitive side was more at the forefront and the control over it was much shakier. My bones popped as my legs shot out. An uncomfortable burn worked its way through my limbs, and I whimpered at the sensation of pins and needles pricking my skin. It wasn't a lie that shifting took longer when you first came into your wolf. And it didn't help that I was sore.

Tears welled in my eyes.

I lay in a panting mess. Goose bumps washed over my limbs, and my nipples pebbled. I was laying here with *all* of it out. Shooting into a sitting position, I tugged the blanket wrapped around me under my arms like you would a towel, pulling it closed with one hand.

I lifted my chin and met nameless mate's glazed eyes. Frowning, I snapped my fingers up, getting his attention off my body. He blinked and then cleared his throat.

His eyes met mine and they widened even more. Red worked its way up his neck and to his cheeks as his lips parted.

I pointed at him and mouthed, *Name?*

He frowned, shaking his head. I repeated the motion.

"My name?" His eyes lit up with understanding.

I nodded frantically. "Kit."

I mouthed his name, and I couldn't help the smile that spread on my lips. I quickly cut that off. No. I couldn't be blinded by his effect on me.

Fur grazed my arm and the gray wolf rubbed against my side. His head dragged across my shoulder and almost bowled me over. He was damn strong.

My heart kicked into overdrive, and it took every fiber of my being not to rub against him. Instead, I pushed my palm against his side and shoved.

Rowan growled and showed his teeth. I snatched my hand back.

*Okay, damn.*

I returned my attention to my other mate who stared at me attentively. He was already on his feet, so I stood. With my hand in the air, I scribbled in the air like I was writing.

He rubbed the flat of his palm against his temple and nodded.

"Watch her, Rowan."

I frowned at the order as he exited the living space. Rowan pushed against my legs, looking up at me without blinking.

I scooted a foot to the side and he followed me. Sighing, I shook my head and angled my shoulders toward the fire. The sun was out, but it was still freezing, so much so my breath formed a cloud.

With the room lit up, it was easy to see the limited decor, although there was a variety of bunched up blankets. In particular, the space in the corner where there were masses of furs in a pile.

Other than that, the carpet was clean and there was only a couch pushed against the wall to the left as you entered the living room.

Muffled steps thudded back into the room. Kit was back with a notepad in hand. On my way to the couch, I grabbed the pen on top of the notepad. The cushion dipped under my weight and Kit sat next to me, making me tilt toward him. I cleared my throat and straightened.

*"Where am I?"*

I had an idea based on his accent and the weather.

"My house?"

I glared.

"Ah, too specific for you, then. You're in Scotland."

I bit my lower lip. Time to plan. I needed to get away from here and contact Nola to get her to send me money. She would understand the urgency. If I called Hector, he'd try to convince me to return, and I couldn't handle rejecting him at the moment. Eventually I would call him to assure him of my safety, but Scotland suited my current needs. It was perfect to lose myself in. Werewolves were all over the world, but since wolves were outlawed here, I doubted many werewolves stuck around.

*"Take me to your closest town,"* I wrote out, and after a pause added, *"Please."*

Kit looked at the note and then at me. My breathing elevated a few increments. He was much closer than he'd been earlier. It was actually getting hot in here. The earlier chill was displaced by the heat flushing my body.

"Why?" Kit asked, his voice low and calm.

Rowan pressed into my leg harder before nudging his nose against my pussy. I smacked his muzzle and he huffed.

This would not be easy. Of course not. They were my mates. They scented my Omega-ness . . . they wouldn't let me go easily.

*"Please. I can't stay here."*

"Why?"

I puffed my cheeks out. Kit was infuriatingly calm and the way he asked got under my skin.

*"Because I'm an Omega."*

"And?"

Okay, now he was trying to piss me off. I gritted my teeth.

*"You're in danger around me. Having me here will put a target on your back. Let me go. I'm not a possession. I want to be on my own."*

His eyebrows arched up and if I wasn't mistaken, there was a little smile tilting the corners of his lips.

"I understand your concerns, but why are you assuming I view you as a possession?" He tilted his head to the side, waiting, but instead of letting me muster up a written response, that frankly hadn't come to mind, he continued, "You're concerned about our safety, but there is no need to be, *mo chridhe.*"

I blinked at his words. So it wasn't that he wasn't understanding. It was that he didn't give a fuck.

"*Why?*" I mouthed. I racked my brain, trying to formulate some logical-sounding response, but for the life of me, I couldn't.

"Because you were made for me." He paused to look at the wolf. "And my brother. Either way, if you attempt to leave, we'll follow you."

My lips parted at his matter-of-fact words. His green gaze dropped to my lips and lust flashed in their depths. My stomach tightened, and the tension spilled into my limbs, waking them from their slumber. I wanted him. Now that I wasn't running for my life or high on the adrenaline, the ache was easy to identify.

My pussy throbbed for him.

I breathed deeply, inhaling the scents of the brothers. Without my consent, my eyes dropped to the front of his pants where his cock bulged. The notepad dropped from my fingertips, and I hopped to my feet.

He snatched my arm, tugging me toward the couch. I landed in his lap with my legs straddling his left thigh. Kit banded his arms around my back and pulled me flush to his chest.

"Don't be scared," he murmured into my hair. His nose grazed my ear and I shivered, my toes curling. He smelled so good—so *right*. My shoulders relaxed and I exhaled, going limp against him. Fear was the furthest emotion from my mind. "You smell delicious," he groaned against my ear, eliciting a shiver from my body. "You're mine. Meant for me."

I was hyperaware of my lack of clothing. The blanket had fallen and pooled around my waist. The roughness of his jeans pressed into my pussy, and I couldn't help grinding against the denim.

I exhaled breathily, sliding my hands to his shoulders and bunching his shirt. Kit groaned, head tilting back.

Static electricity sent a spark to my clit. Moaning, I rolled my hips, reveling in the pleasure of rubbing my needy core against his thigh. Kit cupped my side. His hand spanned my ribcage as his thumb grazed my nipple. He rubbed, once, twice. I shivered, head tilting forward as my breathing became labored. *Oh, sweet baby werewolf...*

His presence and scent drove me crazy. I rolled my hips again, sending pleasure through my nerve endings. He grabbed my hips, stilling my maddened movements.

I wasn't a small person, but he made me feel petite with the ease in which he moved me. His thigh flexed beneath my pussy as he pushed me down in a circular motion.

Oh. *Oh.*

My eyes twitched and a tremble started at my legs and worked to my clit.

A rough wet tongue laved across my spine and then Kit jerked me down.

The oxygen was sucked from my lungs as the wave of pleasure slammed into my pussy, wringing trembles from my clit. It was hard for me to form any thoughts.

I panted, reeling from the orgasm.

Kit's eyelids lowered, covering the satisfaction in his green eyes.

Reality chased away the thrall of pleasure. What had I done? I shoved against his hard chest. I fell back and my ass slammed on the floor. If Rowan's furry body wasn't there to brace me, my head would have hit the ground too.

I blinked and quickly hopped to my feet.

A sopping wet spot stained his jeans and my eyes widened. Heat zoomed to my face. I couldn't believe myself; I was dry humping his leg and I'd come so quickly.

He still watched me with his calm exterior, but there was a questioning edge to the gaze.

Rowan nudged my leg with his wet nose and then his tongue flicked out, licking my inner thigh.

I gasped and smacked him. The darker gray tufts above his eyes lowered, but I ignored the glare and grabbed the blanket to tuck it around myself again.

Swallowing, I returned my attention to Kit. I didn't know my next step, but I ached to shower again, it always cleared my mind.

I mimicked showering and he nodded tightly. He pushed to his feet slowly. Reaching down, he adjusted his cock through his pants.

I swallowed hard and forced my attention away, I was positive my face was fire-red.

"Follow me," he said tightly, jaw twitching.

I scampered after him as we went down the hall. The place was one story, but it was long. The hallway seemed never-ending. We passed a door and the kitchen entrance before reaching the last bedroom in the hall, the russet bedding was familiar. He'd brought me to the same bathroom from earlier.

Striding inside, I slammed the door and locked it. Pressing my palm to the surface, I squeezed my eyes closed.

My lack of control shouldn't have surprised me. Mates were an automatic aphrodisiac. It was normal to want to fuck my mates' brains out.

That truth didn't make facing it any easier, though.

# Kit

I'd be patient. I could tell something bothered her, but it was taking everything in me not to force her to stop saying she was leaving. She wasn't allowed to leave. Did I say that to her? No.

And I wouldn't. She was scared. The shifting eyes, the rubbing of her arms, all pointed toward her leeriness, which meant I had to restrain myself. The only way I managed it was by telling myself it was for her. My wolf normally felt calm, but as soon as she appeared, grappling with him became difficult.

I sighed, squeezing the clothing in my grip.

She'd wasted almost an hour and a half in the restroom. She was avoiding me.

I'd stayed outside the bathroom, fighting the urge to break down the door. But with the memory of her riding my thigh fresh on my brain, it was easier to control myself. That soft, vulnerable look on her face fucked with me.

I squeezed my cock over my jeans. I refused to come until I was buried deep in my mate.

Rowan growled, pacing my bedroom. I hadn't resolved my

complicated emotions around the fact that we had the same mate—an Omega. I wanted to kill him every time he was near her, but as long as she was touching me, I didn't give a fuck who else was around.

She'd already addicted me.

The shower cut off and I pushed off the wall to collect what I gathered for her off the bed. A moment later, the doorknob twisted.

She had her mask back on. That look on her face. Careful and stiff.

Her stare dropped to my hands where the shirt and slippers rested. She plucked them from me and slid her feet into them. She tossed the towel toward Rowan. It fell over his face, draping over his snout.

I didn't spare the wolf another thought with my attention on the swell of her breasts. My mouth watered at the sight of her brown nipples, ready and waiting for my mouth.

I swayed forward and her eyes snapped to mine with a glare. I cleared my throat and handed her a fresh shirt.

Fuck, she riveted me.

The long t-shirt loosely fell to her knees, the forest green material falling over her pert nipples. My cock pulsated. She looked fucking amazing in my clothing.

Her sweet scent had me groaning as she passed me. I snapped myself out of the thrall and followed as she returned to the living room. She marched to the notepad lying on the ground, hugged it to her chest, and made her way toward the door.

Curiosity kept me silent as I padded after her, Rowan beside me. She stepped onto the patch of cement outside the door and swept her gaze across the landscape.

She turned to me and pointed at my old truck.

I shook my head. She frowned, eyebrows furrowed.

The downturn of her lips shouted her dismay. It was honestly cute the way her features became pinched. Her expressions were animated when she wasn't trying to hide her thoughts.

She looked me straight in the eyes, then yanked the pen out of the spiral on the top of the notepad. She jammed the tip of the pen against the paper and dragged it across the sheet with jerky movements. Lifting the pad, she held it toward me. *"I don't want this."*

My lungs tightened. The visual of her leaving . . . not being by my side, struck me like a blow and my heart constricted.

No. Never would she leave me.

Before she could turn around, as I could see what she was about to do, I gripped her wrist and tugged her to my chest. Her warm little body pressed into mine. I dragged my hand down her side. Her shiver told me she wasn't as unaffected as she was trying to act.

Good.

I would use whatever forms of persuasion I needed to keep her at my side.

# Willow

I breathed out slowly. His hard body pressed into my back, and sweet baby werewolf, it was wreaking havoc on my hormones.

I had to fight this. I could hot-wire his car and get out of here, I just needed to yank away from the hold he had on me.

A rumble vibrated from his chest. I sucked in a breath, squeezing my thighs together. Was that a purr?

The motor-like sound vibrating from his chest reached deep into my body and simultaneously squeezed my clit and heart.

My eyelashes fluttered as calm washed over me.

His hard cock prodded at my spine.

I whimpered and my head fell back against his chest. The notebook slipped from my fingers and thudded on the ground.

He wasn't fighting fair.

A delicious heat unfurled in my lower belly and curled around my clit.

I helplessly pushed my ass against him.

He was using his body to stop me, but did I care?

Not much at this second.

"Trust in me, lass," he cooed.

I wanted to. So badly, I wanted to.

His palm slid down my chest, grazing across my hard nipples. My lips parted and my knees weakened.

I wanted to stay . . . but he would be in danger. My shoulders tensed and I straightened my slumped form.

That thought gave me a slice of reality. Yanking away, I bolted toward the truck. There were no hands to drag me back —nothing. My steps faltered, but I continued. They would let me go.

I couldn't deny the strike of hurt working its way through my chest. With my teeth gritted, I jerked the truck door open and bent to pop the compartment where the wires were.

Never thought what Camden forced me to learn would come in handy. It'd be weird driving on the other side of the road, but I'd get the hang of it. My fingers wobbled and one of the wires slipped. I exhaled shakily. It was dangerous for them if I stayed.

Once I wound the wires together, the roar of the engine made me jump. I straightened and hopped into the driver seat, my gaze dropping to the passenger side—Was he fucking serious right now?

I slumped into the seat, blinking at Kit.

"I did nae lie, *mo chridhe*. I will follow wherever you go."

My fingers flexed on the steering wheel, and I squeezed my eyes shut. It wasn't like I could return to my pack . . .

Fact of the matter was, I was lost, had nowhere to go, and my mates lived in a remote place.

My teeth sank into my lower lip.

If I stayed, would that be okay? Kit pinched my chin and forced me to look at him. The mossy green gaze held me in its thrall. His fingers spanned across my chin so he cupped my jaw.

A shiver worked its way through my limbs.

I could take some time for myself, right? Without having to worry about the pack or seeing Camden be with someone.

If it was only that, I would not have to debate, but it was also my concern for Rowan and Kit. The connection with them was undeniable. I wanted to curl up in their lap and have them caress me.

His thumb angled up and brushed against my lower lip. My heart jumped in answer.

There was a loud thump and the truck rocked. I twisted out of Kit's grip to twist around to a panting gray wolf sitting in the bed of the truck.

I sighed and pinched the bridge of my nose.

Who was I kidding? I wanted to stay. The tension in my shoulders loosened.

Decision made, I shoved the door open, pausing briefly to yank the wires apart, and slammed it shut behind me. Making my way directly to the dropped notepad, I scrawled my message to Kit who was already on my ass.

*"If my presence is ever a danger, I'll leave and you will <u>not</u> stop me."*

A myriad of emotions flashed across his face when I held it up. It settled on frustration, and he gave no indication he agreed with it. Honestly, I wasn't surprised. He was my mate, he was hardwired to protect me, as I was hardwired to want him. Realistically, being mates just pointed out who was your perfect match. It didn't force you to love someone or force you to want to fuck them. That was all there because true mates matched biologically and mentally.

"Let's get some more food in you."

I gave a short nod. He reached for me, and I tensed. Kit frowned, but instead of grabbing me as I half expected, he clenched his hand and turned away.

I followed on his heels, studying his stiff back. Rowan rubbed against my bare legs as we walked, hampering my progress.

Once inside, he turned right, the opposite way we'd gone when I first got here. Passing all those doors, he kept on until he reached the kitchen connected to a second living room.

He entered while I stood frozen, watching him open a cabinet. Rowan nudged my legs, snagged the large shirt with his teeth, and tugged me toward the dining table. I didn't bother fighting him.

I pulled the chair out and sank down as I placed the notepad on the table.

Licking my lips, I laced my fingers in front of me and watched Kit pull out a pot and set it on the stove.

"Are you ready to tell me who had you in such a state?" Kit asked, turning the burner on. He said it too nonchalantly. I licked my lips, avoiding his gaze. Talking about it would put him in danger. I would rather that sick fuck remained out there living than have any of my mates in danger. Kit sighed, obviously sensing I wouldn't talk.

I turned my attention to the panting wolf sitting beside me. His focus was so intense that I could feel him watching my every little move.

Rowan was a beautiful beast. His gray coat shaggy and shiny—perfect for sinking fingers into. I wouldn't give into the desire to pet him. If I started, I'd rub myself all over him. He inched closer and leaned against my side.

My chair creaked but held steady.

His nose nudged my arm insistently. Damn it. I licked my lips and finally scratched his ears. A deep groan vibrated through his chest.

The soft tufts at his ears tickled my palm in the best way possible. It rubbed against my skin, shooting strikes of pleasure to my toes. I pressed my lips together to stifle the sappy smile. I arched my pointer finger against the underside of his ear, and he groaned.

Why hadn't he shifted? I had yet to see his human form.

He licked my arm, leaving behind dampness. I grimaced and swiped it away.

Since I was staying, Nola would be a good person to reach out to for advice. She had to have tips on staying hidden even though she'd never allowed her Omega free.

I knocked on the surface of the table and brought Kit's attention to me. I lifted my hand to mimic a cell phone.

"I do nae own a phone, but we can get one from town tomorrow. I need to stock up on groceries anyway." His deep voice was calm and reassured me.

He'd been nothing but caring. I couldn't help but relax after being with them for a few hours. It seemed so surreal. It was such a short span of time, but they felt right.

Kit seemed to hold himself back a lot. He was treating me with kid gloves. Even when his temper flashed to life, at no point had I felt in danger.

I was much too comfortable around him, but I didn't want to get to the point that I couldn't bear leaving.

That was why I kept the distance between Camden and me after having sex. It was the only line I could draw.

I blinked down at my name I'd scrawled on the notepad.

Sighing, I pushed it away and rested my head on the surface of the table. My eyes fluttered shut as a sweet unrecognizable scent filled the kitchen.

I wasn't so cold anymore. My eyelids became unbearably heavy.

A spine-tingling touch grazed my nape.

"Willow . . . Beautiful name, lass."

# Rowan



My mate.

She was forever mine to protect.

Kit settled her on the only bed and dragged the blanket over her shoulders.

Willow kicked at the thick material until her legs were free. She groaned and wiggled side to side, burrowing into the feather mattress. She jostled a pillow and hugged it to her chest.

Her movements captivated me. My tongue lolled out and I gave into the urge to hop on the bed. It dipped under my weight, but she didn't rouse.

Kit met my gaze with his eyebrows furrowed. I bared my teeth at him, nestling closer to mate's side.

I must claim her. That would fix my restlessness.

But she seemed hurt.

I could not understand her reluctance with her mates. We were hers, and I did not like the distance between us.

"I'm going to clean the portable heater. Keep an eye on her."

Not bothering to respond to Kit, I watched her slack face.

Kit sighed and left the room. His restraint was greater than mine because there was no way I would be able to leave her.

Her long leg poked out from the shirt that smelled like Kit and my lip lifted in a silent snarl. I did not like that.

Crawling forward, I pressed my muzzle into her ankle, rubbing against her hard.

I needed all of her covered in my smell.

There was no wolf *in* me. It was just me. I was odd and did things differently, but I just *was*—Instinctual.

I would never think similarly to humans, but I would remain patient for her and learn. She remained in a deep sleep, hugging the pillow hard. Settling closer to her, I breathed her scent it, and I ached for more of it.

THE SENSATION OF BEING LICKED FORCED ME TO wake from my deep sleep. Fur tickled my inner thigh, closer to my knee.

My toes curled at the delicious sensation.

The pressure inside my throat constricted and I shook my head side to side. Was Uggo touching me? I sucked in a breath and pushed to my elbows, blinking repeatedly to rid the sleepiness from my eyes.

Relief loosened the thick fear clinging to me and I exhaled shakily. Rowan rubbed his large head on my thigh, his muzzle perilously close to my core. I sucked in a breath as he inhaled, eyes flicking up to mine, followed by a growl. I should be terrified, but my wolf's excitement at having her mate near, calmed me. Moonlight slipped in through the window behind me, making his pupils glint eerily.

My heartbeat picked up a few levels as the warmth from his overgrown body seeped into my flesh. I liked his proximity, his scent, even the odd way he watched me, and although the gaze screamed possession, it was comforting.

His head tilted to the side and he suddenly burrowed beneath my borrowed shirt, raking up the hem. His cold nose grazed my belly and he sniffed me, moving lower and lower.

I slapped my thighs together, trapping his muzzle. He growled, the vibration sending strikes of pleasure to my belly.

*Sweet baby werewolf.*

The grip I had on the bed sheets was at a strangling level, but the fur against my skin felt phenomenal.

I sucked my lower lip into my mouth, holding back a whimper, and my legs tightened, flattening his ears.

He yelped, pulling back suddenly to shake out his head. The angle of his snout was tipped down . . . was he glaring at me? His fur rubbed against my skin, and the insistent heat in my belly pulsated.

Get it together!

He clicked his very large teeth at me and then shook his head, causing the bed to bounce. The snap of bones and receding fur pervaded the space as he shifted. The bed jostled and as his shoulders broadened, my legs spread with his width which forced free a gush of wetness.

His hair was longer than Kit's and it fell past his shoulders in a shaggy mess. His arms bulged and the indents of his chest dipped.

The moonlight enhanced features identical to Kit.

Kit said they were brothers, but I hadn't realized they were twins.

My observations were cut short as he exhaled heavily, the cool breath tingling across my wet, sensitive flesh. My fingers curled in the bedsheets.

I licked my lips and hiked myself onto my elbows so I could pull myself out of the extremely vulnerable position. Rowan's palms flattened on my thighs, halting my inching backward, and in a quick jerk forward, I was flat on my back.

The quick movement caused my shirt to bunch above my hips, leaving me exposed. Goose bumps rose on my legs, but it had nothing to do with the cold.

Heat flooded my face and pussy simultaneously.

"Mine," he said, but it was almost unintelligible with his growl. His head lowered and he fastened his lips around my clit. I sucked in a hard breath, my chest heaving up and down. Oh, sweet baby werewolf.

I was sopping wet and embarrassed for it, but not to the point that I wanted to pull away. His tongue flicked out, curling around the bud and prodding it gently. Too gently.

I gritted my teeth and wiggled down, trying to get more pressure. Rowan's fingertips flexed on my thighs and his mouth opened wider.

He tasted my core without focusing on one spot, licking everywhere as if he was trying to suck me into him. And by the Moon Goddess, I *wanted* to be sucked in.

My head tilted back, teeth sinking into my lower lip as my heart went crazy in my chest. I couldn't help the quivering of my legs.

Rowan's tongue flattened over my slit, shallowly lapping, then plunging into my core. I tipped my hips up, wanting more. My eyes fluttered shut and the breath was sucked from my lungs.

An orgasm sparked to life. I ground against his mouth wildly. More. Just a little more. My clit throbbed under Rowan's tongue. What was he doing to me?

My mouth parted on a silent shout as my body went taut, neck arching. My hips jerked with each throb.

"Mmm," Rowan moaned as he licked up the gushing release dripping down my inner thighs.

My legs wouldn't stop twitching, which had more to do with the fact that he hadn't stopped licking me. This was too much. I hadn't been touched like this in so long. Too much . . .

Reaching up, I wound my hand in his long dark hair, yanking. He resisted my pulling.

"More," he growled. Rowan lifted his head, face glinting with my juices.

More?

I wanted to shout at him, and I definitely would have if I freaking could. He licked his lips and then his hands spanned my inner thighs, fingers near my pussy. He massaged, thumbs grazing my entrance.

Looking up at me, he grinned.

"Mine."

I blinked down at him, trying to keep my cool instead of forcing his head down, but the possession in his voice did me in. I felt vulnerable, and I wanted to get away before he weakened my resolve to keep my emotions separate.

He was on me again, groaning against my core and causing slick to trickle from my sex.

I missed being touched, last time was with Camden . . .

My heart squeezed for a beat, but Rowan's licks soothed the agony and returned me to the moment.

"More," he repeated, and my chest heaved.

I pressed my fingertip to his lips. His shoulders jerked as if I'd stabbed him.

Rowan exhaled harshly and jerked back on his knees, looming over me. The bed dipped with his movement and then he grabbed my hips, flipping me. The suddenness struck me with panic. I shot forward, scrambling to get away.

It had less to do with fear and more to do with instinct. My wolf came to the forefront and her excitement to play overpowered me. Whatever leftover fear turned into giddiness for the chase. I would have never thought my wolf had such a kink, but did I get why? Hells yes.

I kicked my foot back and hit something hard. Rowan grunted and I took off toward the door at a sprint. I slammed the door shut behind me, the sound echoing. I gripped the knob hard so it wouldn't twist.

Instead of the doorknob rattling like I'd expected, a dull thud shook the entire board. A beat later, an entire fist was through the door. I dropped my hand as I blinked in astonishment.

I tilted my head to peek through and saw a long naked torso and then he gripped the edges of the made hole and yanked.

My heart rate accelerated and I stopped my gawking to take off again. I lost my balance and stumbled forward, catching myself on the wall. Heavy footfalls thumped after me. It was too dark, so I couldn't see where I was going.

Taking a sudden turn, I found myself in the living room I'd been before the bedroom. A fire burned low in the hearth. Shit, I would be stuck in here.

Whirling around, I came to a stunned halt. Rowan stood at the entrance. The intensity of his narrowed gaze pierced into me. His furrowed eyebrows were low over his eyes and his chest pumped with harsh breaths. He lunged at me. My mouth opened on a silent shout as his body slammed into mine.

His arms fastened around me and he twisted his large body

so I landed cushioned on his chest. I grunted on impact as my breath left my lungs.

He rolled us so my back was flat on the ground. Rowan nuzzled me and pressed his teeth into my neck. I shoved at him, but he didn't budge.

With him closer to breaking skin, and without another way to tell him to stop, I slapped him on the shoulder.

It worked, but I received an answering growl.

He glared down at me, but even with the aggression, my wolf was excited. It was taking everything in me not to flop over and rub myself on his cock.

She knew he was my mate and he wouldn't hurt us. I wish I had her confidence. The mix in clashing emotions heightened my anxiety, but my worries were dashed when his hand wrapped around my neck gently.

I blinked up at him.

He lowered his head and inhaled deeply. A rumble came from his chest, and my body liquefied. It was the same calming noise Kit made before.

He was comforting me.

Tears gathered in my eyes, but I blinked them away.

Rowan licked my cheek, and I gawked in astonishment. A wolflike kiss . . .

He palmed my chest gently, a satisfied smile on his lips. The purring ebbed along with my tears.

Running his hand down my stomach, he stopped at my still wet pussy, and dipped his fingers into my sopping core. His digits swirling in my channel elevated my breathing. Extricating the glistening fingers, he lifted them to his lips and cleaned them.

Heat blazed at my core and the still present arousal throbbed through my flesh.

Rowan lifted so he was no longer hovering over me and gripped my hips, twisting me. The long shirt dragged as he tipped my ass up.

I wanted him inside me. My body *ached*.

He slammed into my entrance, and I arched my back. The tip of his cock so deep it hit my womb. The width of his dick was already a stretch, but there was something else happening.

I fisted my hands at the eye-crossing pressure.

Rowan snarled and his fingers dug into my hips. His cock twitched and even though I felt full, he continued to grow, stretching me further.

What was going on? The pain was on the verge of being excruciating, but my pussy clasped at the thickening shaft desperately.

The hands at my hips twitched and grew, palms widening. A stabbing sensation pricked my skin like claws digging into me.

He was so large inside me, he made it hard to breathe.

I looked down at my stomach and there was a rather large bulge pushing outward.

I blinked hard, struggling to wrap my mind around how huge he'd become in his third form.

Nola never said he'd become *this* large, though. She glazed over the transformation mates went through, but I never thought it would be like this.

I breathed hard and attempted to detach from his cock so I could look back. My curiosity was eating me up, but he wouldn't let go. I was left craning my neck to look over my shoulder and looked up . . . and up. From the corner of my eye, I saw him.

He whined, staring back at me with his monstrous half-shifted form. The canine muzzle slightly open as he panted with his gaze fastened on me.

I bit my lip and his attention dropped to my mouth. So suddenly, he extracted the thickness from my pussy. Next thing I knew, my arms gave out and I dropped to my elbows.

My body was made for my mates, which was why the twinge of pain swiftly faded into mind numbing pleasure. My biology was intrinsically different and made to fit their monstrous cocks.

The knot was large, but it would be biggest when he climax inside me.

The wet pop of him removing himself was followed by my juices dripping down my thighs. Rowan slammed into me before I could inhale.

I blew out a breath and my eyelids fluttered as my shoulders lowered toward the floor. Rowan angled me higher, tipping my hips as he ground against me, knot stretching my core.

I whimpered—the sound coming low and breathy from my throat.

He continued grinding into me and the knot pressed against my clit while the pressure of the tip of his dick prodded my insides.

Tears leaked from the corner of my eyes. A wave of pleasure overwhelmed me, the sensation increasing with each little twist of his hips.

My legs trembled so much they gave out. It was a good thing he had a hold on me, because all my muscles were done for.

Rowan remained buried deep, desperately thrusting into me as if he was trying to weld himself to me.

I couldn't say I hated the idea.

The knot expanded, the stretch sucking the oxygen from my lungs and making my clit throb against it.

The wave of release crashed into me, washing over my body and dragging me under. My hips twitched against him with each throb.

Rowan snarled and a loud, long howl vibrated through the room. I felt it in my core. My wolf thrashed, reveling in the claiming.

His movements stilled as my drenched pussy clutched at him and his knot expanded and locked us together as he came.

Claws dragged over my hips, stinging in the best way possible. The end of my release had me weak, but his cum still spurted inside me, filling me to the brim. It was so much it was leaking from me.

The howl turned into a rough groan and his hands flexed.

The knot still hadn't released, so we remained deliciously joined. Rowan dropped on top of me until his furred torso pressed into my back. Sweet baby werewolf that was mind altering.

My cheek pressed into the surface of the cool floor as I lay panting. Warmth exuded the beast on top of me. I drowsily blinked and nestled my cheek against the back of my hand. My gaze snagged a stunned Kit standing at the door, his chest rising and falling in a hard pattern.

# KIT


and had come back to Rowan fucking Willow. I'd been busy hauling wood from the farthest left side of the house and stacking pieces on the porch when I heard the howl.

I was expecting . . . I didn't know what I was expecting, but it wasn't a massive wolfman deep inside Willow. All logic flew from my brain as my wolf sprang forward and pushed through my skin, forcing my fur to spread across my flesh. Before I knew it, I sank my teeth into the gray fur so similar to mine.

Some logical part in the back of my mind understood it was Rowan, but I did not care as jealousy ravaged through me.

Blood spurted into my mouth and flesh gave way to my claws. Rowan snarled and his claws sank into my chest before I flew into the wall. The thud jostled my body, ripping a grunt from my throat. That fucking hurt. He had an advantage in this form, which was only reached after fucking your Omega mate.

Bouncing to my paws, I lowered my head, attention narrowed in on the massive wolfman. I'd studied on Omegas, because unlike many in the werewolf world, my pack knew they hadn't been completely wiped out.

Rowan grunted as he pulled out of Willow and stepped away from our wide-eyed mate. Good, she didn't need to be in the crossfire.

I needed to work fast. One thing about Rowan's fighting skills was that he was a straightforward brute.

My wolf was on the verge of absolute control until a small body slammed into my side. The delicious scent worked through my senses. Overpowering and encompassing—exciting.

I rolled and went limp to cushion her as she fell on me. Willow lifted her palm toward Rowan, trying to stop him.

Usually, once Rowan got started, he was incapable of stopping, so I needed to get in between them. But the unexpected happened, forcing me still. The cloudiness from Rowan's gaze cleared and he shook his head, then he backed up, shaking out his shaggy fur with a growl rumbling in his chest.

I turned my muzzle toward Willow, astonished that this slip of a girl had stopped a monster multiple times her size mid-fight.

Her divine scent seeped into every atom in my body, drawing me to her. She was the sun and I wanted to bathe in her. I forced my wolf back, accidentally shifting from the force I used. Fur disappeared from my skin and the cold floor dug into my side. In our position, she leaned into my naked chest with my cock pressed against her side.

Her lashes fluttered and her hips twitched. Arousal scented the air.

Chin dipping low, she met my gaze with half-lidded eyes. Her tongue flashed out to moisten her plump lower lip. My beautiful mate. Unmatched in every way. My dick throbbed, urging me to take her. I squeezed my eyes shut, tipping my head back. My head pressed into the wood floor, the cold reaching my scalp. I grappled with regaining some control.

I gritted my teeth, preparing to roll away so I didn't invade her space, but then she moved. She settled over my cock with her legs spread to straddle me.

My eyes flew open and I stared at her in awe. A pink flush stained her cheekbones and across the bridge of her nose.

The thread of control I had, snapped, and I cupped her face, forcing her down, nicking my lip with her teeth in the process. I couldn't stop if I wanted to. Her little tongue flicked against the wound, soothing it. The little suckles reached my cock like physical strokes. I groaned, my hips jerking up helplessly.

"Willow," I growled. Her lips parted and a small smile spread over her face as she settled her weight on my jutting cock, wrenching a groan from the depths of my soul as her silky channel enveloped me. She lifted her lips from mine as my body burned with a tugging stretch. A far-off pop filled my ears and she was lifted as I grew beneath her. My dick twitched and an odd ache stretched my flesh. The mix of pleasure and pain was almost too much.

She erased every past sexual experience with simply her presence, but now I was ruined. With one order, I would do whatever she bade.

Moisture dripped from her sex, slicking my cock. Willow's lips parted and she trembled, her already tight pussy tightening around me further. My eyes rolled back. Fuck. Angling her hips, she took more of my dick, yanking away all sense. A roar erupted from my throat as she worked herself down. I'd thought I was already fully in her.

I fixated on her parted lips. She wiggled on my cock, my attention enraptured on the little movements, and when I dropped my gaze, I saw why she was being so careful.

She hovered over the thick knot swelled at the base of my cock. Her juices dripped over the pinkened thickness and she wiggled again, causing it to expand. My claws gouged the floor beneath me and I shuddered, enraptured by the way her pussy sucked at my pink flesh. The bulb at the base of my cock disappeared into her channel and when she lifted, she left behind her honey.

*There has nae ever been anything more delicious.* My hands shook on her waist. *Aye, take me, sweet mate.*

Fur covered my skin, I had shifted when she fully seated herself on me—claiming me. And I had not felt it because she enthralled me.

Her pussy clutched my dick, squeezing it as she shuddered. My jaw slackened, overwhelmed by pleasure. My hips slowed their frantic upward thrusts, and she stilled as my knot expanded. She could no longer move. Her head dropped forward, eyes squeezing shut and lips parting. I couldn't tear my gaze off her as she came all over me. Her pussy released another wave of her liquid honey.

I couldn't hold back anymore. Cum erupted from me and I hissed a breath out between my teeth as she milked my cock. Her pussy took in each jut of release as she remained locked above me.

A growl dragged my attention upward. Rowan neared, burying his nose in her neck. He'd seemed able to stomach sharing her more than I initially could, which shocked me since he was possessive over anything he considered his—Rowan growled and sank his teeth into her.

Willow's mouth opened on a silent gasp and her eyes widened as fear filled them. Her emotions made her body tense up and she clasped me tighter with her pussy. I gritted my teeth, remaining still since I remained locked within her and didn't want to hurt her more.

Attempting to claw to the surface of ecstasy so I could comfort her, I lifted my hand, gently angling her head down to look into my eyes.

Rowan was lucky she was on my cock or I would have decked him. All he saw was his possession. He was his wolf. He only thought of what belonged to him. It wasn't that he was incapable of it, it just meant that his instincts came first. He was trying to claim her.

He didn't register the crinkle between her eyes nor the fear.

I spread my fingers over her belly, making sure I didn't hurt her with my claws, and pressed my furred palm into her clit.

Her gaze swung to mine as her pussy clasped my cock. She shuddered and I couldn't stop another burst of cum.

Fuck.

It was any wonder I could breathe.

Rowan detached from her neck and the blood staining his teeth was quickly licked away, then he licked up the sweat that beaded at her neck. Willow hadn't accepted his claiming bite, so the wound would heal at a normal pace.

She slumped forward, her palms pressing into my abdomen, her fingers scratching my fur lightly. A shiver traveled up my spine and I groaned. A sleepy, pleased smile spread on her lips. Her eyes widened as she touched the damp spot trickling into the fur closer to where we were joined.

Gripping her hand, I brought her wet fingers to my face and

lapped the sweet honey of her release. The taste tightened my cock and the knot shuddered.

My head lulled and her arms gave out. She settled against my chest, cheek pressed to my lower pec. Rowan sighed and lowered beside us, leaning close to rest his head on her spine.

She remained speared atop me as my knot incrementally lessened.

At some point, my knot had released her.

Her words of leaving rolled in the back of my head, haunting me.

I wouldn't let her leave me.

She said she was a danger, but I would show her I could protect her.

I must have dozed off momentarily, because it was Willow's small body wiggling next to mine that dragged me awake.

Her head was pillowed on my large arm. My mate used me for her comfort. A pleased rumble vibrated through my chest. Willow smiled and curled closer. Her movement sparked Rowan's and he inched closer to her back.

He was fucking clingy.

Okay. I understood why, but at least I semi masked my raging need to attach myself to her.

She wiggled again and I frowned. She was on the hard ground. Absolutely unacceptable. I pushed up, careful to curl my large, furred arm under her head, and with my other hand, I slipped it under her waist and lifted her in one swift motion.

Willow gasped and her nose wrinkled. Her eyes fluttered open and she fixed her attention on me, a frown marring her face.

What had her upset to the point of fearing us?

I scowled.

It must have looked fearsome because her eyebrows raised and she blinked up at me owlishly. Fear dilated the pupils and her shoulders jerked backward.

"What is it?" The words rumbled from my throat, vibrating through my body in a half-growl. Was it this wolfman form?

It was a shock to *me* and it was my body, but I must seem a monster in her eyes . . .

A heaviness settled on my chest.

"Let you go?" I said gruffly. She frowned and shook her head.

Her lack of speech made this harder. I couldn't imagine how frustrating it was for her that I couldn't easily communicate. If she used sign language, I could learn it to make it easier.

Willow tugged the fur at my chest, forcing my attention back to her. She tipped her head to the side.

What was she asking?

She lowered her hand and pressed the tip of her pointer finger into my sharp claw, winced, and then pointed toward her side.

I was scratching her! She was precious cargo, I needed to be more careful.

Huffing, I slid my palm until my arm was fully under her lower half. I was large enough that she nestled against me comfortably.

Rowan rolled over, patting around him to reach for her. His eyes sprang open and then he popped up, attention on me. His lip lifted.

"Mine too," he snapped.

"The floor is nae comfortable," was all I said in response and turned my back on him as I carried her out.

My steps thudded heavily as I made my way to the bedroom. I set her on the bed and she automatically reached for the blankets. Once I stopped her, I climbed in next to her, crowding her from one side while Rowan climbed in on the other. The bed creaked heavily. There were hundreds of pounds on the bed with Rowan and me combined, it was any wonder the old thing didn't collapse on the spot.

Tossing my arm around her, I pressed her face into my chest. Our fur would keep her warmer than any blanket. Rowan wrapped his arm around her lower half and inched close. She was tiny between us, almost disappearing in the oven created by our bodies.

Willow rubbed her cheek against my chest and her fingers flexed into Rowan's neck. He groaned, pleased. I frowned and forced her free hand to my side, wanting the same. She automatically understood, silently laughing as she scratched her little digits into my side.

A tremble worked its way down and my leg twitched. What the fuck was that?

She dug it deeper, reaching the flesh near my belly. My leg shook as my stomach spasmed and my cock twitched, hardening against her.

A whine slipped free and I sucked in a breath, looking directly at her.

She shook with laughter. I growled and lashed my arm across her chest to stop her teasing. That smile did vicious things to me.

She blinked, the smile leaving her eyes as doubt crept in. I detested that uncertainty and I was determined to prove to her that with us, her mates, she never needed to worry.

# Willow

Well. I was screwed.

I'd had no intention of staying with them when I'd found them, but their proximity reached deep into my chest and squeezed my heart. The safety they blanketed me with was something I couldn't turn my back on, and I didn't want to. I squeezed my eyes shut, enjoying the fur pressed to my skin.

Something Camden and my dad always threw in my face was my tendency to be rash, but it was more than that. I made a decision and gave it my all.

Did that make me rash?

Sure did, but did I regret it? No. I wanted them, and encased by their furred bodies, I couldn't help but be glad I'd plunged myself into the deep end.

I was no fool. I understood what this was—an opportunity at a life of not living on a ledge. That's how it felt with Camden. As much as I loved him, I could not be with him.

It'd slowly been driving me nuts, and when I'd seen him standing in the forest with Meridith, it'd snapped something in me.

I had blinders when it came to my best friend but never pursued anything because I understood the danger I posed. It would have been fine if he'd been able to accept me as a defective werewolf. I would have just never shifted, but he needed someone who was *more . . .*

And I didn't realize how small that made me feel.

Rowan released a bed shaking rumble and squeezed me. I winced at the tight hold and smacked at his arm, sucking in a lungful of air.

He chuffed and slitted his eyes. Damn, he looked pissed. The dark green was vivid against his gray fur. He flashed his teeth at me, and I jerked my head back so quickly, I ended up head butting Kit in the snout.

The hair at my temple fluttered with his heavy breathing and he released a deep rumbling snore. His heavy muzzle rested on my shoulder, but he was careful with the rest of his body. The furred chest bowed near my side, but it didn't invade my space like Rowan who was crushing me. Lifting my head and torso caused Kit's muzzle to slide off my shoulder. His chest pressed into the mattress and one of his legs hung off the bed. The position was either one of the most comfortable positions or one of the worst. His left side on the bed hugged the mattress as he crowded close to me.

I smoothed my palm over his hand, if that's what you could even call it. Fur covered his skin, the coat thick and warm. My hand looked so minuscule resting over his. I wiggled my fingers into the warmth and studied his claws. Kit's were less curved inward than Rowan's. The rough edges scraped against the palm of my hand. Deadly and dangerous.

I was with my mates when just a day ago, I was being

dragged around by Uggo. The greed from his gaze flashed behind my eyelids. My stomach sank and I sucked in a shuddering breath.

*I'm safe now.*

My shoulders loosened from the tension they'd held for so long. I'd lived the last weeks on edge, waiting for my end, and I could finally breathe. I thought I was fine and back to normal, but I was dead wrong. Memories crowded my head, and I struggled pushing his threats away.

I'd been trapped in that cold place, held on the verge of death . . .

I never wanted my mates to feel this way. A lack of control over their surroundings, this pain—no, numbness. Pressure unfurled from my gut and spread toward my chest until it was too tight. It was getting difficult to breathe, so I scooted back until I was sitting.

My hand shook as I touched the tickle on my cheek and then lifted it in front of me. The cool-toned, dim lighting of the morning allowed me to see the wetness.

Tears started in earnest and I released a shuddering breath, my shoulders shaking on a silent sob. It sucked that I couldn't even cry as dramatically and noisily as I wanted.

Rowan's arm tensed around me as I shivered.

His ear twitched and his blurry form rose in front of me. Rowan ran his tongue across my face, removing the current tears, but more fell.

As frustrating as crying was, it was already loosening the tension in my shoulders. Another tremble accompanied a rough exhale.

"Mate?" Rowan growled with a questioning tilt. His grip

lifted and his hands hovered over my skin, not touching. Without the heat of his body, mine iced over. I pulled my knees to my chest and hugged them tightly, making myself as small as possible.

Rowan shoved Kit's leg once and then twice, the movement verging on frustration.

I wrapped my hand around his forearm and shook my head. Kit should sleep if he was tired.

"Help our mate," Rowan snapped, irritated.

Kit popped up, alarm marking his wolfman face.

"Let me sle—" Kit's snarly words cut off and left the room in silence. I dropped my forehead to my knees and took deep breaths to get myself together. Already the wave of pressure that had blanketed over me was leveling out.

"Willow?"

I shook my head, not meeting Kit's gaze. Licking my lips, I readjusted in my sitting position, sinking deeper into the cushion.

There was a whine from Rowan and then the bed jostled as one of their heavy bodies moved. The fur covering Kit's hands tickled my skin as he slid them under me, and he hugged me to his chest.

My tears quietly trickled from the corner of my eyes. Kit squeezed me harder, thawing me out. My ear pressed to his chest and the pounding of his heart vibrated against the surface.

I peeked at Rowan from the corner of my eye. His muzzle was tight with tension, but satisfaction lowered his eyelids. His head tilted to the side, and I didn't miss the confusion in his eyes. He didn't seem to understand how to comfort me, but Kit would, which was why he'd woken him up. I had no idea why that created a knot of emotion in my throat.

"It's all right, *mo chridhe*."

I rubbed my cheek into his fur, while I reached for Rowan's arm. There was a slight difference in texture. Rowan's was slightly rougher and longer than Kit's and the coloring leaned more toward gray on Rowan.

An image of how we looked flashed through my brain, forcing a smile to my lips: The twin werewolves cuddled me in their beastly forms.

A silent laugh shook my body. Rowan rubbed the flat of his palm against his jutting pink cock resting close to his stomach. It was thick and erect . . .

My toes curled as a shiver traveled down my spine. I'd had that inside me.

It throbbed and I lifted my gaze to find his attention narrowed on my mouth. My tongue flicked out to wet my lip as my breathing became shallow. Need built in my belly. I hadn't had enough.

Kit grunted and his head dipped to bury his nose into my locks. The snuffles against my head lifted the hair on the back of my neck.

The sensual images of me riding him earlier flickered to life and then melded into Rowan fucking me from behind. My nipples pebbled, but it had nothing to do with the cold.

I wanted to be chased by him too, to sate the primal need gnawing at my insides. My wolf was one hundred percent on board. She was all for it right now. This second.

I had to rein her in before her excitement took me overboard.

"We need to get food from town," Kit murmured. "You mentioned a phone as well, correct?"

I nodded, eyelids drooping as I savored their warmth. I had to get the phone . . . but this felt so delicious.

His cock twitched. "Now, or I'll nae release you for a week, minimum."

Damn it.

I jumped to my feet.

# Willow

The drive to town was winding, so I had to massage my temples. I swallowed repeatedly to push back nausea.

It was annoying since I would have loved to absorb the scenery at length. I gawked at the rolling hills and the way they inched over the peaks, spilling into the dips and valleys to fill the crevices. The thin layer of ice covering the knolls glinted so beautifully I hadn't been able to look away even with the whirling of my stomach. I hollowed out my breathing and wet my lips.

The terrifying beauty emulated my feelings toward the twins. I couldn't look away from them and, at the same time, they made my stomach tighten, but instead of nausea, it had everything to do with nerves. As if sensing I was thinking about him, Kit's hand settled on my thigh, setting off a fluttering in my chest so intense it detracted from the nausea that had been my constant on the ride. I licked my lips and peeked at him from the corner of my eyes. His eyebrow was set in concentration as he drove.

My fingertips fluttered over the hem of the huge sweater draped over me, but that wasn't the most ridiculous part of it, nope that award went to the sweats. I'd had to draw the strings, until it dug into my belly and then knotted it.

I rubbed my arms to stave off the chill.

"Cold, *mo chridhe*?" Kit didn't give me a chance to respond before his arm was around me, palm at my hip and scooting me toward him. He dragged me over until my side was smushed to his. Even though he was in his human form, he ran as hot as an oven. Turning my knees toward him, I wiggled closer. This was heaven. A tremble worked down my limbs, lifting goose bumps as it went.

"Cold?" Rowan growled from the backseat, the word tilting up at the end. He reached over and pressed his thick arm across my other side. Unlike Kit, he remained in his wolfman form, and he didn't seem to want to change back even when Kit had snapped at him to shift. I sighed, eyes fluttering as their proximity chased the chill away. I could die in their arms and I'd die happy. The way they fucked, devoured, and claimed my body shattered me. Single-handedly lowering my defenses.

It was me. I craved this . . . this sense of belonging. There was only one person I felt similarly toward, and that was Camden. My stomach dipped. Den was the only aspect of my past life that I would agonize over, and I'd miss Hector, but everything else? Nope. I was sure they'd already replaced me at my job after being a no-show.

Kit and Rowan had been so gentle and caring. If I wasn't careful, I'd fall—

A stomach cramp stopped me from finishing the thought . . . I shook my head so hard that the ends of my hair grazed Kit's shoulder. He peered down at me, but I kept my attention forward and on the mountains. Time to distract myself from those thoughts.

This terrain was beautiful and unlike anything I'd seen back home. The closest I'd ever gotten to them was through a television screen, specifically the show following the chick where she traveled back in time. The show and those kilts, though . . . they chose the cast well.

I peeked over at Kit and took in his features. The main actor had nothing on Kit and Rowan. The planes of their cheeks were sharp and smooth, their jaw broad and stubbornly set. Especially on Kit, I could see the bunching when he clenched his teeth while it was more hidden on Rowan behind his stubble when he was in his human form.

Kit's gaze flicked to mine and my face heated at the rise of his eyebrow before he turned back to face the road. Even through my embarrassment, I didn't turn away. He was my mate, I was allowed to look, plus, he seemed to enjoy it if the tightening of his fingers on my ass was any indication. The hard band of his arm across my back flexed.

I licked my lips and dug my fingernails into my thighs from the rush of tingles that spread down my flesh. It was as if I'd used up every drop of control in the reservoir. It shouldn't have been this difficult. Rowan's wet nose bumped my ear, and he exhaled breathily. My shoulders hiked up as my body clenched. I leaned to the side, but Rowan didn't take the hint and continued to sniff my hair, my strands tangling with his snout. I hiked my shoulders up with a choked laugh and wiggled closer to Kit, gripping onto his arm.

"Leave her be," Kit snapped. The muscles beneath my touch flexed, and I fixated on the thick bulge. My mates didn't lack in muscles . . . I licked my lips. Rowan huffed into my hair again and the tickle distracted me from the raging hormones on the verge of taking over. I reached up and slipped my fingers around Rowan's large snout. He hunched forward, lowering his head so it rested on my shoulder.

My first impression of Rowan wasn't the best. Yes, he was my mate, but the way he'd come at me scared me, and now I could see how gentle he tried to be.

The shaggy fur from his neck fluffed on the seat, so long it almost reached me. He had the longest fur in wolf form I had ever seen, even in my pack. I raked my nails along his muzzle. I wasn't generally a touchy person, but I wanted to rub up against them like a cat does its owner.

I tipped my head to the side, resting my cheek against Rowan's face. Kit shot a frown toward us, and I squeezed his arm. The irritation melted off his face. This urge to calm them was instinct, but I couldn't deny the bubble of happiness ballooning in my stomach seeing how my touch affected them.

I'd always been drawn to Camden, but was it just attraction?

I pressed my lips together, focusing on the dash. I needed to stop mulling over him. Was there a hollowness in my gut when I thought of him? Definitely. But I just had to look at my mates and the sensation was soothed.

"Shift, Rowan, we're close to town, and no one can see you this way." The bite in Kit's words seethed with irritation. "*Mo chridhe*, will you back me up?"

There was that term he called me. I had no idea what it meant, but my body reacted to it, warming. I stopped myself from grinning like an idiot.

I turned my attention to Rowan, who stared down at me. I

blinked up at him as he tipped his head to the side, his fur rustling. With my lips pursed, I tugged at his muzzle.

His heavy sigh rustled the hair framing my face and he retreated. Loud sounds of popping overtook the truck. I stared, fascinated as the fur sank back into his skin and his body shrunk, er, well, in comparison, because he was still massive as a human.

I liked that my mates made me feel tiny even though I wasn't a small woman.

Rowan grunted and his deep green eyes stared back at me as he rubbed his stubble. A frown gracing his lips.

"You should nae have come if you were going to be moody. You do nae like coming to town. I would have kept her safe without you," Kit said and flicked a turn signal. It was still so weird that he was sitting and driving on the opposite side I was used to.

Rowan grunted and I twisted to look at him and quirked my eyebrow questioningly. His nude shoulders rolled.

"I do nae like humans. Or werewolves. Only you."

I huffed out a silent laugh at Rowan's bluntness. Every word he spoke had a gruffness attached that made my spine tingle. It was especially sexy combined with the lilt of his words.

Rowan reached forward to caress my smiling mouth. A flush bloomed on my face, and I nipped his fingers. His lips parted, eyes widening. He matched my grin and swooped forward.

He licked my lips, and I sucked in a breath at the wetness he left behind. My body clenched up and I faced forward, balling my hands in my lap as I tried to reorganize my senses. He was too dangerous for his own good.

I mustn't jump my mates. I needed to show some restraint, right?

I pressed my lips so tightly together it almost hurt, but I had to do what I had to in order to rein in my hormones.

"There should be a t-shirt and a pair of shorts under the seat." Rowan grunted and released the strands of my hair. I fought the urge to turn around and gawk at my mate's rippling muscles.

Kit gripped my thigh.

Oh, fuck, that wasn't helping calm my lust. I tipped my head back and a beat later, Rowan returned to petting me, fingers setting off pleasure receptors.

Kit's thumb caressed my thigh and my eyes about crossed. This was cruel. I had a feeling they knew they were slowly driving me nuts. I groaned and settled into the drive with my eyes tightly squeezed.

The overwhelming pressure in my chest spilled into my stomach. Kit and Rowan wrung this sensation from me. It took me a while but I finally put a word to it—giddiness. They made me feel giddy.

I missed feeling excitement instead of worry and anxiety. It was lovelier than I could put into words. A smile spread across my lips as I lolled, fighting against the raving horniness seeping through me.

The truck bumped and the speed slowed. Opening my eyes, I took in the small village with the squat roofs. A gray blanket shadowed the place as clouds moved over head, shading everything. A few people walked down the cobbled streets, bags in their hands.

The town was larger than I expected.

"Food, a cell phone, some clothing . . . is that all you need?"

I nodded in answer to Kit's question as he pulled into a thin, cobbled lane where multiple cars were parked, and quickly found a spot.

"Will you remain in the vehicle with Rowan?" I frowned, eyebrows furrowing as I followed his attention to my chest. My nipples poked through the long white sweater he'd given me. "If someone looks at you . . ." Kit licked his lips, jaw bunching as a murderous look crossed his face. I plucked at the fuzz on my clothing.

My already wet pussy released another wave of moisture, so I nodded jerkily. He exhaled hard and his shoulders loosened.

I'd had to tie the big ass sweats he'd let me borrow at my hips but even still, they sagged like nobody's business. I'd had to hold them tightly as I walked to the vehicle.

Another big reason I wanted to remain in the car was because I didn't want to be sniffed out by another werewolf. Ever.

Kit flashed Rowan a look and exited. Without his warmth next to me, the chill became more pronounced. It was an odd sensation, considering I was still achy.

"Your pussy smells like heaven." Rowan inhaled deeply, his lips grazing my ear chased away the cold. His hand lifted to my neck, wrapping around the column. My chest lifted and fell quickly as my thighs pressed tighter together. Rowan slipped his palm downward, rasping over my hard nipples before dipping even lower. His fingers slipped under the loose sweats and speared into my weeping core.

I sucked in a harsh breath, my hips jerking.

My eyelashes fluttered, and I wrapped my hand around his wrist, shaking my head hard. It was still light out, and it wasn't like the windows were tinted.

"You want release," he growled in my ear. The vibrations loosened my grip and his fingers dipped into my pussy again. Sweet baby werewolf, he would be the end of me. My head tipped back against the seat as his thick fingers slipped in and out of my sex.

His touch was rough and hard, but it felt so, so good. Heat built in my spine as he swirled his fingers. He worked another digit into my core and the pressure had me sucking in a deep breath.

A soft whine slipped free and he growled, jerking forward to sink his teeth into my earlobe. My body jerked at the roughness. It was criminal how good this felt.

Rowan's fingers dipped deep inside my sex, swirling so the rough pads rubbed against my warm walls.

"So tight and wet," he snarled. "And mine."

Rowan's shoulder rested near my head and his pert nose grazed the shell of my ear before sucking the lobe into his mouth. Sparks shot through my body, firing through my clit. The pressure in my pussy tightened as he added another finger and my lips parted while he worked it inside me. Three of his large digits were stuffed into my pussy, driving me wild. I wiggled in the seat, my hips helplessly jerking to get more from him.

My pussy clamped around his fingers, wrenching a groan from Rowan. I was so close. So close. An explosion set off through my core, squeezing his digits as I tried to contract them deeper into me. My legs twitched with each throb, releasing moisture with each electrifying jerk.

My lashes fluttered, and my neck lost strength. My head lolled to the side, resting near his hovering face. His stubble rasped against my temple. Rowan retracted his fingers with a wet sound. Moisture glinted from his hand as he lifted it, sucking his fingers into his mouth, tasting me on him.

I inhaled sharply at the erotic sight. Another orgasm rolled over my body and I helplessly tightened my thighs. Pressing my lips together, I struggled getting my breathing in line.

I couldn't believe it, he'd gotten me to orgasm just by licking my juices from his fingers.

Lifting my head, I peered toward a thumping noise. A man gawped from outside the car. A flush covered my body and I straightened, immediately crossing my arms over my chest as the guy stood frozen.

Rowan's head lifted and he slitted his eyes.

The furrowed brows, narrowed gaze, and flared nostrils hinted at Rowan's loss of control. He was about to toss himself through the car to get to the man.

I had no doubt he'd kill him.

Before he could twitch, I hooked my arm around his neck and used my other hand to force his face to me. It took some effort, but I pinched his jaw. The slight pain got his attention because he snarled in my face.

Licking my lips, I met his gaze head-on. As much as he snarled, he didn't scare me. I glared right back at him, leaned forward, and bit his lower lip.

That seemed to distract him enough if the shock was anything to go off of. At this point I would try anything to get Rowan not to lose it. Humans couldn't know about us. Fortunately, we were in our human form, so the observer wouldn't have a clue about anything supernatural. He'd simply think of us as a horny couple making out in a truck.

There was movement from the corner of my eye. Shit, I was going to lose Rowan.

I jerked forward and pressed my mouth to his. He froze against my lips, staring into my eyes. At his second blink, I slipped my tongue between his lips.

They parted in a gasp and I didn't stop. Pressing against him more insistently, I swirled my tongue around his, tasting . . . there was a hint of salt and sweetness on his tongue . . . was that how I tasted?

Dipping my tongue in and out, I exhaled into his mouth and tipped my head to reach deeper. Rowan groaned and his hand fastened around my shoulder, forcing my body to turn more.

His head tilted and he mimicked the movement of my tongue . . . as if he'd never kissed anyone. He literally copied what I did and swirled his tongue with mine, licking into my mouth like a drowning man.

If he'd never kissed anyone, he was a fast learner.

My body clenched up again and I detached from his mouth. I stared into his eyes, both of us panting.

"I like that," he growled against my lips.

I was grinning like a lunatic.

My shoulders tightened. The guy that'd been watching! I whirled and scooted to the door, peering out, but the man was gone. He must've dropped the milk if the ruptured container on the ground was anything to go by.

I sighed and rested my forehead against the window.

So much for keeping a low profile.

Lifting my head, I thumped my forehead into the surface again. Damn it. That was just a human, but imagine if it wasn't?

I lifted my head again, but Rowan's hand slipped in front of my forehead and caught it before it thumped.

"Do nae hurt my mate," he muttered.

I snorted and gripped his hand. My anxiety eased a few notches.

The driver side door jerked open and Kit hopped into the seat, shoving a few bags into the back. He started the engine with his lips in a thin line.

"I leave for a moment and you're causing trouble."

My brows wrinkle together.

I'd already made him mad? My stomach tightened uncomfortably.

Kit speared Rowan with a sneer.

"You had one job and instead you finger-fuck her with a human watching."

Oh. Well, when he put it that way . . .

I felt like a scolded teenager which didn't make me feel any better. Scowling, I tipped my chin up, but there was no need, all of his scorn was toward Rowan.

Kit's anger wasn't directed at me, which kind of also pissed me off.

I reached over and poked him in the shoulder. His eyes slowly closed and he exhaled sharply before turning his attention to me.

As I thought, there was no ire . . . at first glance, but he was pissed at me too, if the tightness at the corners of his eyes was anything to go off of.

He was careful about me. He didn't want to show me everything. In my book, that was comparable to him not giving me all of him.

I huffed and crossed my arms, sinking deep into the seat. As unfair of me as it was, I wanted all of Kit. Every single inch, and that meant his temper too.

The truck drove up the driveway and illuminated a woman waiting in front of the house. Her back was to us, and that was all I saw before Kit wrapped a hand around the back of my neck and forced me to lower my face down on the seat.

"Fuck. Willow, do nae let her see you."

At the initial order, I froze. What the fuck did that mean? Who was she? No fucking way, was he mated?

My stomach soured, dropping to the depths of hell as my mind ran wild. My heart rate spiked as my wolf perked up and raked her claws into my chest from the inside. She was definitely not making this feel any better.

Kit slammed the door behind me as I remained down on the seat.

Rowan growled and his bones popped as he shifted while exiting the car. Fortunately, Rowan left the door wide open, so I could hear their conversation.

"Come back to the pack. We need you. Kit." She whispered his name in a small, no, a loving rasp.

*Oh hells no.* I unbuckled my seatbelt, but curiosity kept me in place.

"It is still nae time."

What did he mean by that?! I seethed with indignation. Not time for what exactly?

"The pack made a mistake banishing you. Come back, I can convince them. You haven't even checked in as you promised." Frustration spilled from her tone.

"There was a . . . complication."

I blinked as Kit's words slammed into my chest. It physically hurt to hear that. I was the complication.

Who was this she-wolf he was giving answers to?

My stomach tightened. Dirt crunched, and I would bet Kit's ass she'd stepped closer.

I couldn't take it anymore. There was so much to unpack here, and I was confused, but on the heels of it was raging anger.

This chick seemed to know him *very* well if the intimate way she spoke to him was any indication. I climbed out of the truck and stepped as loud as I could as I approached. Her focus turned toward me. Good. She was lucky I wasn't bum-rushing her ass.

Kit rubbed his temples.

"Who is this?" She side-eyed me with a curl of her lips.

My teeth clicked together, and I stepped closer as my wolf bade. We wanted to attack her, but I was holding on by a thread of indignation with Kit's name on it. How dare he tell me to hide while he spoke to a woman? I turned my attention to him, glaring. The anger was also helping me out with my lack-of-shoes situation. The socks I'd gotten from him were soaked from the thin layer of ice. I hadn't thought this through, but it was too late. I mentally grabbed onto the irritation in my head and wrapped myself up in it.

It was a good thing the headlights were still on, because I wanted him to see how dissatisfied I was with him.

His shoulders jerked straight and he approached me in two long strides. I wrenched to the side, avoiding his touch. Rowan's pelt brushed my baggy sweats, and I leaned into him as he growled at the woman.

I buried my fingers in his fur. She watched with her mouth dropped, gaze bouncing from me to him.

My wolf did not like the vibes she was giving off. I pressed my lips together, unimpressed.

A gust of wind fluttered my hair, and she sucked in a deep breath.

"Sh-sh-he's . . ."

Kit sighed and inched a little in front of me.

"Go away, Bria," Kit growled and turned to me. "You should have stayed in the car." His voice had become a touch gentler.

He wanted me to remain in the car so she didn't find out I was an Omega. I wanted to groan in frustration, but I held my cool, tightening my fingers in Rowan's fur. I was getting as much heat as I could from him because it was freezing out here. How was it possible for it to be this fucking cold?!

"When did you find an Omega?" The confusion in her voice was mingled with shock. Her eyes were plastered to me, but my expression didn't soften.

"She is not simply an Omega, she's my mate," Kit snapped, the brogue thickening his words with a growl.

Okay, I wasn't as pissed at him anymore. Still semi-pissed,

but not *as* pissed. "I ask that you leave and not speak of this. I will return when the time is right."

I frowned. Return to their pack? I thought they were lone wolves. What was he not saying?

I wanted to ask him every question in the book, but I couldn't. I had to take the time to write it out and list them. I exhaled from my nose and the white puff of air ballooned in front of me.

"But you can protect the pack best."

I shuffled from foot to foot, bringing all eyes to me. I wanted to drag my wolf by the ear for forcing me into this position.

I aggressively pointed in her direction. She raised her eyebrows high—at me. I did *not* like that. Narrowing my eyes, I faced her, lip lifted in a sneer.

She took it as a challenge if her stiffening was anything to go by. Good, because it was a challenge. I strode toward her, placing me about five feet from her, close enough that I could tell I was taller than her.

Dominance radiated from her, but I ignored the pull to lower my eyes. As an Omega, I could easily let it fall from me. Other wolves only affected an Omega as much as we allowed it.

Rowan snapped his teeth in her direction and Bria stumbled back a step.

There was an exasperated huff and then I was swept off my feet. My toes curled to protect themselves from the chill.

I glared up at Kit.

"You'll lose your toes, lass."

I pressed my lips together and turned my head back toward the woman gawking. More than anything, Kit pulling me into his arms seemed to shock her the most. Her eyes lifted from him to me and then back again. Her swallow was audible.

I didn't like the way she looked at my mate. My stomach tightened and my wolf took my moment of weakness to jump forward. I turned my head and sank my teeth into Kit's shoulder.

He hissed out a breath and the muscle twitched under my clamped jaw. Blood filled my mouth, the copper taste spreading on my tongue. My eyes widened and I blinked, still attached to him like a leech. His eyes flared wide.

Shit. I slowly drew back with a slight slurp. I'd torn through his shirt with my bite. My wolf was not happy, and she was letting him know.

I swallowed the blood coating my tongue and turned away from him, face burning hot. Rowan chuffed and it sounded like a wolf version of a laugh. I switched my glare down to him and he sneezed, looking away. I was so embarrassed it wasn't even funny.

Kit exhaled slowly and I peeked at him from the corner of my eyes. His jaw clenched and his gaze was fixed slightly over my head. Still, his grip remained gentle around me. A gust of wind lifted goose bumps, and I curled closer to Kit. I was sure it was impossible to feel colder, but I was dead wrong. A speck of iciness landed on my skin and then another.

"You need to leave," Kit said as he strode toward the front of the house. "I'll get the fire started for you, lass," he added in a lower tone. There was no acknowledgment I'd bitten the shit out of him. I frowned. Worked for me, because I wasn't bringing that up.

"If I leave now, I'll get caught in the storm," the woman said, alarm in her voice. Kit's stride didn't stutter. That was what she deserved. Humph. She came here probably wanting to get caught up with *my* Kit.

I shivered from the cool air and peeked over Kit's shoulder as we reached the threshold of the door and saw Bria rubbing her arms and looking around like a lost puppy.

Damn it. *Don't do it, seriously, don't do it*. My wolf shoved up against my rib cage aggressively. I ignored both and peeked behind Kit and snapped my fingers. She looked at me and I waved her toward us. She pressed her lips together, but quickly rushed after us.

Kit's sigh raised his chest, his head shaking slightly, and I frowned up at him. Rowan had passed us and was in the house as Kit headed toward the shower. He balanced me in one arm as he tugged the wet socks from my feet. Once he shoved the bathroom door open, he set my feet on a towel and turned on the shower. He was a werewolf on a mission. He pulled the shirt off me and crouched to pull my sweats down. I licked my lips at his proximity to my flesh and brought my arms up to cover my breasts.

My attention fixed on his bleeding shoulder.

"I'll start the fire for you," he said gruffly and lifted to cup my face. I avoided his touch and jerked back, turning on him as I got in the hot shower. Who was that woman? I still didn't have answers, but I was sure I wouldn't like it.

Was I being petty? Sure was. Did I care? Nope.

He sighed. "Stubborn lass," he muttered. "I'll set another shirt for you to wear on the bed."

I didn't even look at him as he exited.

Pinpricks of heat washed over my arms and to my toes, slicking down my skin. It felt so damn good. Scotland was colder than any place I'd experienced. I sighed and tipped my head back as water spilled down my chest, chasing the chill away. With it came clarity. I'd invited that woman in and Kit was out there. I yanked the body wash from the shelf and poured it into my hands, lathering it before spreading it on my body.

It smelled like Kit. Like bergamot and oranges, but the scent came off his flesh as if he emitted it.

The door creaked as I rubbed the scent into my skin and Rowan lay on the ground, his head near his paws as he watched me finish bathing. Wait a moment. I had someone here who knew who the girl was and could easily tell me.

I tapped on the glass door and Rowan lifted his head, tilting it to the side. I turned my hands in circles, trying to tell him to shift, but he just stared at me. I huffed, turning off the water and grabbed the towel hanging over the stall to wrap it around myself.

I was still chilled but no longer felt like I would freeze into a popsicle.

Stepping out, I used the towel at my feet to shuffle over to Rowan. He tipped his head to the side, watching me crouch in front of him. I pointed at my lips.

He simply stared back. I puffed my cheeks out and rubbed my forehead. Falling to my knees, I lifted my hands to my chest to denote large breasts. Mine were big, but her were another level of big.

I mimicked a larger bosom and pointed toward the door and then shrugged.

He just stared.

I huffed and mouthed, *Bria, who?*

Rowan's muzzle opened on a wolfish grin and the fur sank

into his skin. His head was lowered when he shifted, but his shoulders shook hard. Was he okay?

I frowned and reached forward to set my hand on his arm. When he lifted his head, I saw he was laughing. I stared, stunned by the transformation of his face. The glinting eyes, the flashing white teeth as he chuckled. My mate was fucking hot.

I licked my lips.

Wait a minute, he was laughing at me. I scowled and poked him.

He'd known what I'd been asking. He straightened and my gaze fixed on the toned muscles of his chest. The smooth flesh was enchanting.

I shook my head hard. No, bad hormones.

A flush of heat flooded my gut and spread outward, and I fanned my face. It was awfully hot in here. I rubbed my hands on my arms and shivered, trying to chase the tingling feeling away.

It wasn't working, and Rowan's skin looked so nice. I shivered again. Next thing, I was rubbing my palm against his pec. It jumped under my touch. What would feel even nicer was rubbing against his fur while he was in his monster form.

I wet my lips, a tremble rushing over my arms. Another urge battled with needing them, I ached for a space for myself. Blankets upon blankets, their fur, *oooh* and pillows. Lots of pillows sounded so good right now.

I bounced to my feet. I knew exactly where I wanted to gather my blankets and pillows. Walking directly toward the bedroom, I pulled on the long blue shirt Kit had laid out for me, then bunched my fingers into the bedding. The socks fell to the ground while the pillows rolled onto the sheetless bed. I hugged the heavy blankets to my chest, hiking them up so they didn't touch the floor.

Rowan was frowning at the mattress. I stomped my foot and jerked my head to the pillows. Without waiting, I turned on my heel and inched down the hall, balancing the tall pile blocking my view. I made my way slowly, using memory to not knock into anything. That looked like the entrance of the living room, and once I took the turn, heat from the fire kissed my skin.

I strode near the fireplace and dropped the pile of blankets. I needed to hunt for more to make it comfortable enough for me . . .

My gaze lifted to Bria staring. My eyes narrowed and my shoulders tightened. She was a threat. Why was she in my space? This area was *mine*.

My wolf's emotions rushed forward.

The itchiness still lingered beneath my skin but a new aggression rushed forward. I was nesting. And an unknown female was here. I narrowed my gaze.

"Wow, you smell amazing." She cleared her throat noisily. "I know he probably told you we were lovers . . ." The rest of her words faded into the background. She was going on about how mates were precious and all this crap I didn't care to process.

They'd fucked. Kit and her. My stomach dropped to my knees but on the heels of that was unbridled rage. I lunged at her, shifting midair. It hurt like a bitch, but I forced it forward. She slammed onto the ground, and I landed over her, my still shifting paws thudding near her head.

I shook out my head, fur flying off me.

"Willow!" Kit shouted, and wood thumped to the ground. I snapped my teeth in his direction.

"Kit, help me. I didn't know you hadn't told her we were lovers. I'm sorry—"

"Quiet," he snarled. Her teeth clicked together, and she sucked in a shuddering breath. "Lass, it was a long time ago. We have nothing between each other. And it was nae ever serious. Look at me, lass."

My teeth were still on display and I faced them his way.

"Do what you must to believe me. I worry about only you. If you must kill her, just take care you do nae hurt yourself." His voice lowered gruffly. Fur sprang from his arms and his body grew feet more as he pushed into his monster form.

Kill . . . I wanted to slice her throat out . . . I shook my fur out. The heat flushed through me again. A low breathy exhale shuddered through me. I tore myself backward, stumbling. A tremble worked through my body. I ached down low. A throbbing pulse constricted. I only half paid attention as she scrambled to her feet and tore off toward the left, farthest from Kit, disappearing into the depths of the house.

Kit neared me, flattening his torn clothing beneath his foot, and I rubbed against his legs, leaning hard. Twirling once, then twice as I lifted my tail high, presenting to him. I ached for his claim.

I swished my tail again, flexing my claws into the floor as I shoved my human form forward and my body shifted with pops, the fur bleeding back into my skin. My paws became hands, fingers curling into the ground. My short hair fell forward and around my cheeks.

"Fuck." Kit hissed between his teeth. His fur caressed the back of my thighs. There was a thump as he dropped to his knees. His clawed hands gripped my hips as he tipped me up and retracted, only to slam his thick cock into me. My body shuddered. This was what I wanted. For him to claim me, choose me, ache for me.

A piercing howl rang out as he seated himself deep into my pussy. The sensation of being stretched heightened as his knot grew within my core. Yes. Yes. I wanted him deep in my pussy. He retracted to the tip of his cock, as if he couldn't handle being detached. The sharp stab of his nails burrowed into my waist and then he fully slid his dick back inside me, feeding me his knot.

I clawed at the ground, creating deep gouges into the floor. This was everything I wanted and needed.

"Aye, grip me tight, mate," he half-growled.

I writhed in place, lifting my hips. Moisture rushed from my entrance, and I sucked in a breath. I never wanted to stop claiming my mates. Getting fucked over and over again until I couldn't remain awake.

The insides of my thighs were coated with juices, mine and his.

*More. More*, I mouthed even though he couldn't see me. I hiked higher and he took the clue and pounded into me again. Ramming so hard my body shook with each impact. Heat spread up my stomach, drenching me with more need. My thighs shook within the confines of his claws.

Kit growled and he dragged one of his hands down my spine. The soft fur rasped against my skin, eliciting shivers.

The tremble in my legs hadn't abated. Kit rammed into me with a grunt and his thrusts became earth shattering. He snarled and the clenching on my outer thighs set my orgasm off. My arms gave out and I dropped so my cheek pressed into the floor as he fucked me, wringing out every drop of pleasure. Moisture spilled from me at an alarming rate, but I couldn't feel embarrassed about it because it was too good. I whimpered breathily, wishing I could moan for more.

With a grunt, Kit slammed into me once more and stilled. My channel continued to contract around him, tugging and holding his cock, forcing him to remain while his knot ballooned within my core.

His eruption sent me into another release, and I shook as my pussy throbbed needily. I could happily die from pleasure at this moment.

Kit whined and ground against me, his pelvis pushing against my ass since he wasn't able to withdraw. He dragged his claws from my neck to the base of my spine.

I hummed, pleased that his knot kept us locked together.

A muzzle ruffled my hair and a long tongue lashed across my sweaty neck. I lifted my head to Rowan's gaze steadily on mine, and I propped myself up on my arms.

Rowan followed my tugging and dropped to his furred knees. I shoved his midsection and he fell back, his large, clawed hand catching him as he braced himself. I rested my forearms over his widened thighs and his thick pink cock bobbed near my face. It was so big I didn't have to dip much to get to it, which was a good thing, considering how tired my arms were.

The pink mushroom head dripped with cum. I reached for the base and wrapped my hand around it, the tips of my fingers unable to meet. There was a slight bulge beneath my hands where the knot would thicken when he was in me. I slid lower and cupped the heavy furred sac resting underneath and squeezed lightly. Rowan whined, shuddering.

I licked my lips, mouth salivating at Rowan's twitching dick. I loved the feel of him, warm, moist, and hard as rock.

# ROWAN

Her brown eyes were fixed on mine as she lowered her head. Heat blazed in the brown gaze and I shivered from excitement. What was she . . . Her soft lips wrapped around the tip of my cock, stretching from the size.

This . . . this was—

No one had touched me this way, but I wanted this always. Only from her.

My mate.

It was almost like when she pressed her lips to mine and stuck her tongue inside my mouth.

Kissing?

It never interested me until she did it.

Willow's head dropped forward. That was the last I saw before her mouth sucked the tip of my cock. I breathed in on a groan, my leg twitching from pleasure as I thrust further into her mouth. She gagged at my movement and a rush of liquid spilled from my cock and dripped from the corner of her mouth and down my shaft.

She slurped and flattened her tongue against my dick as she squeezed the base.

A haze fell over my vision. I wanted to pound into her. Fuck her until she claimed me over and over with her little teeth.

The visual of her violence caused my cock to twitch. I'd always had a hole in my life and it was in the shape of Willow—I'd missed her even before I knew who she was.

## WILLOW

Rowan's body shivered and his grip in my hair would've been painful if I weren't in heat. Instead, I leaned into the pain. His muzzle was slightly parted as he panted, looking down at me. His large fangs glinted in the firelight.

The pressure in my pussy let loose slightly as Kit's knot decreased. I pulled forward, wiggling to slip off the rest of the way. With a shove of Rowan's shoulder, I forced him back so he rested on his elbows.

I straddled him. His fur rubbed against my thighs, inflaming my need. The overwhelming rise in temperature in the room overheated me. It burned through me and the only way I could abate this incessant ache was through my mates. Peering directly into his eyes, I gripped his dick and speared myself on him.

Rowan whined and his claws gouged the floor. I gripped his shaggy fur as I leaned forward, settling myself on him. The size of their cocks never failed to leave me breathless.

I trembled, feeling him deep in my core. I looked down to see his knot ballooned at the base. A little more. I wanted to claim him completely.

I worked myself down over it. Rowan yipped and his eyelids

squeezed tightly. Moisture dripped from my pussy and onto his fur, matting it to his body. I ground onto him to take his thick cock.

Leaning forward, I wiggled my ass toward Kit, peering back at him over my shoulder as he watched me fuck his brother. Both of them needed to be inside me.

He lunged forward and gripped my hips. He didn't even need to guide his dick, it was straight up, still slick with our combined juices. The bud of my asshole stretched with his invasion, causing my pussy to tighten. Sweet baby werewolf, I was going to permanently have curled toes.

Rowan bucked beneath me with a growl, and I swallowed hard.

Loving the fullness, I bit my bottom lip and flexed the muscles in my core. They simultaneously groaned. More. I wanted more.

"I can nae control myself, pinch me if it hurts," Kit hissed between his teeth and then he pounded into me. I silently cried out, mouth wide. His movement sent me harder onto Rowan who thrust up to pin me against Kit.

My lungs deflated as I gushed between them. Rowan groaned and his claw dipped to graze over my clit. A second release slammed into me. Tension ran up my limbs, causing my mind to fuzz as I thrashed on them. They seemed just as lost as they pounded into me.

If I were human, they would have broken me, but I was made for them and wanted to show them I could take anything they dished out.

The release only increased in intensity as they continued fucking me, not allowing me to come down. My legs twitched madly as I struggled to regain myself, but it was no use. Another orgasm came on without notice and Rowan and Kit simultaneously followed me, roaring in ecstasy as their knots throbbed.

My lashes fluttered shut and my body panted between them, twitching from the pleasure.

More.

I leaned forward and gripped the fur at Rowan's chest and moved slowly. I twisted my hips with effort, managing to pull myself from his knot. He whined, his eyes squeezing closed. Our liquid dripped down my thighs. Kit pumped lightly inside my ass. I swirled my hips and dropped onto Rowan's shaft. They simultaneously groaned. I was a wet mess, but this was just the beginning. Fire blazed through my veins, ordering me to claim.

"My lass's cunt needs to be wrung dry," Kit purred. I *throbbed*.

Rowan leaned forward, chest rising and lowering rapidly. His tongue flicked out and lapped my nipple. He took the nub gently at the tip of his muzzle and suckled.

My hips jerked as it traveled directly to my clit. I wanted to fuck them until I dropped.

# Willow

I wrapped myself tighter around the werewolf chest. Still unable to go to sleep even after Kit and Rowan passed out. I was smushed between the two slumbering werewolves, and I couldn't help the warmth in my chest at seeing them so vulnerable. They'd matched my hunger, rutting me so deliciously my body was currently mush.

While I could be in heat anywhere at any time, regardless of anything, only my heat could spur on their rut, and they *only* succumbed once their instincts deemed their Omega safe. Ruts never lasted long because a mate's primary instinct was protection. Meanwhile, heats lasted anywhere between three to ten days. It was a gamble. My first heat lasted exactly five days.

Five days of nonstop fucking, clawing, and claiming.

I shivered and Rowan pressed into my back, his semi-stiffy digging into my side. The fire had long since burned away, but my mates had brought out piles of blanket, creating a nest of sorts. I rubbed my cheek on Kit's warm chest, sighing. I wanted to keep rubbing against them. Their fur made the fluttery butterflies take off in my stomach. The scent of their soap spurred to life the memory of them bathing me. They'd taken such meticulous care in drying me off, or at least they'd tried to until I speared myself on Kit's cock.

I groaned, embarrassment getting the best of me.

Even with all the screwing, I still wanted to crawl into their bodies.

"Can I come out now?" a low voice called out, and her head cautiously poked out around the threshold. Her voice was dry and rough. My thoughts froze and I shoved their arms off me to push to my feet. My mates woke up. One moment they were out cold, the next, they crowded in front of me, beastly head lowered, and snarls spilling from their maw.

Bria screamed and dropped to the ground, curling her arms around her head.

She'd . . . been here the entire time?

Heat flooded my face, but I sucked in a breath and lifted my chin. She heard me taking my mates because they were *mine*. Not hers.

I peeked at her through the sliver between my mates.

"I'll leave now. I-I'm sorry for coming." She wouldn't look up as she spoke. Why hadn't she left five days ago? The last interaction with her flashed in my brain and I stifled a wince. I'd been about to choke her out. She moved sluggishly, holding onto the wall. Her complexion seemed sallow.

A smidge of pity spawned. I tugged at my mates' arms. They turned questioningly and I shook my head once. Dipping, I grabbed a pillow and shoved it against Kit's crotch to cover him. It was funny seeing surprise on his wolfish face, but he held the couch pillow when I insisted. An odd stretch to the corner of his muzzle told me he was grinning. I grabbed another pillow and did the same to Rowan, who seemed more irritated at covering himself. Last, I grabbed a blanket and wrapped it around my body. As I approached Bria, she stumbled back, eyes wide.

Grabbing her arm, I tugged her to the kitchen.

I pulled a glass cup out, filled it with water, and shoved it into her hands while she gaped at me. Then I rifled through the semi-empty fridge and pulled out the juice after checking the expiration date and poured it into her now empty cup.

Bria quickly swallowed it down, watching me with wide eyes.

I rustled through more cabinets until I found a granola bar and handed it to her. She tore it open and scarfed it down.

My stomach growled, but I ignored it. My mates had fed me while I'd been deep in the throes of my heat, but with all the energy I'd used up, it wasn't enough.

"I'm sorry." Her accent tilted the end of her statement. Ugh, I hated how it was kind of cute. "I think I have enough energy to leave. I'll hunt for some food while I'm a wolf."

She cleared her throat, awkwardly backing away. Kit was near the door, and she scooted as far from him as she could.

"I apologize, Alpha, I hope you return, many regret your banishment." That word again. Banishment . . .

With a final nod to me, she scurried out of the house like I was chasing her. I kind of enjoyed her leeriness over me.

She disappeared around the corner.

"That was kind of you," he murmured, now in human form. His chest rippled as he lifted the grocery bags onto the counter. I'd forgotten we'd gone shopping before I'd gone into heat. "I threw out the stuff that went bad, but we have a good amount of food here." He set them on the counter and pulled out the writing pad I'd been communicating with and handed it to me. "I'm glad we had a box of granola bars. That was all your attention span allowed you to eat."

My gaze dropped to the low-slung sweats and tight shirt molded to his body. It was unfair how he filled clothing out. He tugged a shirt off his shoulder and pulled it over my head, then wrapped me back in the blanket. Taking care of me.

He invaded my space and his orangey scent made me hum in pleasure. I sucked in a breath. The man was big and it was unfair how much I liked that. He dipped down and pressed his lips to my forehead. My eyes fluttered shut and a shiver worked down my body. The simple press of his lips caused my knees to shake.

The click of nails and heavy steps pulled my attention toward Rowan as he shuffled into the kitchen still in his monster form. He pressed into my back, his warm, shaggy fur warming me. A sappy grin spread on my lips. This was the life. If my chest was hollow at times, then that's how it was going to be. Whenever Kit or Rowan loved on me, that sensation was soothed.

My stomach chose that moment to growl.

Kit stepped back and ran the tip of his finger down the arch of my nose, staring me directly in the eyes.

"Can nae have my mate hungry," he said and pulled away, gripping my arm to force me into a seat. In a swift move he had an apple in my hand and was at the stove, turning the knob.

A grin tipped up the corners of my mouth and I sank my teeth into the apple. A crisp crunch filled the kitchen as I munched away. The apple helped abate the gnawing hunger. I continued eating as Rowan pulled a bar seat out beside me and lowered into it. He was fortunate it was such a huge seat.

I snorted out a laugh at the sight we made. It was so . . . domesticated.

The seat Rowan rested in creaked. Oh shit, I could tell where this was going, but he was too busy sneering at Kit. The legs cracked and shattered, taking him to the ground. I couldn't even shout a warning.

Rowan sprawled in his wolfman form with his deep green eyes wide.

His slow blinking was what took me out.

My shock turned to full-out body-shaking laughs. Rowan let out a short growl, which only set me off even more.

I couldn't breathe because I was laughing so hard. He pushed to his feet and stalked off, shaking his head with his ears flicking.

I wiped my blurry eyes to find Kit grinning at me.

"I never knew he was so sensitive." Kit tsked and turned back to rifle through a pantry. I pursed my lips. Rowan was so stinking cute it was killing me.

I reached for the little pad and wrote out the question that had been gnawing at me. Knocking on the surface of the island, I called his attention. Kit turned and his eyes moved as he read the question I'd written out.

*"What did she mean, you were banished? How long were you Alpha?"*

His set down the pan.

"About fifteen years."

I gawked at the number. That meant he was older than I thought, unless he became Alpha as soon as he shifted. There was absolutely nothing wrong with him being older, considering our life spans were longer than humans.

I quickly scrawled out my question. *"You're thirty-three?"*

"Add five years."

Even then he looked much younger. A gift of the werewolf genes. The good thing was we aged so slowly, it'd hardly be noticeable. I knew of a hundred-year-old werewolf that looked no older than a human version of midfifties. Usually, werewolves shift at eighteen which was when aging began to crawl. Werewolves' lifespans weren't an obscene length—one hundred and fifty was as old as it got, but at least we had a smidge more time than humans.

"There were . . . situations with Rowan. Everyone lived in fear of him. He'd killed a few packmates and the pack had enough. They'd banded together to request I put him down."

I sucked in a hard noisy breath as my hands fisted. How dare they want to get rid of him?

"I obviously did not. Instead, I agreed to leave to try to get him under control."

*"And you want to go back to your pack?"* I held it up, trying to keep my expression even.

That was the exact opposite of what I wanted. I wanted out of pack life. This, here, just us and no other responsibilities, or having them put anyone over me, or me having to socialize, that's what I wanted. It was my heaven.

Kit frowned, meeting my gaze pensively, hesitating. I saw the caution in his eyes and it made my heart tighten.

His lips parted but before he said anything, I hopped off the seat as I wrote out my next phrase. *"I'm going to shower."*

I twisted on my heel and rushed out of the room like a coward. I didn't want to hear him say the words because when he did, I would have to state my position, and that would put us at a crossroads I didn't want to consider.

It was unfair of me to impose my desires on him. I didn't

know if he'd go back as Alpha, or worse, give it up for me. Both sounded like a nightmare.

On the way down the hall, I hesitated in front of an open door on the way to Kit's bedroom. I nudged it open. The room was completely bare. I sniffed and the remnants of Bria's scent wafted to me. So this was the room she locked herself inside. Backing out, I closed the door and continued to Kit's room.

Once the shower was on, I tossed the blanket on the bed and shucked off the shirt. Even though they'd bathed me in the last five days I'd been lust driven, I still had cum dried between my legs from the last round.

I stepped into the warm spray, closing my eyes as water pelted my skin.

Rowan's unpredictability was why they lived out in the middle of nowhere and why they were banished. Poor Kit, having to choose between two things he cared for. He was much older than I thought, and he'd been Alpha for so long. No wonder it was all he was thinking about returning to . . . My teeth sank into my lip. It would be selfish of me to ask him to choose again.

I finished washing up and speared my fingers into my wet hair. This mate stuff was harder than I expected. I scooted the curtain to the side and grabbed a fresh towel off the hook. Each time I used the shower, there was a fresh one waiting in the exact same spot.

It was becoming clear that Kit was a silent giver. He'd just give and give to the point that he came second. I imagined him as a fair pack Alpha.

After donning my slippers, I trudged back into the room and froze at the threshold. The bed was made and a fresh set of clothing lay on the bed.

There was no longer evidence of the mess I'd made when I'd come in.

I frowned. Even the curtains were drawn back. I lifted the clothes. They were my size. I swallowed, trying to lessen the thickness in my throat. Beside the bundle was a cell phone.

I dressed in the sweater and leggings, then pulled on the thick coat and socks. The cell phone was in a box and the screen flickered on to a battery image when I pressed the button. I pulled out the charger and hunted for a plug until I found one near the large window.

Layers of snow blanketed the trees and ground. The way the sun fell over the fresh sheets and glinted in the crystals was gorgeous. Giddiness swept through me.

There was never snow in Redwood Pack.

I rushed around the bed and knocked into a pair of boots.

Shoving my feet into them, I wiggled my toes. Only a *little* big, but much better than going without. I continued rushing out, zooming past the kitchen.

The cold air slapped me in the face but it felt glorious. My heels sank into the snow with a satisfying crunch. Even though the coat was thick, I could still feel the chill through it. My freezing nose was testament to the weather. I had no doubt it was red.

I stepped forward, eyeing the pile of snow a few feet away.

"Careful," a growly voice intoned. I whirled to find Rowan peering at me from near a tree. So, he'd come out here when he'd run off.

In answer, I dipped and grabbed a handful of snow, balling it tightly and then adding another layer until it was a well-sized beast. Rowan tilted his head, watching me.

I positioned and tossed it right at him.

The snow splattered across his chest and dropped to the ground. His head jerked back, muzzle falling open, showing his fangs from within his maw. The gawking was hilarious on his wolfman face. I lifted my hand to my mouth as I broke out in silent laughter.

Rowan snarled and bounded close, baring his teeth at me in a vicious display. It just set me off harder. He loomed over me and growled warningly, eyes glinting with humor.

I grabbed a handful of snow and aimed it at his face. He closed his eyes and I took advantage by tossing myself at him.

Rowan lost his balance and stumbled backward under my attack, then thumped hard into the snow, sending a flurry up around us.

He growled and I scurried off him. A wicked wolfish grin lifted his muzzle and it looked more like a baring of teeth. He fell to his hands, legs bending easily in his wolfman form, then he used his huge furred hands to dig into the snow, aiming at me.

I sputtered and put out my hands to ward from the snow attack. No fair, his claws were an advantage.

It was only a few swipes and my legs were half buried. He paused and peered at me. I huffed, pouting as I poked my finger at him and then dragged it across my neck. He was dead meat.

He must have seen the intention in my gaze because his head tipped back and he released a short bark and took off at a sprint.

Dragging my feet out of the pile, I hoofed it after him.

Damn him for being so fast. If these weren't new clothes, I would have shifted.

I screeched to a halt to pull my clothing off as his gray tail disappeared in the distance.

THE CRUNCH OF SNOW BUNCHED UNDER MY PAWS AND my nose was ready to chip off. I couldn't feel much of anything, but still, I moved forward. I had to. My wolf fueled me with energy despite my exhaustion. I'd been running on fumes, hardly stopping for anything remotely relating to rest.

When I found her, I would spank her ass until she understood she couldn't leave my sight. Right after that, I'd bite her all over to stake my claim.

It was enough. If I'd learned anything in the last few weeks, it was that I couldn't live without her, even if it meant forcing her to face her feelings.

I'd bided my time. I went along with Torrin's orders as he sent me away to do one thing or another, convincing myself to be patient. And she'd slipped from my hands. I wouldn't allow her to push me away *when* I found her. There was no if. I had enough of acting like we hadn't fucked so good I'd never touched another.

But enough was enough.

I had to find her and if I didn't, that was it for me. At least I was somewhere I could easily end it. I had no desire to continue without her.

I tensed at the sound of huffing and clicking teeth. My ears twitched to listen. I'd been on her trail. Or at least I'd thought I had been, but then the snowstorm came and wiped all traces I'd scented. Snow was a fucking nuisance.

My wolf was on edge, and he'd been especially itchy these last few days.

I'd had to hunker down in a small cave to wait out the blizzard and I counted it as wasted time. At this point, I was going in circles. Or at least it felt that way on this vast fucking land.

I took a sharp turn and picked up the pace, letting my wolf rush forward and take the reins. His excitement bled into me, overtaking my flesh and causing my stride to widen. It took my human mind a second to comprehend the delicious scent.

Familiar, yet not. It was stronger, more intense—mine. I sped up.

Weaving around a snowy knoll, I bounded over a fallen log and careened to a halt, snow spitting up around me.

My lungs stopped functioning and I froze, my wolf clawing at my insides.

*Please don't let this be an illusion.*

I shook my head and blinked hard as the girl tossed a shoe to the side and hopped on her bare foot to reach for the other.

Here she was *finally*.

She turned, a huge smile fixed on her face. Her scent filled my senses, and I groaned.

I found her. Days, weeks had passed without her.

*And she was my mate.*

I sucked in a hard breath as the ground shook.

Willow was mine.

A ragged exhale exploded from my chest as a childish grin fixed on her lips as she looked through the trees.

*How the fuck was she so happy while I'd suffered looking for her?*

It was an illogical jealous response, of course, I didn't want to find her suffering, or worse, dead, but the intense churning in my gut overwhelmed my senses. I shifted and my popping bones called her attention.

As soon as her gaze met mine, she exhaled with a heavy puff, eyebrows raising high on her forehead.

"*Camden*?" she mouthed and lifted her hands to her chest. She stumbled forward and my ire faded. I caught her before she fell.

My arms wrapped around her torso so tightly she grunted. A few beats passed as I absorbed the heat from her body. It seeped into my flesh and thawed the iced over organ that had stopped functioning properly when she went missing. I clasped her face, shuddering at the feel of her skin.

She inhaled deeply, eyes fluttering as she swayed toward my chest.

My mate was as enthralled by my scent as I was with hers.

I squeezed her face so tightly her lips pouted. I had a severe urge to squeeze her tighter and keep her glued to me.

Her scent overpowered my nostrils. It was still her but slightly different and . . . she was a wolf?

How was that possible? No one shifted past eighteen and she was already twenty-six.

"How could you be so foolish?" I snapped, pent up frustration exploding.

She remained frozen as she stared at me. Her temper flashed in her gaze.

My shoulders tightened as a scent of a male filled my nose. "Do nae speak to her like that."

Shock locked me in place. Who was he to demand anything, especially about *my* mate?

His smell was all over her. My already overstimulated wolf wasn't having it, he ripped forward, fur exploding out, and I lunged at him.

He shifted midair, twisting and snarling. I skidded through the snow but quickly got my footing, setting my gaze on him. I mirrored his lowered head and flicked back ears. His shoulders bunched and then he took another shot at me which I avoided. In the same motion, I lashed out, dragging my claw across his leg. Blood splattered across the white blanket of snow. He lunged forward, spit dripping from his teeth as he opened his maw. I wasn't going to be quick enough to avoid it.

He suddenly careened to a halt, his muzzle wide open.

Snow sprayed in my eyes and then Willow was between us. Chest heaving, her lips were set in a thin line. *She was pissed.* Practically spitting obscenities with her gaze.

The gray wolf's teeth clicked together, and he growled but didn't move forward to continue our fight.

I wasn't liking this—

A sudden force rammed into me from the side. My body thumped against a rock, a sting radiating from the gash in my side. Shoving off the pain, I faced my attacker.

What the ever fuck was that?

It was similarly colored to the other wolf but much larger. The form monstrous and standing on slightly bowed legs. His face remained wolf, but with a much larger muzzle and the teeth to go with it.

Willow threw her hands up in . . . exasperation? Then charged at the creature. I sucked in a breath, instinctively trying to call out to her but my wolf form wouldn't allow it. She pulled back her arm and released a sudden fist into the *thing's* side, but it didn't even budge. It just looked down at her and roared.

My heart was about to pound out of my chest, but this wasn't the time for me to lose it. I'd taken down big opponents before, but nothing like that. I was already hurtling through the snow, my aim to get *it* away from her.

I expected her to jump out of the way when she saw me coming at them, but instead, she put up a hand, forcing me to careen to a stop.

The wolf beast lowered his head, snarling teeth coming right at me until Willow gripped its ear and twisted it. He roared, body hunched as he tried tugging free, but she wouldn't let go.

I gawked, watching it happen.

Then she yanked at a wad of fur on the back of my neck. If I tried pulling away, I'd just rip a hunk of my coat out, but I was more concerned with hurting her. I begrudgingly fixed my glare on her. Her mouth moved with an obvious *no*.

She shoved as she released me and turned her back to me, facing the beast. She'd released its ear and pressed both palms to his stomach and pushed. I didn't know what shocked me more, her calm in the face of it or how it let her force him to retreat a step. The monster sneezed hard.

"Enough, Rowan," the wolf I'd fought with ordered, the

dominance lifting the hair on my body. Before I could pounce on him, Willow signed.

*"What are you doing here?"* Willow's teeth clicked together. It was a gamble, but I needed to communicate with her, so I let my shift pulse over my body. I stood before her naked, my cock pointing toward her. The way her gaze dropped to it and her pink tongue flicked over her lip didn't escape me. *"Don't you have a chosen mate to go back to?"* The color was high on her cheeks, flushing them pink. Those angry sparks in her eyes and the jealousy peeking out made my chest expand. A smirk tilted my lips. She cared. Why had she acted like she didn't when we argued? Even telling me to go to another woman. *That* concern had taken second place while finding her swallowed me up. With that one look, all my doubts about her feelings for me evaporated.

The dark-haired fucker who'd shifted into a human was still looking at me. His lip lifting in a sneer.

"Step away from her," I snarled. My wolf felt restless and although hostile toward the other males, there was also almost a . . . begrudging acceptance?

What the fuck was going on?

*"Please stop, Den. They're my mates."*

No. They must have tricked her. She was *my* mate. Why was she protecting them?

"Lies," I hissed, striding forward and gripping her shoulder to jerk her toward me. She resisted and pressed her hand into the other man's stomach, way too close to his dick. Up close, the creature was larger than I thought.

My body shook with restrained rage. I wanted nothing more than to hold her tightly to my chest, but I refused to trap her hands when they were her only form of communicating.

*"I'm an Omega."*

Her signed words echoed in my head, rounding and rounding torturously. What the fuck?

The title sounded familiar. As an Alpha I'd learned about all sorts of shit, but the details avoided me. I never despised myself more for rushing through shit that didn't keep my focus.

Her brown eyes stared up at me through her long lashes. Her sharp, defined look—short-cropped hair, a beautifully pointed nose, and sharp features—remained still. She used to insult her looks and height, but after I'd snapped at her about it, she stopped. She was beautiful.

Her scent hadn't escaped my nostrils. A sweetness that lifted the hair on my arms.

Resolve tightened my spine. Despite what she was about to explain, she would not push me away again. The first time I'd allowed it and bided my time, but it would no longer work that way. She wouldn't leave my side again.

# Willow

My arms twinged from signing so much. It'd been so long since I'd been able to communicate like this.

As I finished explaining Omegas, a glint of understanding flashed through his gaze. I curled my toes inside the boots, the cold still clinging even after I pulled them back on.

"And they had multiple fucking mates," Camden muttered. "I remember thinking how shit it'd be to share your true mate—"

My shoulders jerked back, forcing him to cut off.

My heart shuddered at his words. He *would* be the one to have a difficult time with it. How could he not? It was him and me for the longest time. In his eyes, I would bring two new werewolves into the picture. He'd be the mate to ask me to come away with him. A choice I wouldn't make.

Camden shook his head as he looked at Kit and then Rowan.

"And I'm assuming since they had their *other* form—they fucked you already?"

My eyes slid closed at his comment. It was posed as a

question, but he didn't mean for me to answer it, since it was pretty damn obvious.

Sweet baby werewolf, this was giving me a migraine.

He was having a difficult time, but I was on cloud nine. It was taking everything in me to not ask them to hold me. The hollow feeling in my chest that occasionally haunted me was soothed with Camden's proximity.

"How dare you put your filthy hands on her?" Camden's chest rumbled, and the snow crunched under Kit's steps. I slipped between them, ending up smushed between them.

Rowan paced, but didn't get involved.

The only two that seemed to have real beef were Kit and Camden. The hate-filled looks they exchanged over my head weighed on me.

I slapped my hands against their chests and stamped my foot once.

"Willow Suarez, you're going home with me."

*"Don't full name me! Enough is enough, Camden. I want you to translate my next words."*

Camden's jaw bunched, and I tipped my chin up. He was generally rash and angry, but he'd listen to me.

*"Do not hurt each other. I don't expect you to get along, but hurting one another will hurt me."* The red flush deepened on Camden's neck. His tell when he was pissed. *"Translate that, Camden."* I shoved his arm. He scowled.

"She said she's leaving with me," Camden said instead, and I gasped.

"No," Kit snarled, grabbing my arm in a punishing grip.

I whirled and shook my head at Kit. His gaze was wide and frantic. Turning back to Camden, I shoved him.

His jaw twitched.

"Fine," he snapped. "She said if we hurt each other, it'll hurt her."

I nodded quickly, looking at Kit.

The hard grip he had on me relaxed, the tension slightly melting away.

My brain hurt and an overwhelming pressure compounded on my chest.

This was too much for me.

I needed space.

*"Give me a moment."*

I whirled on my heels and rushed back toward the house, snow kicking up around me.

My brain was in shambles and it was pissing me off. I wanted the calm. Not all this drama. I wanted to live in peace.

My third mate was someone I'd always wanted and loved, but could never be with. And now he wanted to take me back to Redwood Pack.

One mate wanted to return to be Alpha to his pack and the other one wanted to get me back to our pack. It was a fucking mess. I didn't want to live in either. I'd never been happier than I was in the middle of nowhere with my mates.

I slammed Kit's bedroom door open and headed directly to the cell phone connected to the charger, plucked it off, and powered it on.

The date . . . Just as I'd thought, it'd been two months since I'd been snatched from that parking lot.

I licked my lips and tugged the collar of my shirt.

It was too stifling in here. I punched in my mom's number as I exited the house. She was the only one that would understand my fears.

There was no sight of my mates. Good, they needed to give

me space. Now that I made my stance clear on them not fighting, I needed to be alone for a moment.

The snow crunched under my boot as I stalked away from the house.

> It's Willow. I'm calling, so be ready.

A few moments later, my call went through. I exhaled shakily and chose a random rock to drop onto as I took the call on speaker so I could text as she spoke.

It was how we always communicated, since it saved tons of time.

"I thought you were dead," Nola said, her voice tight. A thickness in my throat made it hard to swallow.

I understood the underlying question. She wanted to know if I was calling for help.

> No, I'm safe. I shifted.

A gasp and then silence.

"Why are you calling me if you shifted?" Panic filled her voice. "I have sons, Willow, one is a baby. If someone catches wind that I know what you are, they'll use my family to get to you. How could you be so selfish?"

Her words had taken on a frantic edge. I hadn't considered that, but now that she mentioned it, guilt hit me. I licked my lips.

> No one knows I'm an Omega.

"It won't be long until they find out. Your aunt thought the same and they burned down our house when I was a child! They killed everyone but me—" There was a shuffle.

"Is everything okay, Nola?"

It was male's voice.

"Yes, love, just handling some business, I'll be done soon."

She'd always hidden me from her human husband. Her voice came clearer, as if she was hunching close to the phone.

"Although Hector and I are no longer together, I worry for his safety if you're around. I hope you make the appropriate choices. Please take care and don't call me again."

The call clicked off and the phone fell out of my limp hand. I'd meant *that* little to her?

When she ditched me as a kid, she drilled it in my head that I must never shift, but I hadn't expected her to cut me off completely.

The only reason she'd agreed to keep in contact was to answer my questions, stipulating that if she thought us speaking was a danger, she wouldn't be able to keep a relationship with me. But I never thought she'd meant it. My lip trembled, and I closed my eyes, breathing deeply to get it together.

I shouldn't feel this level of hurt and shock.

Wrapping my arms around my stomach, I hugged myself.

Still, she was my mother and I'd craved our conversations. Even if our interactions were short and far apart.

I didn't want to contact her again. That feeling of being small . . . I hated it. I'd always had that knot in my throat after communicating with her and it made me feel like shit.

A tear got caught on my eyelash and I sucked in a breath as it dripped off and plunked onto the snow.

I pressed my hands to my face, shaking. Arms wrapped

around my waist and Camden's familiar cedar musk filled my senses, causing a shiver down my spine.

"Don't listen to her bullshit."

I remained tense in his arms, using every drip of control to not fall apart.

"Let's go back and forget all this—"

I straightened, frowning.

*"Did you forget I'm an Omega?"*

"I'd want you even if you were a worm, Willow," he snapped.

Even as a worm? A warmth flooded my chest, but I forced my brain back on track.

*"I'm not leaving. I don't want to live in the pack. Any pack."*

"That's fine. It works better for me. I accumulated a healthy savings account. I'll buy you a place wherever—"

*"I am not leaving."* I was responding belligerently, but I couldn't help it. My heart was still throbbing from the hurt after the talk with Nola. *"Weren't you going to be Alpha? Your life was all set for you, why are you even here? Did my dad send you?"* I pushed to my feet.

"No one sent me." Camden's jaw bunched and he stood too, I had to tilt my head to keep eye contact. He had the whole unkempt caveman thing going for him. "I wanted to be Alpha of the pack for you."

I scoffed. *"For me? Did you take Meridith to our spot for me too?"* My hands shook with restrained frustration. This was the last conversation we should have right now. I was feeling explosive, angry, sad. It was all too much. I kicked snow at him, and it smacked his bare chest. His eyebrows were high on his forehead and that telling flush crept up his neck. *"How do I know you don't want me just because I shifted? How convenient that it's now that you're making a move?"* It sounded illogical, even to my ears, since I pushed him away first. It was stupid. It was fear. He'd always had my back, and I'd never not felt cared for by him. But was he only saying this because he discovered I was his fated mate?

"Do you have such little faith in me? After everything we'd been through? *I was planning our future together,"* he hissed.

*"You know what? Leave. I don't need you. I have two other mates."*

I didn't stop signing and I really should have. It was messed up. Mean. Hurtful. I wouldn't go back with him, and it was best we have a clean break.

"Enough," he roared.

I gaped up at Camden. His chest heaved as he stared down at me.

I'd pushed him too far. Rage morphed his expression into something terrifying.

"Willow," he breathed so low it made the hairs lift on my neck. "You have always and will always belong with me."

His muscles twitched, chest swelling in a rough gust.

*"Den, please, give me space."* I hurried away, hugging myself.

Nola didn't deserve my emotions. I knew where I stood with her all along, but it stung like a bitch.

And now Camden was here, upending everything.

He was my mate. I swallowed past the thick ball in my throat. And he didn't get along with my other mates.

I exhaled, quickening my stride. A short walk to release the energy and then I would take another shower. Sitting in the hot water with the door locked sounded perfect, but I needed to clear my mind before returning because as much as I hated admitting it, I was weak for them.

As I stalked around the trees, I kicked up snow, watching it descend with a satisfying plunk. It was oddly relaxing. Snow crunched as someone approached. Which of my mates was coming?

A palm pressed over my nose. The same scent that filled my nostrils when I was taken from my car. No! I jerked my elbow backward and hit something soft. I couldn't go so easily like last time.

My worst fear . . . I was discovered. Were my mates okay?

I whimpered. If they were attacking them, no, killing them while I was being taken—I would never forgive myself.

I should have left instead of allowing my selfish needs to overpower me.

# WILLOW

My cheek pressed into a soft surface. A cloying scent lingered in my nose. Not again . . .

"Her breathing changed," a male voice said.

My lashes fluttered open and I lunged at the man staring at me. He winced as my fist hit his junk. There was no way I was letting him take advantage of me. Spurring his anger until he killed me was the only option because if I had my heat under their thumb . . .

Never. My fist shook as I slammed it into his stomach. His breath puffed out and I pulled back, sweeping my eyes across the room.

"Stop!"

I frowned. *Bria?*

"Sorry, Willow, I didn't know he'd do this." I narrowed my eyes at her. After I gave her orange juice . . . I shook my head. Conniving bitch. "You're scaring her, Alpha."

I turned back to the male and scowled. He was still rubbing his dick with his nose wrinkled.

He seemed *really* young.

Ah, that was what Bria meant when she asked Kit to return. He seemed sloppy.

"Sorry, Willow. I did nae mean tae scare you."

His eyes formed small halfmoons full of pain.

"I told him we should have asked Kit, but he had a point, he would nae let you leave his side." Bria approached and handed me a notepad with a pen hooked into the sleeve. "Alpha didn't bring you here in the best way, but after seeing you were an Omega, there really was no choice."

Shit. Were they going to force me to do something or, or—

"Can we come in now?" A woman with salt-and-pepper hair poked her head around the small door opening. What was going on here?

The room I was in was like any bedroom, if very bland. It didn't seem occupied based on the bare mattress and blank walls. The woman pushed the door open the rest of the way, holding the hand of a little girl.

What? . . .

She looked to be around eleven years old, but that wasn't what forced me to step back, it was the intense scent of lavender and another smell uniquely like *us*. My wolf pushed forward, sensing someone similar.

Omega.

My mouth dropped open. The dark-haired girl's eyes widened on mine and she tipped her head to the side.

A man with silver hair shuffled forward with her and he shared a look with the salt-and-pepper haired woman.

I scribbled across the notepad.

"*When*?" I lifted it.

"She shifted when she was seven while Kit was our Alpha," Bria responded. I gasped. I knew we had the ability to shift early on, but fuck. There were consequences of not being informed. "Morag and Clyde adopted her."

How was she still safe?

*"No one hurts her?"* I gripped the pen so tightly that it burned.

"The entire pack knows. Kit made sure to dispose of anyone he thought would be a threat a long time ago. Now that it's my job to protect my pack, I figured you could give us some pointers for when she's older."

I lifted my brow at the Alpha. I could see why Kit was overall okay to leave the pack in his hands. He was sloppy, but he seemed to care.

"Alpha Jace was only following my request, Willow," Morag said, fingers flexing on the girl's shoulder.

The things I knew about Omega's flashed in my mind and I quickly scribbled.

"She's never had a heat." My shoulders relaxed, relieved. It made sense since she hadn't had her period. "What we were wondering about was matings. How did you know?"

It wasn't something I could explain well. It was something I *knew* based off scent and my reaction. As for them not asking her to use her ability was shocking . . . and reassuring. The Omega Call was a coveted ability where we could call forward the wolf of any defective werewolf. It was a big motivator for keeping hidden, because although helping was good, the consequences of being used and abused were much too high.

Omegas were thought to be gone, so if a desperate pack heard of another having an Omega, it would create chaos.

"We found her when she was a babe," Morag said. My face must blare my questions. "Introduce yourself, little lass," the woman prodded, in her thick accent.

The young girl blinked up at me.

I wiggled my fingers at her and she smiled, huddling behind her mother's arm.

A roar from outside shook the wall.

"I knew it would nae take him long." Bria grimaced. "He's going to be pissed."

"I'll escort him in," Clyde said and left. He was only gone a moment before Kit stormed into the room, Camden on his heels and Rowan's wolf head lowered with his teeth bared. Morag pulled the girl back.

Clyde stumbled back in, palming his cheek.

Jace stormed forward, going chest-to-chest with Kit.

My mate's eyes spat fire and he sneered. "I'd kill you if you hadn't left me that message that you took her." Jace stumbled back, catching himself. Rowan prowled in front of me, attempting to block me from the fight. I shook my head, sighing.

"I don't owe him any consideration." Camden stormed forward and slammed his fist into Jace's other cheek. He grunted, stumbling back. He snarled and shot forward, but Camden easily slammed him back down.

Before he could continue the pissing contest, I threw the notepad at Camden, and it hit him in the face and fell to the ground. The girl giggled and I couldn't help the grin spreading across my lips.

Camden glared at me and I motioned for him to stop. Clyde stepped in front of the girl, focusing on Rowan.

Frowning, I slipped my hand over Rowan's neck. Clyde's jaw tightened and looked away.

"Rowan killed his brother," Bria stage-whispered toward

me. "And killed Jace's cousin." I winced and tugged Rowan's fur. No wonder.

Jace stood back up, brushing himself off.

"I was doing it for the kid, Kit," he muttered belligerently. "You made your choice to leave the pack to me. A little respect would be nice."

"You took my mate," Kit snarled, rage molting his expression.

"We didn't harm her, and besides only the people in this room know!" he retorted belligerently.

"I'm going to knock this kid out." Camden wasn't helping the situation and the girl looked terrified.

I huffed and clapped my hands together once. The slap resonated through the room and everyone's attention turned toward me. Briskly stomping forward, I stepped in front of Kit, forcing him back.

"*Why didn't you tell me you knew an Omega?*" I smacked my opened palm into Kit's chest.

Clyde, Morag, and Jace gasped.

His brows furrowed and his lips thinned.

Kit looked toward Camden for translation but he smirked and crossed his arms. I smacked my hand into Kit's chest again and his shoulders jerked back.

"Camden," he snapped.

"That was quite a rude demand, Kit." Camden lifted his hand, tugging at a very familiar band around his wrist. *That was my hair tie*!

"Please," Kit gritted out.

"She asked why you're such a fucking dick." He smirked. "And why you didn't tell her you knew an Omega."

Kit scowled. "I wasn't intentionally hiding it from you."

I huffed and lifted my hand, palm up. I turned back to the shocked expressions of our audience and mouthed, *Sorry*, staring directly into the girl's eyes. She grinned at me.

"Would it be all right if Pen contacts you if she ever has questions, Willow?" Morag tentatively asked.

I adamantly nodded and her expression slackened, her shoulders lowering with a deep exhale.

"We're leaving," Kit snapped and gripped my wrist.

"Do you nae miss being Alpha?" Jace taunted. Kit tensed, his fingers flexing around my wrist. He released me and slammed his fist into the kid's face.

Camden shuffled me through the door, his palm flat on my spine.

"It's a pretty small pack, but I want you out of here before anyone catches your scent. They might not hurt the Omega kid, but you're fresh meat," Camden explained, rushing me out. I stumbled over my feet and he pulled me into his arms, hurrying to the old truck a few feet away. My mind wandered as he buckled me in.

Kit never responded to Jace's comment, did that mean he missed it? Was I holding him back?

As soon as Kit parked the car in his driveway, I hopped out. My mind overflowed with information.

"Lass," Kit called gruffly and Rowan whined. I slammed the door, ignoring them.

"I got her," Camden said and the crunch of his footsteps followed. I rolled my eyes up at the sky. What, now they were communicating? I scoffed.

I was completely on edge. I couldn't get Kit's look out of my head and it burned in the back of my corneas.

And the tension in my throat wasn't helping.

I needed *something*.

Scrubbing my fingers into my scalp, I attempted to calm my heart rate.

"What is your problem, Willow?" Camden snapped. I ignored him and continued trudging. A small part of me was glad he followed because this was what got me kidnapped the last time. "I bet I know."

My teeth clicked together at his mocking tone.

"Do you fear one of your mates rather remain with his pack than with you?" My shoulders jerked and I lowered my head, continuing my stomping. "I saw the way you looked at him after the taunt. It was pure fear—"

I whirled and pushed him, my chest heaving. Camden smirked.

"You have this tendency to run from things that scare you—"

I shoved him again and signed, *"Whatever Den!"* A sudden stillness washed over his muscles and I licked my lips, clenching my thighs together. That covetous look in his eyes . . . I hadn't seen it in so long. I exhaled, the breath shuddering from my lungs. I needed him. Ached for him to fuck me. The restlessness eating up my insides was all for it.

I took off running.

The snow slowed me down, but I used all my energy to push my legs forward. I weaved around a rock and turned sharply.

His rough exhales reached my ears as I ran and a gush of

wetness throbbed through my core. Fuck, this was turning me on.

My wolf thought we were playing. Her excitement bled into me and if I was in her form, I'd be wagging my tail.

His heavy weight brought me to the ground and we grappled, tossing up snow with our efforts. I shoved at his chest, but I wasn't fighting and if the sneering smirk on his lips was anything to go by, he knew it.

I panted as he gripped my clothing and tore in two. I yanked back, rolling to my feet as he tossed the ripped sweater, the shirt along with it. Backing up, my back flattened against a tree.

Den approached with wide strides.

"I've missed you," he growled, gripping my hips. Another gush of arousal pulsed through my core. The tree braced me, and I didn't remove my gaze from him as I unbuttoned my jeans and shoved them down, kicking them to the side.

I was blistering to the point of not feeling the cold. He gripped my thighs and hoisted me up, spreading my pussy as he balanced me on a thigh. My lips parted as he stared at my glinting flesh. Camden was messing with my insides and unraveling that knot in my throat.

His finger dipped into my entrance, swirling slightly. When he retracted his hand, he spread my juices on my lips.

He leaned forward and took my mouth, sucking and nipping.

"I love you," he said against my lips, ripping the breath from my chest. Camden slid his shaft into my channel and groaned. "I missed this."

I missed his cock. It was as I remembered, with a slight curve upward. My breathing stuttered and I writhed my hips, taking every inch of him. Camden shook, his hips slapping against my thighs with quick pumps.

His shoulders curved forward and bones popped. I cried out as his length twitched inside me and my channel clutched at him needfully. Sweet baby werewolf, that felt too good.

Camden groaned, lips parted as I wrenched forward his monstrous shift. His teeth elongate as his jawbone popped and stretched forward. Red fur exploded from his skin in a beautiful ripple, tickling my inner thighs near where he speared me.

His cock thickened, sucking the breath from my lungs. The slight curve to his dick made the expansion toe-curling as the tip prodded my g-spot. I jostled, my clit rubbing against the shaft, setting off an orgasm. My belly tightened and my head fell back as it shuddered over my spine. *He loved me.*

My legs twitched in his hold, flexing around the wide spread of his hips.

His knot swelled, stretching my channel even more. Pain mingled with ecstasy. Looking down, I stared at the base of his smooth pink cock.

He withdrew slightly, making his knot pop out. The sensation rocked through my senses. Den slid back the pink flesh of his bulbous knot back inside me. He slowly slid out, moisture dripping from his shaft as he poised at my entrance.

Stillness came over my muscles and I held my breath, waiting for him to move. Another moment passed as he panted, then he pounded into me. The tree shuddered and my mouth parted on a silent cry.

Again and again he thrust, mercilessly driving his knot in and out of me as it thickened. Snow fell around us from where it'd collected on the treetops. The small flakes landing on him, melted into his fur. Another orgasm flooded my veins, and I couldn't stop moving on him.

"Fuck," he snarled, stilling inside me.

Camden's head bowed, exhaling so hard my hair fluttered around my cheeks. He whined, shoulders and legs shaking. His clawed hands spread my thighs wider, and his knot ballooned.

A shudder wracked his body, and my thighs jerked with each jut of his release. It filled me to the brim until it seeped out around his knot.

My head fell forward, thumping on his chest. My fingers buried into the fur at his stomach, rubbing. How did my mates still have fucking abs in this form? It was like the fur moved in the pattern of the slopes.

I didn't want to move.

His cum dripped down my thigh and he dropped to his knees, keeping his grip on me. My thighs widened, lifting with the change in position. He shuddered, sniffing into my hair.

I moved, but the pressure stilled me. His knot was still swollen. A wave of pleasure squeezed through my channel and Camden groaned. I scratched his fur, spawning a purr in his chest.

I never thought I'd be in this position with Camden.

Now I just needed all my mates wrapped around me.

I rested my cheek against his chest and looked into the forest. The snow was truly beautiful, though I may have been singing a different tune if I wasn't wrapped around my oven-hot mate.

Wait a moment. The tree shuddered.

*Crack.*

I tossed my body to the side, tearing myself off his thickened knot.

*Fuck, that hurt.* I squeezed my thighs together, wincing.

Camden gawked at me before he disappeared under a huge pile of snow that fell from the tree we'd just banged against.

# Willow

A SHADOW MOVED OUT OF THE CORNER OF MY EYE and the hair on the back of my neck lifted. My wolf clawed forward and I gave in to her, trusting her instincts.

I bounded away from a sputtering Camden as he clumsily clawed free of the pile of snow. The shadow moved farther away and I took off at a sprint directly toward it.

My sides heaved as I pushed myself harder, running faster than I had before.

I careened around a mossy cliff and climbed up the incline. The tobacco scent was familiar. I pushed harder, seeing a dip in the snow about five feet long. I needed to catch him.

With my hind legs, I shoved off the edge, jumping to the other side. I slowed, lowering my head as my ears twitched.

"You shouldn't have run from me."

Snow kicked up with how fast I turned. That was why the smell was so familiar. I showed my teeth, lowering close to the ground as I inched to the side. A naked man watched me, those dead, evil eyes roving over me.

He'd been the one that held me in that basement. He

continued moving in a slight angle, and I kept my eyes on him. My wolf wanted to lunge and tear his throat out, but I needed to bide my time for the perfect moment.

"I saw you fucking that thing." His eyes were small pinpricks. He licked his lips, an odd tension on his face. "You're an Omega," he breathed. That expression was of reverence.

I stopped my momentum forward. I thought that was why he'd taken me. That he hunted down Omegas. He shifted and charged me, teeth dripping saliva. Shit. I scrambled back on instinct.

A red-furred wolfman slammed into him so hard he went flying.

Camden clawed downward. Blood exploded with the wolf's cry as his body slammed on the ground. Kit appeared, stomping on the wolf's tail, wrenching a cry from him. He bared his teeth at Rowan, stopping him from slicing his claws into him and finishing the job Camden started.

"Shift," Kit snarled. The wolf trembled.

I stumbled to my feet as the man shifted.

"Please don't kill me. Please," Uggo whimpered. He curled on his side. Sick fascination swirled in my gut. I hope their attack hurt him.

A heavy furred palm rested on my shoulder, and I looked up at Camden.

I signed at Camden to translate for me.

"How does that—" He turned to the man. "Why did you take her?"

"Answer," Kit said, growling as he stepped on the man's ankle.

"I bought her," he shouted, hiccuping.

"You bought an Omega?"

"I didn't know she was an Omega," he yelped. If he hadn't known I was an Omega, then what? He just purchased a werewolf for fun?

The look on his face told me that was exactly it. My stomach churned from the memory of the dead body I'd been locked up with.

"What about the dead girl you locked me up with?" Camden asked the question for me, his jaw clenching tightly.

"S-she couldn't satisfy my needs," he said high-pitched. This gross piece of crap. What a sick individual.

"Who did you buy her from?" Camden's hands shook.

He whimpered when Kit pressed down harder. "I don't know."

A snap tore through the air with his scream. Rowan bent over and tore through his neck, detaching it from his body with a pop.

I stumbled back into Camden from the sudden bloodshed.

"He hurt mate," was all Rowan said. I couldn't deny that Uggo's spasming muscles were satisfying, but I *wanted* to know why he had me and who he had purchased me from. I avoided looking at the stringy meat from his torn neck and pulled out the cell phone he had tied to his ankle.

"Let's go," Kit's voice rumbled.

Camden scoffed and I turned to glare at him.

*"Weren't you leaving?"*

He growled and gripped my arm, pulling up. I dangled from his claws as he swung me on his back. I wrapped my legs and arms around his body, hanging on as he took off running.

Kit sprinted past us in wolf form. I'd rather hop on one of them in that form. They were fucking huge anyway, they could definitely carry me like that.

It didn't take Camden long to get us back to the house. He strode inside, ignoring the dirty look from Kit, and lowered me to the ground.

I took off toward the room and sank into the edge of the bed, swiping at the phone. Shit, it was locked. I tried a few combinations, guessing the simplest numbers . . . but nothing.

I gritted my teeth, squeezing the device.

"Of course you're looking through it." I jumped, the phone flinging from my palm. Kit caught it and attempted to swipe through. I didn't miss Camden's expression of irritation.

"It requires a passcode?" Feeling Kit's gaze on me, I shrugged sheepishly.

"I understand your need to find out who sold you, Will, but you need to talk to me about it." I could hear the irritation in Camden's tone.

"I'll find out for you." I scowled at Kit next. And that was exactly why I didn't want to involve them. They'd want to protect me.

"I like that idea, now we're speaking the same language," Camden said, a smirk on his lips. I rubbed my palm across my face. Oh, great . . . "I have a guy in England that can unlock the phone. I'll make a few calls so we can meet up with him tomorrow." I perked up. "You can wait here—"

My teeth clicked together, and I grabbed a pillow and tossed it at him. It smacked into his chest.

*"Nope. I'm going with or without you,"* I signed.

"You don't know my contact's number."

*"You think I don't know you direct message. I have your social media passwords. I can find out."*

Camden sighed, lips twitching. It meant that if they tried to leave me behind, I would find a way to go, which Camden knew.

"I don't need the translation to understand what that means. I'll grab the luggage from my storage to pack some clothing for you," Kit said gruffly and exited. "Let's go, Rowan."

I watched him depart, his spine like an arrow. A weight settled on my chest. His tone was low and tight. Upset.

Did he want to let me go now that I had another mate? He wasn't showing me any of his emotions. He hadn't even addressed how he'd known an Omega, and not only that, protected her. I scowled and quickly caught myself. There was no need to be jealous over a child. Maybe he thought I was too much of a problem to keep around, and he wasn't wrong. My body stiffened at the thought of not having him.

"He's efficient, at the very least."

Ignoring Den, I pulled open Kit's drawer and plucked out clothes for Camden, which he tugged on.

"You dropped your cell phone after your conversation with your mom, I left it on the stand near the door." It had completely slipped my mind, and although grateful, I held back my thank you and continued digging through the drawers.

I pulled another open to find him some socks and stared at the contents, stunned. My nose burned seeing the carefully folded clothing in multiple shades. Kit had purchased a lot more than I'd expected.

I cleared my throat to calm the swell of emotion.

"We weren't done with our conversation."

Well, I was. My shoulders dropped and I sighed.

*"What else do you have to say?"*

"Why didn't you trust me with this?" The accusation in his

tone was gone as opposed to earlier. He'd calmed enough to process. "You could have shifted a long time ago."

*"What part don't you get that Omega's were hunted to extinction, or at least to the point where any surviving Omegas went into hiding?"*

"You don't think I could have protected you?"

*"Why is it even relevant? It feels like you wouldn't have wanted me if I hadn't shifted."* That visibly took the wind out of his sails and he sighed.

"That's not what I mean. I hate the thought of you hiding something from me. Even when I didn't know you were my mate, you had me," he said gruffly and stepped into my space.

His cheek pressed against my face and I shivered.

"We've always argued. But now I can kiss you until you forgive me."

And I was goo. His palm pressed into my spine, forcing my back to bow toward his heat since he was still bending down, pressing his cheek to mine.

He groaned against my ear and pulled me with him to the bed. The mattress creaked under his weight, and he spread his legs to accommodate pulling me between them.

His lips pressed to mine, tongue slipping between my lips. His thick cock nudged my stomach, twitching. I mimicked his groan.

If I continued down this path, I was going to fuck him again. I yanked away from him, breathing hard. There were places to be and getting distracted by dick needed to hold off.

I scurried away from him.

# KIT



My stomach did that somersaulting thing it had done since he'd shown up. Then it had all worsened after my old pack took her. If she leaned more on him, it was my fault. I should have told her more about the kid, but the primary thing on my mind was Willow. Now she would turn to him because of my lapse in judgment.

I had watched them, my limbs tensed and stomach cramped. The way they moved around each other and how she treated him with such ease . . .

It made me feel like an interloper. My stomach tightened.

There wasn't anything I wanted to fall back on. Not my role as pack Alpha, not my brother, nothing. Jace's comment got under my skin and I'd let anger overrule me when I should have swept Willow out of there as Camden had. I rubbed my palm over my hair.

I just wanted her to look at me the way she looked at him.

Rowan growled as he yanked the shirt down, making his hate for clothing evident.

He seemed to take Camden's arrival better than I did.

Was he the true reason she was so reluctant to remain with us? When she tried so hard to leave us at first?

A bitterness crawled up my throat at the thought.

I envied the ease of his communication with her.

I wanted that.

Resolve loosened the knot in my gut.

I'd already decided to learn sign language, so it *would* be similar for me too. I scrubbed my fingers through my hair, pushing my fingertips against my scalp.

She was dead set on finding the people behind her kidnapping, but her resolve did not outshine mine. They caused her leeriness when she first slammed into my life and they must pay for that.

She didn't mention it, but the way she popped out of bed, or suddenly tensed up when she woke up wasn't lost on me. My lovely mate struck me as the sort to push through, never showing anything got to her. She appeared to be someone who had to keep many things to herself. Willow needed to learn to rely on me, but I would take it day by day as to not spook her.

Since she came into my life, I didn't spare a thought to returning as a pack Alpha—no longer was it an incessant longing gnawing at me like it used to be.

I'd been going through the motions the entire time, knowing my past pack, Invern Pack, would eventually need me. As much as Jace cared, he was still too young of an Alpha, but now . . . he must truly take on the role because I would never return. It shouldn't be difficult for him. He'd learned everything underneath me, which he'd taken advantage of by taking my mate. My cheek fluttered with how hard I clenched my teeth. He was lucky I had not killed him.

When Willow showed up, for the slightest second, hope bloomed that a return to my role as Alpha would be possible. She controlled Rowan . . . but the pack was full of old-fashioned werewolves that would have an issue with how I put Willow's needs first, and I wouldn't subject her through any conflict.

A low chuckle came from my bedroom, and I gritted my teeth. Camden was too comfortable with my mate.

Accepting the leftover scraps may be the only option I had, but it caused a block in my throat to thicken.

If she went back with him . . .

I couldn't allow it.

# WILLOW

The sharp mix of air freshener and cleaning products in the public bathroom stung my nose. The airport had me on *edge* and Kit, Rowan, and Camden were making it worse. Each time I twitched, one of them was scanning the area. The fortunate part was it wasn't badly crowded, so the concern of a werewolf finding me was low, added to that was their extreme caution whenever I entered a new area.

Even going to the restroom by myself had been an argument. What was worse was getting Camden to translate me exactly and not use his own little twists and turns of phrases. But I eventually got my way.

I pounded on the little knob again to get the spout to continue to spit out water. It shut off too quickly. I hurriedly rubbed the soap off my hands.

I couldn't stop thinking about Kit's tone. Was there an underlying sadness he attempted to hide? A sick feeling churned in my gut.

Yanking the paper towels from the dispenser, I quickly dried my hands and tossed it as the water from another sink ran.

The hair lifted on the back of my neck. My wolf was sensing another werewolf nearby. I whirled, prepared to slam my foot out and take off running. I wouldn't have much of a choice, considering I couldn't shout out for help.

"You're an Omega, what are you doing not hiding your scent," a girl asked, leaning slightly forward with her hands behind her. I had to turn my head down to peer into her gaze. She grinned up at me, approachable. Nice.

I squinted at her and swept my gaze around the bathroom.

"Don't worry, I checked if anyone was here before I asked," she said, lowering her voice a few octaves. "I'm Evie," she added, smiling wide. Her eyes glinted with happiness and mischief.

I licked my lips, on the fence on whether I should take off running. Evie gripped the straps of the small sage-colored backpack.

I'd never seen coloring like hers. Her skin was a shade paler than mine and straight, dark hair framed her face.

"I'm not a murderer or anything."

Well, that was good to know. My shoulders relaxed at her use of humor.

"I'm an Omega."

That was probably more shocking than anything else she could have said. I fished out my cell phone and rapidly texted. I inhaled deeply and frowned.

*You don't smell like one.* She only smelled of werewolf. I didn't scent her Omega, yet my wolf was on edge. I lifted it to her and understanding flashed in her gaze as she caught on quickly.

I worried being found by other werewolves, but the need to know who was trying to kill me overpowered my concern. It wasn't like I wasn't taking precautions though. Kit swept through the airport before I came in to make sure there were no other werewolves. Looked like didn't check the bathrooms.

"A recipe was passed down in my family. My cousin taught me when we were kids. It *really* came in handy," she muttered the last bit. "Actually, do you want some? Because, let me tell you, you best hide your Omega unless you want to be someone's toy or breeding factory."

She unhooked the strap from her shoulder and pulled out a small vial similar to perfume testers.

She held it out. "Make sure to drink the whole thing. It should last around a week and a half. It tastes like shit, though, so I recommend pouring it in coffee or tea."

I believed her more by the second, but honestly, the possibility of it being true was too much of a temptation. Peering into her gaze, I held it. She seemed guileless. Damn it, I hoped I wasn't wrong. I uncapped it and chugged it. A bitterness coated my tongue and I gagged. Forcing myself to suck it up, I swallowed until the taste was gone.

"Damn girl, you're wild. I did that once and threw up."

*"You're not from here?"* I showed her the phone. It was more of a prompt to get her to tell me where she was from. Her lack of local accent made it obvious she'd traveled here.

"Canada. I just came down to get a breather from my stifling pack." Her cell rang and she pulled it out of her pocket and silenced it. Her button nose twitched. "It's already working."

Her phone rang again, and she sighed with exasperation.

"I turn it on for *one* second," she muttered, and the light flicked off before she shoved it back into her backpack and tugged it over her shoulders. "Damn, I wanted to see a bit of the city before I'm dragged back to my pack." She started to turn and then stopped. I met her eyes and she seemed to be grappling with something. She sighed. "Hand it over," she said, jerking her chin. I hesitantly handed it over. "Text me your address and I'll mail you some."

She fiddled with it and handed it back.

*Thank you*, I mouthed.

"We Omegas have to stick together." She started out of the restroom.

I was a few feet behind her when she yelped and froze. My boobs smacked into her backpack. Rowan stared down at her with an angry glint in his eyes. His head lowered, long hair falling across his cheeks as he stalked forward. He looked like some long-haired, vengeful god come to life.

So, *Rowan* followed me. I sighed and pulled her behind me and put my hand on his chest.

With a hard shake of my head, I bunched his shirt. He huffed. I smiled slightly at Evie as she gawked. Approaching her, I pointed at the hairband around her wrist.

"You want it?"

I nodded and she placed it in my outstretched palm.

*Thanks again*, I mouthed. Rowan growled, making her back up. I could have stolen mine back from Camden, but I kind of liked him wearing it.

"Text me," she whispered, waving as she scurried off. A glare practically burned into the side of my face and I peeked up at Rowan.

I wiggled my fingers at him with a smile while his eyes slitted. He was so suspicious about everything.

"Kit and Camden checked outside for any *others*." I got the gist. "They are waiting at the entrance." Rowan's eyebrows furrowed and his inhale was audible. He sneezed and pinched his nose, observing me with his head tilted.

He roughly brushed his hair back. He'd been struggling with it for a while. I reached up to his shoulder and tugged. Rowan leaned down, getting to my level.

Reaching over, I collected the top half of his hair into a half ponytail and tied it off. I nodded to signal I was done, but he buried his nose in my neck.

"You smell odd." I huffed as he rubbed his smooth human nose against my throat. My eyes widened and I caught the gaze of a woman with her hair cut in a bob watching us with judgment.

I clicked my tongue and gripped his hand, tugging once. He still seemed puzzled but took the lead guiding me out of the airport. The doors slid open to the cool moist air. Camden leaned against the front side of an unknown vehicle, while Kit sat in the driver seat.

*"Where'd you get the truck?"*

"The guy is scarily organized." Camden opened the door for me to slide in.

Of course, it was Kit.

Before I could pull myself up, Rowan wrapped his hands around my waist and easily hoisted me into the seat.

I just let it happen at this point. Rowan climbed in behind me and then we were driving out of the roundabout.

Kit frowned at me from the rearview mirror. All of them kept shooting me glances and rubbing their nose.

"Will, why do you . . . why is your scent different?" Camden inhaled deeply. "It's dulled."

*It worked.* I wanted to bounce in place, but I kept my excitement tempered down.

*"This werewolf girl gave me some concoction she made. It's supposed to hide me as an Omega, so I think it just gets rid of the Omega phermo—"*

"You took something a complete stranger gave you in the bathroom?" Camden asked incredulously. He was twisted toward me, his arm braced on the seat as he turned his torso. Kit's sigh was audible and he rubbed his forehead.

Heat rushed to my face. Okay, that sounded more stupid than it was . . .

I licked my lips and pouted, crossing my arms.

Whatever. It worked and that was all that mattered, now all we needed to do was get to Camden's connection.

# Willow



*"This is wasting time."* I glared at the back of Kit's head. He pulled the breakfast diner door open and waved me in as the other two shuffled me inside.

Rowan rubbed at his neck. Being in his human form *really* wasn't his favorite.

"You have to eat, Willow," Camden said, gripping my shoulder. "And how is it a waste of time? The contact can't meet with us until tomorrow morning."

Rowan pushed into my side, invading my space.

"Just the four of you?" the middle-aged waitress asked while chewing gum.

"Yes." At Camden's words, she shuffled the menus in hand and gestured for us to follow her to a booth.

Rowan got in first and Camden motioned me in next. I slipped onto the pillowy, leather seat. The other side dipped and my eyes widened. Camden was trying to sandwich me in.

I glared and pushed both palms into his arm. He paused and looked at me, red brows pulled tightly together.

*"We don't fit,"* I signed. He was going to ignore me. With a

huff, I continued, "*I want to eat without my elbows being trapped in by you guys. You two aren't small.*"

"Fine," he snapped. Kit waited near the seat across from us, with his arms crossed. Camden nodded for him to get in first.

"No, thank you, I do nae like being closed in."

"Me neither, you bag of—" I slapped my palm on the surface of the table and glared at them. People were staring. Camden sneered and pushed into the booth.

I didn't miss Kit's triumphant smirk.

I rolled my eyes. They were still such pups.

Rowan's arm wrapped around my back and his palm pressed into my side, scooting me flush to him. I attempted to stifle my smile but couldn't.

My lashes lowered in pleasure as he used the tip of his fingers to rub on the patch of skin he held me at beneath my shirt. A flood of arousal built at my belly.

"Are you fucking serious," Camden muttered, eyebrows lowered with his attention on me.

Kit moistened his lips and a red flush spread on his cheeks.

I loved the way they looked at me.

"Ready to order?"

I wrenched myself out of the thrall of his gaze as Camden ordered the food I wanted. Something called Eggy Bread.

The rest ordered two portions each, and by the time the waitress completed the order, her wide eyes almost bugged out of her head.

She went off to put in our order and I was left with my mates. Two of whom seemed to really not like each other. I didn't miss the sneers and side-eyed glares they exchanged.

"If this guy manages to get into the phone, what do you expect to do?"

*"I want to find them and ask why."*

"You can't go off half-cocked to find someone after they sold you. There are steps you take." Concern lined Camden's expression.

"You can nae needlessly place yourself in danger, Willow. If you allow me to find them for you, I will drag them to your feet." Kit's words were low and rumbling. The clinking of silverware accompanied his words.

I cleared my throat, overcome by the tension in my esophagus. His intense sincerity blared through his tone.

This *would* be their take. Of course it would be, but I didn't want to be a backseat participant. I needed to put a face to the culprit and put them down, only then could my anxiety cease.

I just tilted my head down in a short nod. I didn't want to get into it right now because if I did, I was dragging out *everything* Kit kept hidden and it wasn't the time or place. Our drinks were thumped onto the surface, and I wrapped my hands around the coffee mug.

I hummed, eyes closing as I sucked the liquid down. It also gave me the perfect escape from their pushy concern.

"I'll drive the rest of the way," Camden announced.

"I don't have faith in your driving, American," Kit said. Camden's lips tightened and I settled in for an argument.

# Willow

The rental truck roared down a road, passing four other homes with about an acre between each. The area had no trees, it was an expanse of greenery. A light drizzle fell on and off throughout the drive. Kit was bringing us to their house on the English countryside. It'd been news to me that he had another home, which made me realize I knew very little about them. Rowan or him.

After knowing Camden so long, it was natural that I knew him like the back of my hand, but I wanted the same familiarity with my other mates.

Rowan's fur tickled my arms as he pushed against my side, invading my space. As soon as we'd gotten on the road, he'd shifted into his wolfman form. He exhaled into my neck, and I leaned into him, burying my fingers into his shaggy fur.

A soft rumble rolled through Rowan's chest. The frantic thumping of my heart slowed. Sinking my teeth into my lower lip, I turned my face into Rowan, inhaling his pine and rose scent.

I needed more time in their arms. The truck hissed to a stop and Kit peered back at me, his eyebrows lowered, gaze unreadable.

His attention on me was like a stab to the chest, so I avoided his gaze, pressing my lips together. Camden was already out of the car and pulling my door open. I slid away from Rowan and jumped down.

The home was wide from the front, but from the side, the build was narrow. It stretched into two stories and was built with bricks. Moss crawled up its sides, adding to the charm of the house.

Kit pushed the door open and looked back at me. I trailed after him and pressed my fingers into the crook of his arm. The muscle twitched as he tensed, and he avoided my gaze. I felt uneasy about us already and he wasn't making it any better.

Did he not want me anymore?

The next breath I dragged into my lungs hurt. I studied his profile, taking in the taut lines of his jaw. It only took two strides for him to surpass me and my fingers limply fell off his arm.

It was a good thing if he didn't want me, then he wouldn't be embroiled in the shit following me.

If I told myself that enough, maybe I'd believe it.

The chasm grew between us, causing a fissure in my heart.

The front door opened to a small hall, about ten feet deep and then opened to a living room. I followed him as he flicked the lights on. I didn't have time to study the room before he dragged me to the side and pulled open the last door down the hall.

"I figured you'd like your own space, so I had this room remodeled." Kit's arm stretched out and I stepped into the bedroom.

A floral upholstered settee rested in the middle of the room with a crystal coffee table in front of it. A plush cream carpet lay beneath both pieces of furniture. Swirls were carved up the poles of the four-poster bed and the curtain frills matched the lining of the bed. My wolf writhed in my chest. She was happy with the space, and she ached to toss herself into the mounds of pillows and rub her face all over them.

"I also have a cozier space for your nest upstairs, but I wanted you to set that one up yourself." A grin tugged at the corners of my lips, and I whirled toward him.

Kit watched me, guarded.

It deflated my excitement. He'd been careful with me . . . I puffed out a breath and ran my fingers through my hair. What was wrong with him—no, what *had* been wrong with him?

A thump from down the hall echoed to us and he turned away, frowning. I rushed forward to grip his wrist tightly. An uncomfortable tension squeezed my chest. His eyebrows lowered.

"What is it, lass?"

I pursed lips and released his wrist. My Kit—always so patient. When he looked at me, I had his entire attention as if no one else in the world existed.

Withdrawing my hand, I shook my head and stepped back. A small indent formed between his eyebrows.

"Kit," Camden roared. Kit pivoted toward the yell, but paused, peering back at me. I pressed my palm into his shoulder blade and waved my hand to prompt him forward. A curse from outside had him striding away as I watched his wide shoulders disappear down the hall.

Palm at my chest, I rubbed in small circles to soothe the ache. Was Kit pulling away from me? No way, right? He wouldn't have brought me to his house . . . given me this room if he wanted to leave. Or maybe, he was helping me find answers and then leaving.

Shit, my chest and head hurt.

I hugged myself, attempting to hold my whirring emotions at bay. A distraction would be great right about now. Turning away from the door, I swept my gaze across the bedroom and inched close to the bed, sinking my fingers into the cream silk sheets. So soft. My attention lifted to the mass of pillows in the middle of the bed and I dropped facedown into them. I swept my arms out, hugging them close and squishing them. The bed frame creaked with my wiggles. The space was perfect for us. I froze. *If* they wanted to stay with me.

I groaned and scooted back, resting on the corner of the bed. Elegance bled from every inch of the room. My fingers traced the lace lining of the comforter. It was nice in here, but I needed all three of my mates to make it perfect.

Thumps pounded down the hall, too insistent for me not to bound to my feet. Camden poked his head in, his shirt wet and splattered with mud.

"Will, a pipe broke. Kit's shutting the valve off, but we need to head into town for supplies to fix it."

I nodded quickly. "*Okay, be careful,*" I signed.

He turned but pivoted to face me. In a couple strides, he stood before me and bowed to press his lips to my forehead, his wine-colored hair rustling with his movements.

"We will be back soon. Rowan will be here to protect you. He's staying outside until we get the water running so he can wash the mud off."

I stared up at him, taking in the planes of his face and those lips. *Do not jump him.* I laced my hands behind my back and cleared my throat.

Camden gave me one more lingering glance and left. My shoulders slumped.

At least I had Uggo's cell phone to distract myself with as they did all that. I fished both cells from my pocket and set mine on the coffee table, sank into the settee, and kicked off my shoes.

The screen was fresh for me to try again. I'd been mulling ideas on the plane ride and all I could think of was his tendency for straightening his sleeve. Uggo loved straight edges, uniformity, but no way it could be that easy, right?

He wouldn't be dumb enough to—

The phone unlocked and my eyes widened.

I popped out of the settee and bounced on my toes. I needed to tell them I'd gotten it open! A step forward and then I froze, they weren't here and Rowan was outside . . .

Nibbling on my lower lip, I dropped to the couch. Looking through it was probably best done with my mates, but a peek wouldn't hurt.

These were some *raunchy* exchanges and after each interaction, it showed he deposited money to the person he was talking to. There were so many . . . This man had *bank*.

I swiped through each conversation and the majority were sexual . . . Then I reached a conversation from weeks back.

*I have a Redwood Pack female I have to make disappear.*

My breath stalled in my lungs, and I scrolled to the top. It sounded like the two people conversing were . . . friends? It was also clear the other person was a mercenary who'd gotten other girls for Uggo.

It was the guy that snatched me! He described the coffee

shop he plucked me from. My eyes scanned the rest of the messages and I sucked in a breath. Uggo asked to make sure no one would look for me once he had me because he didn't want trouble. I snorted at that. How quaint, he didn't want trouble for holding a woman hostage.

*Nope, I looked into the account and number that contacted me and it came from the Alpha of the pack. T. Wyatt.*

My fingers went limp and the phone slipped out of my hand.

Camden Wyatt . . . The letter in front of their last name . . . Torrin.

*Why?*

I rubbed my face.

My Camden . . . my mate's father . . . ordered my kidnapping? A cramp shot through my stomach.

The only reason I could think of Torrin wanting to get rid of me was because of Camden. He wanted his son to become pack Alpha as he'd been training his entire life, and that wasn't happening because of me, but why would he go this far?

I stumbled to the restroom and pressed my palms into the counter and met my gaze in the mirror. The strands of hair were uneven and fell to about my shoulder blades. I stared into my brown eyes and lifted my fingertips to the frayed edges. Camden. I didn't want to tell him. It was horrible to even think about, and his reaction . . . I was already a main reason for their strained relationship. He never verbalized it, but Camden never forgave him for my injury. He blamed himself as much as he blamed his father.

If I told him . . . Camden would kill him, and if he killed him, it would leave Britt alone, and she didn't deserve that.

Rowan and especially Kit . . . it was already strained between my mates; this could cause them to blame Camden.

If they knew, shit would explode and they'd try to keep me out of it even though it involved *me*.

The room spun so I gripped the edge of the sink. If I went alone, I risked him hurting me, but Hector was there and as Beta, he had sway. There was no doubt in my mind he would protect me. It was enough of a safety blanket.

It was dangerous to go, but I needed to know why he would do such a thing. I needed answers, but my mates couldn't come with me.

Why would they want to be involved with someone who had so much shit following her?

Kit had already pulled away from me and Camden . . . a sharp strike of agony pierced my chest. They didn't deserve this. I needed to give them one final opportunity to bow out of my life.

I should bring up going our own ways. Maybe Kit had been distant because that was what he wanted.

*If they didn't want to be with me.* My heart shriveled at that.

First, I needed to calm myself and think.

I SAT in the sparsely decorated living room with Rowan's head on my thigh, combing my fingers through his long brown hair. His gaze hadn't wavered from my face.

By the time Kit and Camden got back, I'd already spent what felt like ages agonizing in my room. The moment the water was turned on, I stepped beneath the hot stream, hoping to clear my head. Only then did I step out of the bedroom to wait for them.

Camden walked in, rubbing his hair with a small towel, face clean shaven.

*"Call Kit, please."*

Camden frowned but called out for Kit.

I tapped Rowan for him to sit up.

Kit entered, a quizzical furrow to his eyebrows, hair still damp from his shower. Peering at Camden, I waved for him to sit and after a beat, he did. On the other hand, Kit remained standing—stubborn wolfman. My gaze bounced from one to the other.

I inhaled sharply, pulling out my phone and typing in my message. I wanted them all to hear me at once. Camden had an advantage with understanding ASL, and I could see how that hurt Kit. I clicked the button for it to read out what I typed.

"Do you guys want to be with me?"

Heat flushed my face. The voice was high-pitched and cheerful and considering what I wanted it to convey, it was not the vibe I was going for. Their gazes bore down on me. I cleared my throat, wiggling my toes within my shoes.

Camden burst into laughter and even Kit smirked. I narrowed my eyes at them.

I furiously typed the next part.

"I'm serious. I'll leave you guys alone if you want nothing to do with my baggage."

That shut them up, although there was still a slight smirk on Camden's lips.

"You want to leave with him?" Kit strode toward me, and I shot to my feet, shaking my head. His steps were precise and intimidating. I was already leaning back as he pressed into my space, rage contorting his features.

The hair on my arms lifted and I licked my lips. Electricity seemed to crackle through the air. He was *pissed* off. I cleared my throat.

This would not work.

"No. I'm talking about all of you," the cheerful voice announced.

His presence crackled, even with the space between us, and he dragged his fingers through his hair. My insecurities roared forward and I furiously typed my fears.

"Think about it, you're already acting weird with me. Detached. Is it because you want to return to your pack? You never denied Jace's claims. This will never work, Kit. I don't want to live in a pack and that's been what you've wanted." I shook my head. "It's already a mess."

Kit's jaw twitched and his eyes narrowed. His incredulity pounded at me as I furiously continued typing. "Then I find out you lied about the Omega child—"

"Enough," he snarled, his clothing bursting from his body as he grew into his monster form. "I. Did. Not. Lie." My face flushed and I gritted my teeth, getting fired up in the face of his anger. Okay, he never lied, but still! My wolf perked up at his anger, taking interest in his passionate reaction.

"You're right, you didn't lie, but you weren't forthcoming. You could have told m—"

"Excuses," he roared. The phone clattered to the ground.

"I'm surprised you caught on to her tendency, Scot."

Kit ignored Camden, continuing his tirade. "There was nae opportunity tae explain my past to you. If we'd had more time before they stole you from me, I would have explained everything." His words verged on snarls in his monster form. "I do nae need a pack. What matters is you."

The thickness in my throat returned with furious vengeance.

"You are not going anywhere without me."

I was already shaking my head, trying to wrap my brain around this.

"I will nae leave mate," Rowan's voice rumbled through the room.

I licked my lips.

I used to think I had steel will, but my mates made me weak. My chest heaved as I took deep breaths. Kit's green gaze burned into me, the color flashing with anger and frustration.

I understood the look. It reflected the hurt I struggled with. He was letting it all out after attempting to hold back the emotions he'd been dealing with. Kit was finally showing me all of him.

I bunched my hands into Kit's fur and tugged him down. Fortunately, he gave into my demand.

Wrapping my arms around him, I hugged him tightly. He straightened, with me hanging off him and my feet dangling. I buried my nose into his neck, pulling my legs up and around him.

He shuddered and his arms constricted around my body as he walked with me.

The tip of his cock prodded at my jeans with each step. I couldn't see where he was walking because I kept my face in his fur.

There was a thump and I lifted my head as he entered my new bedroom. He gently laid me on the bed, taking care with his claws. Pillows scattered and thudded to the ground. My gaze dropped to his hard dick, pink and glistening. He saw me watching it and it twitched. Kit groaned and placed his claws on the bed, hunched over as he inhaled.

"You'll make me lose control," he hissed.

I wanted that. Bad.

Hooking my fingers under my sweater, I hiked it off, exposing my breasts to the cool room. He hadn't bought me a bra, so that made things easier.

My nipples hardened.

His attention fixed on them as I unbuckled my jeans and wiggled them down my hips along with my panties. Once I kicked them off the rest of the way, I scooted back, holding myself propped by my elbows and spread my knees, exposing my wet flesh to his gaze.

He inhaled deeply, shuddering.

Sinking my teeth into my lower lip, I smoothed my hand down my stomach, going lower and lower until I reached my core.

Using two fingers, I spread my pussy. My toes curled, hips wiggling.

Kit's breathing turned ragged and the tip of his cock released pre-cum.

"Touch yourself." I lifted my half-lidded gaze to Camden who watched from behind Kit. I was so drawn into Kit I hadn't registered him coming in.

That meant Rowan was close by, but they were giving me time with Kit.

I returned my gaze to Kit and dipped my pointer finger into my channel. The walls of my pussy fluttered around my finger, making my leg twitch. Another gush of wetness dripped down the crevice of my inner thighs.

My head tipped forward and I whined breathily.

Kit's restraint snapped and he lunged forward, burying his snout into my pussy. I sucked in a harsh breath.

His cool nose spread my pussy and he opened his mouth, stretching me with his snout. His tongue lapped against the walls of my core, and I jerked helplessly, causing his beastly muzzle to retreat from my entrance.

A hand pressed into my shoulder, stilling me. My head dropped back, and I met Camden's eyes. A red flush spread over his neck, but it wasn't anger, if the parted lips were anything to go by.

Rowan's forearm settled over my hips, his claws out and resting against my belly. I sucked in a breath at the sight of the gray fur against my skin.

Kit grinned, showing his teeth and I gawked at the evil look. His head lowered, ears flicking back as he stuffed his muzzle into my entrance.

My lips parted on a gasp, and I struggled to move as my other mates held me down. Kit opened his maw slightly, stretching me open to slip his tongue deep into my pussy. My walls constricted and I whimpered.

A gush of moisture dripped down my thighs. Kit continued licking, driving me to maddening lust.

"She likes that," Camden murmured huskily. I glared at him, and he smirked, lowering his head to press his lips to mine. I moaned into his mouth as Kit continued doing that little flick upward.

A wave of tingles flushed through my body. I whimpered, legs shaking.

Rowan dragged the back of his furred hand across my belly in repeated motions. The added sensation shot me over the edge and I crashed into a release that worked through my clit all the way to my belly button in ripples. My pussy clasped his tongue as he continued to move it inside me, dragging out my orgasm.

My limbs finally relaxed from the pressure holding taut, but he didn't stop. Kit took his time licking all the juices clean.

"My turn," Rowan growled, the tone mixed with excitement.

*Wait a minute,* I mouthed pointlessly. I lifted widened eyes to Camden and he smirked.

Kit gripped my thighs, holding me still as he moved to the side. The fur on his muzzle was wet from my release, darkening the gray color.

Rowan didn't even let me take a breath before his long pink tongue swiped across my sensitive flesh, sending me into a spasm of twitches. He flattened it at my clit and then flicked it over the sensitive bud. My toes curled and my legs shook from the intensity. Another orgasm washed over me, and I struggled against the grips they had on me.

Sweet baby werewolf, they were settling in on driving me to insanity.

# Willow



I was a whimpering mess by the second time Rowan made me come simply by playing with my clit.

My limp noodle legs easily bent when he shoved them up. His tongue slipped down to the bud of my ass. I kicked my leg at the invasion.

Rowan snapped his teeth at me.

Kit gripped one of my thighs, forcing it up for his brother to have better access to my ass. The tension gave way and sucked the air from my lungs.

"Relax, Willow," Camden breathed. His cock was hard as a rock under my shoulder blade, pre-cum spreading by the second.

The pressure worsened at my ass, making it difficult to breathe. Kit pressed the back of his claw into my clit, rubbing it. The combined sensation sent shockwaves of electricity to my toes.

Rowan's tongue stretched deep into my ass and I helplessly arched my hips toward it as the pain turned to pleasure. He finally gave me what I wanted and thrust his tongue in and out in shallow pumps.

My head jerked side to side. He was fucking my ass with his tongue, and *oh*.

Kit rolled my clit again. My legs shook and a release crashed into me. My spine arched, lips parting as I squirted across Rowan's face. It continued until the gray fur darkened from my juices.

"Fuck," Camden breathed, and his cock throbbed beneath my shoulder.

I went limp as Rowan lifted his head, grinning wolfishly.

Kit released his grip on me and laid back on the bed, legs sprawled and hanging from the edge. Once he was settled, he ripped me away from Camden and Rowan.

With my back to him, he easily lifted me, kneeing my legs wide so I straddled him backward. His cock prodded my asshole and Kit dragged me down, claws digging into my hips.

My eyes fluttered shut, head tipping back as my channel constricted around him. The thickness of his wolfman cock stretching me.

Camden stood at the end of the bed, hovering near and I gripped his shirt and pulled him to my lips, kissing him as I ground on Kit. He seemed hesitant, but he got into the kiss, cupping my cheeks and angling his head to deepen the reach of his tongue into my mouth.

My eyes fluttered and with each shutter, images of when he'd first made love to me played in vivid light. I tugged his cock free and wrapped my hand around it.

It twitched as I guided him toward me.

Since I was perched on top of Kit, I was elevated enough for him to reach me easily. Spreading my thighs further apart, I pushed his cock into my warm, wet channel and arched my back. His eyelids lowered and he shoved forward, seating himself. Fur spread up his arms and his body shook as he shifted into his wolfman form. Both of them inside me . . .

I groaned at the girths stretching me.

A few months ago, I never would have expected to be here.

Camden's thick cock pooched my belly out with each thrust. His head bowed forward as he pumped into me, slamming so hard that it drove Kit's dick deeper.

I enjoyed watching him lose control. His flashing gaze, snarls, and teeth excited me.

I dipped my fingers down to my pussy and petted the thick, hard knot ballooning at the base.

Camden whimpered, his pupils becoming pinpricks. His hips rammed into me in frantic pumps, his teeth bared. A whine escaped his throat and he stilled inside me, knot ballooning to the point of fastening me on his dick as his release jutted into me.

Camden's shoulders trembled as his hips twitched. The pressure of his knot pressed into my clit and he wrenched out my orgasm. I tensed, thrashing between them. Kit snarled.

Rowan leaned over and lashed his tongue across my neck, his warm cock rubbing into my side. I gripped it in hand, palming it as Kit's grip bordered on painful.

His claws sliced into my waist and cum spilled from his cock, dripping out of my ass and making it easier for me to grind down on him.

How would I survive this?

Camden snored deeply and Kit's arm twitched. A smile stretched the corners of my mouth and I met a deep green gaze steadily watching me—as it had since I'd met him.

Rowan's head rested on my thigh. I loved this . . .

The lump in my throat returned with a vengeance. I sighed and shut my eyes, rubbing my cheek into Kit's fur.

*I wanted to be theirs.*

A sharp stab sank into my leg, causing my clit to tighten. A small orgasm washed through my pussy in comforting waves, lulling through me.

My head dropped back as warmth spread through my chest and from the bite as he lapped . . .

He'd bitten me! What an asshole. The dull throb of pain pulsated through my thigh.

Wait a minute.

I lifted my head and gasped at the blood and the indents from Rowan's teeth.

Camden mumbled in his sleep and I stilled.

If I woke them up, they'd get pissy and do it too. Fuck. Fuck.

I swallowed my anger and squeezed my eyes shut.

Rowan had just claimed me. It was irreversible. I ached to be claimed when he'd sank his teeth in me.

He caught me in a weak moment and took advantage as any possessive wolf would. I gritted my teeth, but softened my glare since Rowan's attention on me remained unwavering. I scratched his side and he groaned. I continued petting him. Once he fell asleep, I would sneak out.

It took another hour for me to slide away without waking them. I paused at the room threshold and Rowan rubbed his face into Kit's side.

No wonder he'd watched me, he probably sensed something was off. I fisted my hands and turned away. I wanted to be upfront about my plan, but that was foolish because they wouldn't let me place myself in danger.

# Camden

I rubbed my grainy eyes and flexed my arm around Willow's torso. It felt too big and furry . . . had she shifted?

My eyes sprang open to see I was cuddling close to Kit. I jerked back so fast I fell to the floor.

I shoved up and froze. There was no sight of her. No. Fuck, no. I had such a bad feeling. I rushed out of the room and peered out of the window facing the truck. It was gone.

A ball of dread weighed in my stomach.

One thing about Willow was her stubbornness.

I understood this and I'd still passed out. Fuck. I knocked into a stand near the front door and a piece of paper fluttered to the ground.

*Please trust me. I will be back soon.*

*PS Don't be mad.*
*PPS Don't fight with each other.*

She was fucking gone.

I was already half out the door when I hesitated at the threshold. The other two were still asleep. I rubbed my face. Why was I hesitating?

I didn't owe them anything.

But the way she looked at them . . .

They were part of her happiness.

*Fuck.*

I disliked it, but I hated the thought of her not being happy and they were a part of that.

Mates were sacred and once you found yours, the ache to be near them was indescribably painful.

I didn't want her to be in pain.

That made my decision. Striding back to the room, I slammed the door open. Kit shot into a sitting position, while Rowan bounced to his feet. They immediately searched the area and simultaneously turned their attention to me in alarm.

"She left, didn't she?" Kit snarled and shoved off the bed, shifting back into his human form. I didn't bother responding, it was obvious.

Kit snatched the letter from my hands.

"Trust her? While she places herself in danger?" he roared.

Same.

"Left," Rowan snarled and was already charging past me, I caught myself before I slammed into the wall. *Fucking dick.*

"Rowan," Kit snapped. "If you don't want to run around like a headless wolf, calm the fuck down, we need to figure out where she went before we run out without a plan."

Rowan roared and shifted into his wolf.

"She took the truck."

Kit sneered and broke a door as he opened it. I watched

him, eager to *move*, but the guy had a plan, and I would wait if it would help us to find her. The cell phone we took from the man that purchased her rested on the nightstand. It had to do with that. She must have discovered something.

I tugged on the clothing Kit tossed me.

"Since the car is a rental, there's a tracker on it," he said, grunting as he bent to shove his feet into work boots. "I will call the place and get the location."

"How are we getting there?"

"There's a car behind the house."

The pressure in my shoulders loosened.

*We're coming, Willow.*

## ROWAN

They were idiots.

I needed to be with my mate, and they kept arguing back and forth. I was close to tearing throats out, but my mate would not like that.

I grumbled, skin itchy in this *clothing*. Uncomfortable shit.

"Why is she at the fucking airport? Where did she fly off to?" Camden hissed as the car turned up a road toward a lot. "Wait until I wrap my fucking hands around her neck."

I snarled at him.

He turned to glare at me, and I snapped my teeth. No violence toward my mate.

The car screeched to a halt beside a van. Camden's contact agreed to meet us to get into the cell phone we found.

"How sure are you he will know how to get into the phone?" Kit asked.

"There is no other option," Camden responded grimly.

I ground my teeth, fingers flexing to release the building energy.

"If he doesn't—"

"Stop talking," I snarled. "Where is mate?"

"We're trying to figure that shit out!" Camden shoved the door open.

I clicked my teeth at him, snarling, and followed him to the van.

# Willow

I hadn't missed this place. The Uber driver entered the invisible line marking pack lands. Glinting eyes stared out at me from the woods, but they wouldn't intercept the car yet.

"Looks pretty abandoned out here."

I pressed my lips together, nodding tightly. I'd put a note I would not be speaking, so I didn't feel too bad not trying to communicate with her. Getting a hang of the app to order a driver had been difficult, but the airport fortunately had Wi-Fi I could connect to.

I stayed quiet for another five minutes. The coordinates I put in would get her to stop soon. She slowed, turning her head side to side as she took in the surroundings.

"Are you sure this is your drop-off?" she said, eyeing me through the rearview mirror. I nodded and she pulled to the side. It'd been disorienting coming back to the driver being on the left side.

I slipped out of the car. She still seemed skeptical but said nothing else as she turned the direction she came.

I'd purposefully waited for the sun to start setting. This was when Hector was traded out to do the rounds. He was the only one I trusted to get me to Torrin without informing him ahead of time.

I waited with my arms behind my back until the car disappeared into the distance. After another beat, I started down the road. It didn't take long for wolves to circle.

"Willow," Hector shouted.

I stopped, scanning the rustling forest. A dark shadow detached from the depths and my father rushed toward me. "Where have you been?"

I squeezed my eyelids tightly and hugged him back. I was so thankful for Evie giving me the liquid to block I was Omega.

He tensed and pulled back, hands lightly squeezing my arms.

"You've shifted."

Shock bled through his tone. I knew he had questions and was worried, but I didn't want to waste time. I was here with a mission.

*"I need to see the Alpha."*

Hector frowned but seemed to sense my desperation. He slowly nodded.

We weren't far from the pack house since it was the first building at the end of the road. Alpha liked things widespread and private, so there was a healthy distance between all the homes.

I pulled my cell phone out and checked the time.

It was the time of year when it got darker sooner in the day, and twilight descended, casting a low gray light through the tall redwood trees.

I kind of missed the wet mossy scent of Scotland. The snow was beautiful too.

"I told your mom you disappeared," Hector started gruffly, eyebrows furrowed.

All I hoped for him was he'd be willing to give happiness a shot one day. Either search for his true mate or take the leap and choose someone else. He'd never mated my mom, so he still had the option, fortunately. I guessed it was a good thing my mom was leery about being tied down.

"Have you contacted her?" His question was hesitant. I could understand why. He never wanted me to talk to her, but he hadn't stopped my attempt to connect with her.

He even kept her contact in his phone, something he vehemently disliked.

I nodded tightly in answer, not looking at him.

"What did she say?"

I shrugged.

The thickness in my throat had lessened since she'd spat her venom at me. I shouldn't have expected much from her.

"She only looks after herself, Willow." I blinked away the sheen of tears that obstructed my sight.

He was right. That was the harsh version of what he'd been telling me since I could remember. His warning to be careful, his disgust toward her veiled, but easily discernible. It was a realization I'd had long before, but I'd had hope. Even after what she'd said before ditching me at the gas station. *"You'll be the death of anyone you care about."*

I was a danger to have nearby, but the concoction gave me the confidence to be near my mates. Nola's words were just that —words. The fear she'd instilled in me haunted me enough, but I trusted my mates.

I'd had enough of wanting to shoulder everything as Nola did. Her mentality was toxic, and I was accepting that it was okay to block people from your life if they made you feel shit about yourself, even if it was your mother.

I peeked at Hector from the corner of my eyes and sighed before signing, "*You're right.*"

# Willow



With my wide stride, it didn't take long for me to near the Alpha's home.

"Wait, Willow, I'm going to have to check if Torrin is okay with speaking to you, but we should wait until he finishes dinner."

Unlike other packs, Torrin liked eating without disturbances and while he still had pack members provide food for those of us that didn't have mates, he didn't host them in his home. Instead, he had a community hall deeper into the lands where any mass meeting or gatherings happened.

Blaze, a pack enforcer that switched with Hector when they did the rounds, jogged up as we strode to the front of the house. His wide shoulders hardly moved from the exertion.

"Willow," he said, chest rumbling as he inclined his head. "Glad to see you're okay."

I signed, "*Thank you*" to him. Most everyone in the pack that did associate with me understood the basic pleasantries of ASL, something I appreciated more than they knew. Blaze was one of them. He was always kind and polite.

"I'm sending a few of the guys to run the perimeter. I already checked with Alpha." Blaze kept talking but I inched forward more. When he didn't turn his attention to me, I quickened my stride.

"Wait, Willow," Hector called, but I ignored him and climbed up the house steps and shoved open the door. I stormed in with Hector on my heels. He was trying to go in first to let them know of my presence, but I wasn't having it. I knew the house like the back of my hand since Camden and I had grown up running through the place. I turned through the living room and entered the kitchen.

The sweet, buttered scent of bread and ham filled my nose, immediately tossing me back into my memories—Britt cooking for me when Camden had me over for dinner. Spending time with them while my dad patrolled.

My gaze lifted to Alpha's, his eyebrows lifted and he was standing.

"Willow?"

Yeah, be shocked, bitch.

I licked my lips and nodded tightly.

How could he have done this? It shouldn't have stunned me, he was the tough-love sort, which wasn't necessarily the worst thing, but he took it too far. That was how I ended up mute. Even so, I never thought him capable of selling me just because he didn't think I was fit for Camden.

"Where have you been?"

Was he really asking me that as if he didn't know? I hadn't realized what good of an actor he was until now. I couldn't deny it kind of stung that he would go to these lengths. As dismissive as he'd been to me, he was still Camden's father *and* the pack Alpha. It was also eerie how similar Camden and him looked. Torrin was just a pale-haired, older version.

Wood screeched against wood as Britt shoved to her feet. Her red mass of hair swishing over her shoulders at her quick move.

"Is Camden with you?" Britt's voice rasped with anxiety. She rushed toward me and gripped my arms, her expression beseeching. Her fingernails dug into me, even through the sweater. "Please, Willow, you're the reason he left. Did he find you?"

I frowned as I stared down at her.

"Luna, Torrin told him to leave, it's unfair of you to blame my daughter." This was the first time I'd heard Hector speak like that to her. He was always painfully respectful of the Alpha and his Luna. But then again, there'd never been cause for him to not be respectful. He'd never wanted or needed to challenge anyone. The only time I'd seen him close to that sort of anger was when I got hurt, but Torrin smoothed that over with him.

Torrin bristled, stepping forward with a scowl.

Omegas are to be loved, taken care of, and cherished . . . but that didn't mean I was a fucking push over.

I gently pulled my arm away from Britt, making sure not to hurt her. She didn't release for a beat, forcing her nails in deeper to that point that it burned. The scent of blood filled my nose, but I turned away from Britt and faced Torrin.

Everything I experienced, the gut-wrenching fear, the unknown, the uncertainty, all rushed to the forefront. Being stuck in that small space for so long and not knowing what that werewolf would do to me. Every possible scenario had crossed my mind of how bad it could have gone.

I had a small chance of surviving an attack from Torrin, but that's why I was here, that was why I left my mates. They didn't deserve to be dragged into my crap, but I needed to face it.

I needed justice.

Slowly, I signed, "*Why did you sell me?*"

My heart thundered in my chest, raging to get out as much as my wolf did. She bristled to escape.

Hector frowned and looked from Torrin to me.

"Sell?" His lips thinned. "What do you mean, Willow?"

Torrin's eyebrows remained furrowed, the only response was increasing anger. He didn't understand me, but *I* needed to ask the question.

"I have no idea what you mean. But there is a time and place, Hector. Take her out and we will discuss this at another time." My dad stiffened beside me. The pompous words, the sneer to his lips, it ground on my gears.

My wolf raged forward, and I let her. Fur burst from my skin and my bones popped as they extended. Scents filled my nose. Sweat, butter, woods . . . My ears flicked as a rush of noise filtered through them, everything becoming enhanced. Red filled my vision. Bunching my thighs, I lunged at him.

He was much larger than me, but in my wolf form, I had a smidge of a chance. My paws smacked into his chest, claws sinking into his pale shirt. With my momentum, he went flying backward. The dinner table buckled underneath him. I lost my balance and fell to the side.

Chaos ensued. There was a scream, shattering glass and then the Alpha shifted.

He swiped out and I avoided the hefty paw in time for it not to slice across my face. In a quick dash forward, I sank my teeth into his hindquarters. Blood burst onto my tongue and he roared. My heart pounded in my chest.

"Kill her, Torrin," Britt shouted, her pupils shrunk into pinpricks. Hearing that come from her lips made me freeze. I went limp, looking up at her as my side lifted and dropped in rough inhales and exhales. It was both of them? My heartbeat pounded in my ears.

The thinned lips and the sweat dotting her forehead . . . She'd never shown me she hated me. *And she loathed me.*

Teeth sank into my throat. Torrin jerked down and my legs buckled as he pinned me to the ground. My paws scratched against the floor helplessly, eyes flicking around.

Two pack mates attacked my dad and dragged him to the ground.

No! This was my fault. It had nothing to do with Hector! I wanted to scream. I struggled harder, but it only forced Torrin's teeth deeper into my throat.

What had I caused?

Hector snarled, blood matting his mocha fur so similar to mine. I'd attacked the pack Alpha—a move punishable by death. But what hurt was I'd brought my dad down with me and that my mates would never know what happened.

I was never more thankful that I hadn't let Kit or Camden claim me, but Rowan . . .

Tears leaked from my eyes, seeping into my fur.

I squeezed my eyes shut.

There was a pop and pounding steps accompanied by snarling. The pressure around my throat disappeared as a russet wolf slammed into the pack Alpha.

I gasped, pushing to my knees as Kit shifted in front of me and cupped my face. My brows furrowed and tears pricked my eyes.

"Shh, *mo chridhe*," he murmured roughly, pressing my face

to his chest. I'd researched what his endearment meant on the plane ride, and it'd taken hours since I couldn't get the spelling right. *My heart* . . . He was my heart too. All of them were.

Sweat slicked his skin and his orange scent filled my nostrils. I sucked in as much as I could.

There was a yelp and I lifted my head. Rowan rounded the area Kit and I knelt, head lowered, blood dripping from his maw.

"Camden," Britt said roughly.

He ignored her, fur lifted at the back of his neck as he watched Torrin. The dining room was an utter mess. Shattered dishes littered the ground.

"Why are you being aggressive toward your father?" Her eyes flicked to me. "She challenged the pack Alpha, that's a death sentence. You can't blame your father!"

Rowan's teeth flashed and he snarled at her, neck becoming taut.

"Look at how she's hanging all over that man," she spat, side-eyeing me, venom spitting from her gaze. Camden shifted, fur slinking back into his skin.

"Enough, Britt," he snarled. "We're both her mates." Her lips smacked together, and she glowered, shaking her head. I could tell her thoughts were going a mile a minute. I shifted into my human form, remaining propped against Kit.

"Impossible. That only happens with Omegas." Her eyelids widened. "No, no. The selfish bitch. She can't do that to you, Camden."

Kit tensed against me and leaned down. His lips pressed against my cheek as I struggled to process. Her hate hit me like a fright train. I didn't even feel him detach from me until he'd neared her.

How could she? She was my substitute mom. She was always kind to me. How could she be saying this right now?

Camden's mother, the woman I believed cared for me . . . she had betrayed me. Sold me off like I was trash.

I'd been thrown away by my mother and now this?

My hands shook with barely restrained rage.

# Willow

women willing to do anything for their own gain. She claimed she was looking out for her son, but I couldn't believe selling me off was her only option.

Rowan twitched at my side, and I bunched his fur. He growled at me, so I squeezed it tighter. He huffed but stayed at my side.

Even if her warped intention was to protect her son, that didn't make what she did right. I didn't want to understand—not after the trauma. I didn't want the memories of a dank, cold room, where I didn't know if I would live or die.

I faced Camden. *"She was in on it."*

"You knew Torrin sold her off?" Camden's eyes flashed.

"I didn't sell anyone off," Torrin snapped. I froze, staring at him. He was an arrogant, willful Alpha with a fuck ton of pride. He wasn't the type to hide behind his mate.

So that meant . . . My lips parted. Britt was the only one who orchestrated the kidnapping.

Camden seemed to reach the same conclusion. His expression tightened, lips thinning.

"You don't get to stare at me like that," she hissed at me. Kit lashed out and gripped her throat. She kicked her feet. I rushed forward and grabbed his arm, shaking my head. He scanned my face and his eyes softened.

Inclining his head the slightest bit, he dropped her. She fell to her knees. Camden placed himself between us and Torrin.

"Don't think of touching her," Camden spat.

"I shouldn't have allowed that little bitch to stay in my pack," Torrin snarled.

There was a rush of movement from the corner of my eye. The slightest ripple in the air as Britt's arm jerked back. A glint of silver and the arching angle toward Kit's chest. In an instant, I threw myself to the side, jumping in front of Kit and smacking into her arm—ruining her aim. I met her gaze as she slammed the knife into my upper chest. Horror widened her eyes and then resolve. She bared her teeth and twisted.

Agony burned through the wound, striking outward.

Where it would have hit Kit in the heart, it sliced into a weird angle downward near my sternum. It all happened so fast.

Rowan's shaggy fur flashed before me, and he jumped, teeth bared as he tore into her throat. He yanked his head to the side, and a sick gush exploded across my cheek. With a toss, he sent her head to the other end of the room. My vision warbled and my knees gave out. Kit caught me against his chest. Red fur flashed and all I managed to catch was Camden sinking his wolf teeth into his father's throat. He shook hard, snapping his neck.

If not for me . . . My heart constricted, throbbing for my mate. Killing his father . . . *Camden. I'm sorry, Camden.* It was all my fault.

My vision became increasingly blurry, and strength leaked from my body. Kit trembled against me.

Thundering steps approached, but I struggled to keep my eyes open.

## KIT

No. Not her. No.

My wolf clawed for freedom and fur exploded from my skin. My body rippled and stretched with the shift into my third form. Nausea crawled up my throat, but I didn't let go of Willow. My hands shook as I clasped her tighter. I couldn't think. In my long fucking life, I'd never needed to keep control more than now, but I could nae.

Camden shifted back into a human, hands shaking as he dropped to his knees next to me, shouting something. All I could hear was a sharp ringing.

Camden's hands hovered over her.

"Get help," he roared.

Rowan paced, whining low in his throat, his lips curled to bare sharp teeth.

A female ran into the living room and gasped at the bloodshed. Her attention dropped to Willow and her eyes widened. I didn't think they could get any bigger but then she looked at me.

"Let her through," Camden snarled at Rowan. "Fix her."

I watched, detached from myself, struggling to breathe. Willow's head drooped too much and all the woman did was stare.

"Now!" Camden roared.

She dropped to her knees a few feet from my mate. My

fingers flexed and I bared my teeth, growling. She stilled, horror filling her gaze.

Willow's breathing rattled.

It snatched my soul from my body. A low, choked whine ripped free from my chest.

"I'll try to help her," the woman whispered roughly. This time I didn't stop her.

Rowan hovered next to me, his body hunching so he could watch. His focus uncanny. "I'm going to lean close to her chest. I need to listen to her breathing."

She lowered her head and pressed her fingers to Willow's wrist.

"Place her flat on the surface."

I hunched to place her on the cold ground. Camden disappeared and came back, gripping an armful of blankets. We pushed them against her body.

"It's not looking good," she said, not looking up as she ran her hands over her. Rowan trembled and swayed. His sides moved harshly. He leaned into my side heavily and whined.

Camden lunged forward and gripped her around the neck.

"Save her," he spat, teeth flashing.

"S-she's holding on, but it's not enough. I think the knife punctured something vital." My mind rushed. I couldn't think of anything. If she was gone, I was done. I would follow her to the afterlife.

"Don't remove the knife!" Her shout stopped Camden's reach. "She'll bleed out faster."

"There has to be something we can do," he snarled.

"A mate bond might force her to fight," a male voice intoned nearby. His voice was rough and grainy. "Camden, complete your bond with her." It was the male that smelled like my mate.

"I don't know much about Omegas' mate bonds, but if you have any chance at all of getting her to fight through this, I'd say that's your best bet." The woman's grim words weighed down my shoulders. I should have convinced her to accept my claim. Tears stung my eyes. "We need to wake her up to get her consent for it to grasp, otherwise you'll just damage her more."

"My mate." Rowan shifted into his wolfman form, leaning heavier into me. His clawed hand hovered over her lower half. My gaze dropped to her bare thigh. Beneath the rivulets of blood were healing teeth markings. They hadn't been there the last I spread her thighs, and the healing was too far along. Willow's eyebrows furrowed at Rowan's touch.

Rowan claimed her? Jealousy tightened my throat, but I shoved it away. It was what held her to me. That was why she reacted to his touch. He was tied to her.

He licked her cheek and whined in her ear. A soft purr thrummed through the room, making her lashes flutter.

"Mate," Rowan growled. The corner of her lips tipped down slightly.

Camden leaned near her ear. "Love, accept me." Her lips twitched. "Willow." Her lashes twitched on her cheeks.

Camden lifted her wrist to his lips.

I lowered to press my muzzle into the side of her face and then gripped her other wrist. Her shoulders relaxed and a slight smile twitched on her mouth.

I sank my teeth into the tender flesh.

Her only reaction was hissing out a breath between her teeth.

Her tart blood spread on my tongue and I lapped the punctures.

She exhaled and slipped back into sleep as a warmth bled into me. The sensation of fullness, completeness. Her sweet scent filling me and wrapping around me.

"Should we remove the knife?" Camden asked gruffly. We knew the risks of completing the mating bond, but it was the only thing keeping her with us. The only chance. Our sheer will pouring into her would help her fight and hold on. If she felt us with her . . . our bond, then she'd fight. And if she chose not to, then she was taking all of us with her.

"Yes," the interloping female finally said after studying the wound for a while. She'd been feeling around the area and nodding as she did. It was obvious she hadn't encountered anything terribly concerning. "I don't think it's hit anything vital." She bunched a cloth in hand and nodded at me.

I wrapped my hand around the sleek silver handle. Exhaling, I yanked it out quickly. The female immediately pressed the cloth to her stomach.

Willow whimpered, scrunching her face tightly. I bit back my sounds of pain, tossing the knife aside. The female lifted the cloth, and she nodded.

"That's a good sign," she mumbled to herself. She looked up. "Keep it tight to her wound, I'm going to fetch my medical kit." Camden swiftly took her spot, and she ran off.

"I want her more comfortable," I croaked.

"Move slowly, I'll keep the pressure steady." Camden slid his other palm under her as I gently scooped her up.

He jerked his chin toward a nearby open bedroom.

I settled her on the mattress, gently lifting her arms flat beside her and setting the blanket over her, tucking the edges under her legs. I nestled as close to her as I could without hurting her.

The door opened and the man smelling like my mate limped inside. He sucked in a breath. Not only did he smell like she'd been around her, but they had similar features. She never told us about her family, but Camden filled us in on the plane ride here. I'd taken advantage of his knowledge about her. I wanted to know everything.

I'd also gotten him to give me the resources he'd used to learn American Sign Language but . . . would I be able to show her?

My heart squeezed.

"Camden. The pack Alpha's dead. We're going to need to deal with it."

Camden's jaw tightened, jaw flexing. "I can't deal with that, Hector. I won't be the pack Alpha and I *will not* leave her side."

Hector sighed, rubbing the back of his neck. He kept shooting Willow looks and his gaze continued to bounce over me and a pacing Rowan who'd turned into his wolf form.

"Fine. I'll handle it."

They stared each other down for a beat and then Hector turned on this heel to leave, passing the woman who came in with a kit.

# Willow



M MY MOUTH FELT LIKE COTTON. My EYELIDS REMAINED closed, twitching a few times before I could force them open. I took stock of my surroundings as awareness seeped into my consciousness. I wiggled my uncomfortably numb legs.

Rowan's head lifted from my stomach and he whined, lapping my cheek frantically.

"Willow," Camden rasped, his palms pressing to my face and forcing my mouth to his. His tongue plunged between my lips, kissing me fervently as he groaned.

A rough, large palm settled on my belly. Camden released my lips and Kit claimed them quickly after. The way he cupped my cheeks . . .

His hands shook.

The desperation in their touch made tears prickle my eyes.

Heat engulfed my chest, spreading down my limbs. I'd never felt more whole. Any hollow sensation was obliterated as my wrists and thigh pulsated heat. I was complete.

"How dare you?" Kit growled into my mouth. "You stupid girl. How dare you leave?"

My lip trembled and I dropped my gaze. I was going to come back . . .

Camden spat out, "I think I'm speaking for all of us. Don't ever fucking do that again." He dragged his hands through his russet hair.

"You are never to leave me," Kit growled, the violence in his tone lifting the hair on the back of my neck in the most delicious way.

Rowan huffed and opened his maw to gently tap his teeth on my belly, the anger in his gaze unmistakable. The wolf was heavy. I wiggled my toes and could hardly feel them with how numb they were under him, but I couldn't bring myself to force him off.

The thickness in my throat reached excruciating levels and tears leaked from my eyes. I exhaled shakily. Kit sucked in a harsh breath, his body trembling. In an explosion of fur, his wolfman form pushed to the surface and the hands on my face stretched much larger to engulf my head. The bed creaked and tilted to the side, forcing me to slide toward him.

A pinch in my chest had me hugging myself.

"Fuck," Camden shifted, his fur and thick arm pushing into me as his weight balanced out the unevenness of the bed. I settled between the wolfmen while Rowan, who lay on my legs, remained unfazed.

A soreness at my wrist brought my attention to them. My eyes widened and I patted it, rubbing at the healing wound. I winced. It was real, not my overinflated imagination. Shit. *Shit.* This worked against everything I was trying to do to protect them.

"You must have wanted it as much as we did." I could *feel* the smirk coming from Camden.

A hazy memory surfaced. It was a dream! My hands shook. This wasn't supposed to be real. It was my deepest desires, but I was never going to act on them. It was bad enough I'd slipped up with Rowan.

I lifted my head and angled an accusing stare at Kit and then Camden.

*"How could you guys do this? It's dangerous being tied to me."*

"A fucking letter, Willow? Seriously?" Camden snapped. "A little faith would be great."

"Aye, *mo chridhe.* Trust us to protect you."

Their words were accompanied with a gutturalness due to their shifted form.

I frowned, crossing my arms. They were ganging up on me but a tiny piece of me was ecstatic they seemed to be working together.

Trusting them . . . that was what it came down to.

Had Nola trusted anyone to protect her? No, instead she'd chosen to leave.

Maybe it wasn't just leaving for safety, maybe it was selfishness too. She hadn't faced anything or chosen to trust Hector who would have made sure she was safe. Instead, she abandoned us.

*"What if you die protecting me?"*

Camden growled. "She's going on about the same shit."

Kit huffed and used his claw to gently force my chin up so I faced him.

"You belong to us. Not a question."

His green gaze settled on me, unwavering. His muzzle hovered near my face. They'd proven they would follow. I took a beat to consider more than myself. I was behaving like my mother. Acting like I knew best instead of trusting those around me.

Hope bloomed in my chest. I could . . . keep them?

I didn't want to be away from them, and stubbornness hadn't helped me much.

The corners of my lips twitched up and I tilted my head back and pressed my lips to Kit's wet nose. Rowan lifted from my legs and sensation washed down them, shooting tingles to my toes. Rowan whined and ran his tongue up my cheek in a swift swipe. I reached over and buried my fingers in the fur behind his ear. He groaned and tilted toward my hand.

The door creaked and in a swift move Rowan bounded off the bed, growling at the door.

Meridith cringed back but quickly straightened with a scowl.

I smirked, enjoying her fear. It practically radiated from her pores. Camden made some odd noise between a laugh and a snort, his hand engulfing the back of my neck, taking care with his claws.

Meridith remained near the door, hugging the bag to her chest as she glared at us.

"Hector was asking for Camden and Kit."

My shoulders immediately tightened hearing their names from her lips and my eyes narrowed on her.

She licked her lips. "I can't even say their names?"

I continued looking at her and winged my brow upward.

"Fuck, fine. Willow, can you inform your mates that the Alpha is looking for them?"

The shock of the title took me off guard. She just said Hector was looking for them.

I turned to Camden and raised an eyebrow. He leaned forward and pressed his nose into my temple.

"Later."

I nodded slowly. Kit flexed his grip and then released me.

"Let's get it over with." Camden stood, cock semihard. Meridith's face flushed, eyes rounding.

I clicked my tongue and yanked the pillow he'd been laying on and threw it at him.

A tightening burn stung my chest. I winced.

"Willow!" Kit growled. I struggled sucking in a breath, but I tugged the other pillow and shoved it at his chest. His claws flexed into it, tearing the fabric.

He huffed and straightened.

"Watch her," Kit growled at Rowan. "Do nae let her move."

Meridith inched farther and farther away as they neared the door, clutching their pillows over their dicks. Their tipped ears flicked across the top of the doorframe even though they ducked.

Kit lingered outside the door. Camden growled, "Faster we finish. Faster we're back."

They disappeared and Meridith exhaled and inched over to me. Rowan paced.

"Same deal, I won't help her if you get near."

Rowan bared his teeth and remained on the other side of the room as she perched next to me on the bed.

"We had the pack doctor in here but your mates almost murdered him, so I was sent in his place." She didn't sound happy about it. "Lean forward."

I did as she said. The position hurt like a bitch. Sweet baby werewolf. *Ouch.*

She reached behind me and the bandage around my chest flexed as she unwound the material.

"Honestly, I don't think you could have hung on if they hadn't completed the mating bond."

So she was the one with the brilliant idea.

Cool air pricked my skin, and she tugged the rest of the bandage free.

Her finger pressed into my shoulder, and I leaned back. My breasts on full display. She may have been a werewolf for a while, but nudity was still odd for me. I stared down at the stitched gash on my chest. Yellow surrounded the area. Blood dried around the wound, crusted and dark. It was way too close to my heart. The knife had punctured smack dab between my breasts and the wound was about two inches long.

She zipped open the bag and rifled through before pulling out a tube and some wipes.

"This will sting a bit but try not to move."

She cleaned off the wound and I focused on not twitching in pain.

"Uh, since we're here." She trailed off and licked her lips. "I just wanted to apologize about what I said before you disappeared. I wasn't in the best place. I knew how Camden felt about you and it stung."

I studied her sincere expression.

"Everyone knew. And if they didn't, they definitely did after he almost murdered Riley when we were teens. Man, it was a whole thing. Alpha Torrin and Hector worked so hard to bury it. Riley's dad was *pissed*." Murdered him?

He did what? Was that why Riley avoided me after kissing me?

I scoffed, shaking my head. I had no clue.

"Why do you think no one approached you, like ever?"

I could only gawk. "Now let's get you bandaged up so your mates don't rip my head off."

She continued cleaning the wound, but I was officially on auto pilot, still trying to wrap my head around her revelation.

# WILLOW

I STARED AT THE CEILING, BLINKING IN A MIX OF astonishment and anger. No way. Here I thought no guy liked me. It didn't help that the one guy who came onto me, kissed me and then disappeared. Yes, realistically I didn't care because I only had eyes for Camden, but it was the principle! The only reason I'd frozen when Riley kissed me was because I was pissed at Camden. All the she-wolves were on his ass when he went through his growth spurt and it was annoying. There would have been nothing between Riley and me anyway, but I couldn't even address it since he'd avoided me afterwards.

I still hadn't said anything to Camden because grinning like a lunatic when I scolded him wouldn't get him to feel bad.

Unfortunately, I had all the time in the world with my mates. Even if I seldom saw them, and when I did, they just passed out. They were on some sort of rotation. At first, Rowan remained with me, but he was slowly dragged into whatever was going on outside. Curiosity was killing me, and Meridith wasn't helpful in giving me information other than mentioning my mates were vicious and she'd hate to see anyone on their bad side.

I wiggled into the bed. Meridith had helped me shower and change into clothes, but my skin itched with the need to see my mates.

I gingerly scooted to the end of the bed and put on my slippers. As soon as I was upright, the room spun, so I took a moment. Once I felt like I wouldn't fall over, I shuffled to the door. There was no one in the living room, in the kitchen . . . I shuffled through the house on my way to the door leading outside.

Blood stained various spots throughout the house.

I'd focused on not thinking about Britt and Torrin, because I didn't want to consider the repercussions. I struggled with their deaths, but Camden hadn't said anything. He wouldn't, but I couldn't help the guilt eating me up from the inside.

I pushed the front door open. The sun hung low in the sky, and the cool breeze caressed my face. There was more blood scattered in spots around the house. Movement caught my attention, and I turned in time to see Rowan running at me. He slowed as he neared, growling and pressing into my side.

He shifted into his human form, something I knew he hated doing.

"You're hurt. Lay down."

His muscles rippled, hair rustling around his face. The texture looked soft to the touch. I reached up and twirled my finger in some of the strands. I loved the feel of it.

The corners of his lips twitched and he lowered, pressing his head closer to my hand. It reminded me of how he liked getting pets in his wolf form. I shook my head and untangled my grip, clearing my throat.

He rumbled grumpily, the noise coming deep from his throat.

I ignored him and trudged down the veined path. It was like a ghost town. A pack mate was a few yards down near the road and I turned toward him. He saw me coming and his eyes widened. Turning on his heel, he fled.

I skid to a stop and narrowed my eyes at Rowan. He turned away so he wasn't looking at me. Scoffing, I took off down the road. I'd keep going until I bumped into someone, then.

What was going on?

Rowan huffed a few minutes later, shifted into his wolfman form, and pressed his palm into my spine, navigating me to the left instead of the right, leading me toward my house.

There were a few men hanging around outside, their expressions tight. Jay, Lee, and Brian. All except Lee looked away. He lowered his head slightly.

My shoulders tensed up and I sniffed myself. I didn't think the scent concoction Evie had given me had worn off, but I had to text her soon to have her express ship some to me.

When I looked over my shoulder at the glaring Rowan, I realized they weren't acting that way because of me.

I climbed the creaky steps to find the living room packed. I stopped in place, staring toward the far wall where my mates sprawled in wolfman form, clothed in shorts with the tattered edges at different lengths. They looked like some Hollywood version of a werewolf in that form, but with the shorts, it brought it all together.

Even with that, I could see the outline of their shaft, which left little to the imagination.

At least they'd tried?

I sighed and stalked up to them, ignoring the looks.

Accidently getting too close to a male, he jerked back so quickly he fell out of his seat.

I glared at my mates and walked straight toward Hector. He'd been keeping his distance because of my mates. His eyebrows furrowed and that was all I saw before I threw arms around his midsection.

He patted my shoulder, but I didn't even get a full five seconds before my shoulder was tugged back.

"I know it's your father, mate, but instincts are difficult to calm," Kit said, teeth flashing.

I frowned and stepped away from Hector.

"I'll walk her out," Camden offered and then my legs were swept out from under me. I scrambled to grab hunks of Camden's russet fur as I glared up at him.

"Willow," Hector chided and I frowned.

An eerie silence fell over the group gathered in the living room. I slowly released his fur, sweeping my gaze across the crowd.

A mix of emotions were reflected in every gaze. Fear, worry, and anger were among them.

I cleared my throat. Avoidance seemed like my best bet.

My attention settled on Riley's leery expression. Our eyes clashed and he blushed. Camden's claws flexed into my skin and I winced, narrowing my eyes at him.

*"I know what you did."*

Camden's brows furrowed. Seeing the twisted expression on a wolf face was terrifying.

He made his way toward the door with me cradled in his arms. I angled my head toward Riley and wiggled my fingers at him. The white of his eyes shone and Camden snapped his teeth at me.

"That's what you meant?" He snorted. "It wasn't a secret."

I shot him a side-eyed glance.

"You best hope Rowan didn't see you waving at that mutt. He's harder to convince to chill out."

As the door shut, a man spoke up about the home-building permits.

They were in the middle of listening to grievances.

I swayed within the comfort of his warm embrace. I exhaled, wiggling my toes as I rubbed my cheek into his chest.

A large mound caught my attention. It was covered by dark tarp-like fabric and I wouldn't have known what it was if it weren't for the limbs poking out of the side.

Shit. How many people had died?

When an Alpha battled, many others followed in his defense. Torrin had many people loyal to him. My stomach soured. He'd lost both of them . . . he'd *killed* his father.

It was on me.

Every death weighed on my shoulders. I peeked up at him.

Camden took a sharp turn and the crunch of his steps echoed as he went up an incline. I knew exactly where we were headed. A few more yards of crackling brush under his feet and then we were at our spot.

He perched on the wooden table, and I wiggled to get out of his grip to sit beside him, but he didn't release me. There was a slight dent between his eyebrows as he looked out into the forest. The swaying trees rustling with the wind.

I tipped my head back, looking at the tree arched over the table. It was the very tree I saved him from when we were kids. If those jerks hadn't trapped him in that net and if I hadn't cut him down, would we have been the same?

The corners of my lips tilted up. *We would have found our way to each other anyway.*

*We'd known one another for so long . . .*

I licked my lips, clenching my hands once before trying again.

*"I'm sorry about your parents."*

Camden frowned. "She chose to do something so heinous and Torrin supported that. He protected his mate and I did the same. It's not your fault, Willow." I was already shaking my head. "It's not and I don't blame you," he said roughly. "I know you, so I know it will take you a bit to understand, but I will be next to you for as long as you live, honey."

*"What about the pack?"*

"Hector will handle everything here." Hector never wanted to lead, but he was taking over?

"Stop your crazy worrying, everything is okay."

I eyed him in blatant disbelief.

# Camden

It'd taken *weeks* for me to finish teaching Hector everything about the pack and to get things back in order. And just as I'd told Willow—everything was okay. I browsed the snack section, striding down the isle of the mart and looked over at my girl as she perused.

She was beginning to believe it, because I could see the weight falling off her shoulders as each week passed. She'd spent most of the time hanging out in our room watching television and getting checked over by Meridith. I was starting to think they liked spending time together more than they let on. As long as Meridith didn't harm my mate, I was fine with her having a friend, not that my being against it would stop Willow.

Any day now, we'd be able to leave everything without worrying someone would turn on Hector. He was a good Alpha and he more than had it in him, but I'd needed to squash some of the ways he was trying to deal with things. It'd been an entire week without me needing to step in and tell him something or other about running the pack or investing the finances he'd inherited from my father since taking over.

Soon we could finally go back to that place Willow liked. Kit's home. She turned her beautiful face up as she told me her plans, her hands moving wildly.

*"I'm still open to coming back and forth between here and Kit's place, but I want some alone time with you guys without having to worry about when I get to see you. You're always so busy."*

Red flushed the crests of her cheeks and she fanned herself again. The fluorescent light of the store highlighted the pinkening of her skin. I frowned.

"I forgot something," I said and turned on my heels to get the electrolyte-infused water bottles from the farthest aisle. I hoped she wasn't coming down with something.

It took me only a moment, but by the time I was back to where I left her, she was gone. My heart rate quickened and I whirled, but there was no sign of her.

Had a werewolf taken her while I wasn't looking? Fuck, I should have agreed to Kit and Rowan coming. We'd come out during the night for this very reason. The concoction to mask her scent that girl had given her was set to arrive tomorrow, so she'd waited and stayed out of everyone's path. Did some werewolf in the pack leak the information? Fuck. We'd taken out any potential traitors and instilled fear in all the others. Willow's existence was not to be leaked.

My wolf rushed to the surface and the scents enhanced. A sweet berries scent reached my nose and I sucked it in, following it.

I skid to a stop in front of a large metal container housing a ton of furred, circular pillows. It was like hitting a wall. It was filled with her potent smell. My fingers clasped the wires and they bent under my grip. Fuck—the scent was delicious.

It took my eyes a while to really register that she'd crouched to the bottom and was wiggling around. Multicolored circular pillows undulated with her movements.

"What are you doing, Willow?" I gawked at my mate swimming in the sea of pillows.

She popped up so fast, I jerked back. I cleared my throat as her head appeared from the masses. She grinned sheepishly, her cheeks bright red. She stood, rubbing her arms frantically as she waded through the sea of pillows toward me. Her expression tightened and she looked at me with shock.

Her scent slammed into me, and my cock *ached*. Without a doubt, she was drenched for me.

I needed to bury my nose in her warmth and lap—

*Fuck. She was in heat.*

I sucked in a harsh breath and scooped her out of the container. Her legs immediately wrapped around my waist, hugging my torso as I held her up with one hand at her ass.

Willow tipped her hips to rub against my cock—practically dry humping me.

My steps stuttered as my dick twitched.

"Sorry about this. She had a few too many drinks," I wheezed, nodding my head to the store representative. The can the man held dropped from his limp fingers and his head craned to watch my frantic exit.

The lot was fortunately empty except for the vehicle I assumed was the cashier's. I yanked open the truck door as Willow sank her little teeth into my neck.

My knees buckled and I sucked in a harsh breath. I wrapped my palms around her waist to pull her into the seat, but she tightened her hold with a hiss.

"Fine!" I left her clinging to me and pulled myself up. She settled against my cock, perfectly nestled.

I groaned, brows furrowing.

I started the engine and settled my shaking hands on the steering wheel. She licked up my neck and nuzzled my ear before sucking it into her mouth. The move sent shock waves to all my senses.

Damn. Fuck. I needed to get an award for not bending her over here and now. I pulled the car into reverse and sped onto the road.

Willow's hands wandered over my shoulders, little nails digging in. She tugged at my shirt and with a sudden yank, ripped it. Her hands wandered down my abs, following the dips and hollows until she was at the waistband of my jeans.

She angrily hissed again and rubbed the thick bulge through the denim.

She was going to force me into a shift.

I needed to get her back to the pack. I couldn't have her unsafe, and if I was too preoccupied fucking her, I couldn't protect her.

I yanked my cell phone out and pressed the last number I called.

"Yes?"

Fuck, it was Hector.

"Can you do me a solid and send Kit and Rowan down Oak Street before the Sycamore cross?" I said, strained.

"What's that sound, Camden?" Hector's voice seemed too fucking loud.

"Please make sure no one stops us on the way to my cabin."

"What's going—"

Fuck, I would have to say it.

"Your daughter's in heat, Hector."

The silence was ringing.

He cleared his throat.

"I'm sending them to you." The call clicked off and the phone slid out of my limp hands in time for her to unbutton my jeans and tug out my dick.

Pre-cum beaded at the head and she used her thumb to smooth it. She gripped the sides of her shorts and used the slight tear to rip them in half. No fucking panties?

I groaned.

She spread her legs and the sweetness of berries permeated the air. Fuck, it was delicious. The best thing I had ever smelled.

She dipped her fingers into her core, slicking them with her juices.

I was going to explode.

I yanked the wheel to the side, driving as deep into the forest as I could without hitting a tree. Willow poised herself over my cock and I slammed on the breaks. I pressed my palm to her spine so she wouldn't hit the wheel and it forced her to slam down on my dick.

The roughness sent her over the edge and her pussy gripped my cock in rough squeezes, dripping on me with her need.

My eyes crossed and I roared, head tipping back as my body shook and grew, fur spouting from my flesh. My knot ballooned, adding pressure at the base.

My little mate's lips parted on a breathy gasp and her fingers flexed in the fur on my chest. My arm bumped into the door and my body took up more of the seat as I expanded.

Fuck. Fuck.

Willow ground down on my cock, taking all of my knot, her brows furrowed and lips parted with pleasure.

I was going to come. And by fucking god, I didn't want to come yet.

I slammed my fist into the door and metal crunched. It creaked and fell to the side, useless.

The roar of a vehicle neared and I attempted to grasp some sanity. Headlights fell over her tan skin and I gritted my teeth.

"Get her in here," Kit shouted. Thank the Moon Goddess it was him. I didn't think I'd be able to tear myself away from her.

My claws grazed her spine as I held her on my cock, pulling her up and down on my throbbing dick. I definitely could not stop fucking her now. The backseat door was wide open for me. I squeezed her hips to lift her, but she yanked my fur, jerking herself down. My hips moved without my consent, and I thrust.

She was going to end me.

My knees buckled as my cock stuck inside her wet pussy and strings of cum exploded from the tip, filling her up.

My mouth watered as cum leaked from where we were joined.

Willow pressed her lips into a thin line, rubbing her hands over her hard dark nipples. I leaned forward and lapped them.

"Hurry." My ears flicked and I curved over her, my clawed hand cupping her head as I looked over my shoulder.

Kit.

His gaze was narrowed as he stood behind me, keeping aware of the surroundings. His face was flushed and from here I could see his pulse jumping at his throat.

I struggled to slide into the backseat but pulled on every ounce of strength I could to sit. Her legs settled around my waist.

Willow writhed and ground on me, short-circuiting all my senses.

# WILLOW

EVERYTHING WAS A FUCKING BLUR AFTER THE HEAT took over. My last 'logical' decision was to toss myself into the basket of pillows. It was the only way this heat would desist. Now I was a bundle of need as Camden fucked me.

I couldn't stop the helpless grinding onto him until more cum jutted inside of me. I was so glad his knot hadn't let loose; I didn't want it to. I wanted it to tie us together. Now all that was left was to have Rowan and Kit inside me. I shivered. Their scent surrounded me, and I wanted them after Camden.

The engine shut off and Camden shoved open the door. There was a brief flash of his cabin, but my eyelashes fluttered shut as his stride caused his cock to rub in my channel.

He gripped my ass and remained locked inside me as he walked. I didn't even care where we were going. I just wanted him never to leave my body.

The thud of steps over floorboards was the only sound before he propped me on the end of the bed, exhaling raggedly. My shoulders pressed into the mattress and my spine bowed from the angle. I clenched my thighs. They ached from the wide span of Camden's waist.

"You're going to kill me."

I wanted more. I needed more pressure. More filling me. I peered at Kit from beneath my lashes and held out a hand. He strode forward, standing next to Camden and gripped my fingers. They stared down at me and their heated gazes set off flutters in my belly. Camden grunted, hips thrusting shallowly as I arched my back. I squeezed Kit's hand tightly and reached for the waistband of his sweats.

I tugged them down and he pulled them off the rest of the way. His cock bounced in front of my face. The thick mushroom tip glistening. I wanted it inside me too. With my other hand, I pushed at Camden. His thick knot popped out of my pussy with a squelch, releasing a slew of moisture down my thighs. He sat on the edge of the bed, and I crawled over him, swinging my leg over his waist, then sank down on his dick. I tipped my chin down as I lowered over his twitching cock, wetness gushing from my pussy. That look on his slack face . . . my thighs trembled. *More.*

I wiggled my hips up and peered over my shoulder at Kit, presenting to him.

His cock was prodding at the bud of my ass within seconds, but I reached between my legs and gripped the length. Without warning, I pushed it in next to Camden's cock.

My pussy sucked at them, the pressure excruciating as Kit's body shifted, making his dick widen.

They simultaneously groaned, hips jerking to seat themselves deeper into me.

"Take me, honey," Camden growled under me while Kit

gripped the back of my neck. My pussy gushed at the demanding touches. I liked that very much. Was it possible to die from pleasure?

I shuddered at the sensitivity as they fucked me ruthlessly. My arms lost feeling and my face pressed into Camden's furred chest.

Their thrusts turned disjointed as their breaths sawed out of their chest.

Rowan . . .

The bed dipped and a slight pressure at my ass joined everything else, wrenching the air from my lungs.

From the side, Rowan's dick bobbed near my face, and it was distended and large enough for me to pop the tip between my lips. I arched to the side and did just that.

My hips wiggled and I rolled my tongue over his warm tip. A gush of pre-cum filled my mouth and I groaned, lapping up the salty taste. I hummed, wanting more.

Rowan bowed over my body so his warm wet tongue dipped into my asshole as Camden and Kit simultaneously thrust. Claws grazed my spine, dragging down my back until they rested at my head. A hard thrust of hips forced more of the thick cock into my mouth and a pinch in my jaw forced me to relax the muscle. Rowan's dick obstructed my exhale. Fuck he was so wide and thick I couldn't fit him.

Camden and Kit continued their pace and I breathily whimpered as the pressure throbbed my clit. I hummed around Rowan, legs trembling. I couldn't hold myself up anymore. Knees buckling, my legs splayed, slamming me fully on Camden's dick, his knot stuffing me. I twitched, tears gathering at my lashes. *Sweet baby werewolf.* Furred palms gripped my thighs, a different touch of each as Kit spread one leg wide and

Camden spread the other in the opposite direction. It allowed more space for Kit's hips to jack between them and shove his knot into the tight space. My legs twitched in their hold as I huffed and wiggled. They gutturally moaned.

Kit's and Camden's knots stretched my entrance until they were seated. My palm slapped into Camden's chest, and I pulled his fur as my eyes rolled.

Rowan forced my mouth to remain on the tip of his wide cock as I writhed. Kit's and Camden's roars rang in my ears as stars burst behind my eyelids.

My channel was so tight and needy for them. It wanted to clutch them forever.

Rowan filled my mouth with his cum, to the point that it dripped from the corners of my lips. I swallowed as much as I could. He wrapped his palm around his dick and popped it from my mouth and creamy cum jutted across my cheek. He guided the tip over my neck and warmth spread across it, dripping down my breasts.

Camden watched, half-lidded. He rasped a claw against the tip of my nipple, massaging the cum into my flesh like it was lotion.

Fuck. Shit.

My body was too sensitive for this.

I whimpered as Kit gently ground in me, adding to the fullness. Both of their swelled knots in me? There was no way they'd pop out without ripping me in half. Cum and slick leaked from my throbbing channel.

Kit hummed, and a claw scratched across the swell of my ass as he dragged his furred hand down and carefully caressed the pads of his fingers at my leaking core.

What was he doing?

My question was answered when his fingers slathered my ass with the cum trickling out. As if he was trying to push it back inside me.

They'd overstuffed me. *Sweet baby werewolf.* I was going to die from pleasure.

# WILLOW

Camden was right. Everything turned out okay. I didn't tell him that, though, because I didn't want to see that smug smirk. We were fighting if I saw it.

I tilted my head, staring at my nest.

It was not here earlier, but someone kept moving things around, and it made the hair on the back of my neck rise. My wolf was not having it and her dissatisfaction irked *me*.

They were most definitely messing with me and I had a feeling it was Rowan and Camden. As innocent as Rowan tried to come off, he liked pressing my buttons more than anyone. Mostly because it got me fired up and then he liked screwing me while I was pissed, while Camden liked seeing me irked in general.

I'd learned that after setting up my nest at Camden's place in Redwood Pack for when we visited.

I glared at the displaced pillows which I had artfully arranged exactly how I wanted a few hours ago. Sharply turning on my heel, I stormed down the steps and outside of the house where my mates were checking the tall fence surrounding the first story of the place. Trees were going in next week to provide more privacy.

I'd have to tell Pen, the young Omega, about this itchiness to keep a nest when the time came for her. Hopefully her life was much easier now that she was taking the concoction for her scent.

I inhaled the cool air, and when it would normally soothe me, it did nothing for me now.

Narrowing in on my mates, they talked for a bit as they looked at the fencing. They were marking off the places they'd put the trees. Rowan was the only one in his wolfman form as he waited. I stormed directly up to him.

I gritted my teeth and wiggled my finger in a come-hither motion to Rowan. He huffed, eyes narrowing, but eventually leaned down. In a simultaneous motion, I hopped and reached. I had to put in extra oomph into my thigh muscles to catch his ear, but missed.

"I'll help you, lass," Kit announced gruffly from somewhere and then Rowan's leg buckled and he dropped to his knees. He snarled and was about to yank sideways if I hadn't tugged on his ear. He showed me his teeth, his growl so vicious it would have made any sane person reel.

I thinned my lips, eyes narrowed. Even on his knees he was much taller than me, so his spine was bowed toward me.

"I believe our mate is ordering you to stop messing with her." Kit's words were matter-of-fact, but the humor beneath his statement wasn't lost on me. My lips twitched. I clicked my tongue against my teeth and nodded.

"Okay!" Rowan growled. I released him and he yanked back, cupping his ear.

Camden tsked. "How do you hold so much fucking violence in that small body?"

I turned my torso toward Camden.

*"Easily."* I looked at the holes they'd already dug deep into the ground. *"When will everything be done?"*

"Should be in a few hours, we just have the backend of the property and near the gate area left to finish," Kit answered.

Kit hired a company to put up the gate before we arrived, so things were progressing quickly.

*"What about the trees, are you guys planting them?"* There would be a lot of trees circling the property.

"Yes, they'll just deliver them for us but the three of us should be able to get it done within a few days," Kit continued.

Wait a minute . . .

No one was translating for me and he was answering everything.

I rounded so quickly the world spun.

Kit stared at me, a proud glint in his eyes.

*"You know what I'm saying?"*

"Yes," Rowan said with a grunt in his deep grating voice.

I gawked.

*They'd learned ASL.* Tears sprang to my eyes, blurring them out.

Every bone in my body liquefied and I grinned sappily.

"Are you okay, Willow?" Camden smirked. Very much in on it.

The fact that they made the effort and then surprised me with it, my heart couldn't handle it. I hadn't told them how I felt because I didn't want it to be translated for me. I tried showing them every day, but now they could all understand me.

My chest ballooned.

*"I love you."*

I grinned at them, blinking the blur away. Rowan's teeth flashed and he pressed into my back, his purr vibrating up my spine. Camden and Kit exploded into their furred wolfmen forms, their gazes heated and needy.

"We love you as well, *mo chridhe*." Kit grinned toothily.

I licked my lips, a heavy, needy warmth flooding my system. Elation rushed through my limbs and I slipped out of Kit's grip, taking off at a sprint. Snarls and growls followed after me.

It was a good thing the fence was up because I was about to get fucked by my mates in my yard.

THE CAR SWERVED BEHIND ME, TAILING ME AS I careened down, desperate to lose them. I shouldn't have gone out alone . . . but time was of the essence and I couldn't reschedule my appointment. I'd had it all planned. Go get the package Evie sent to the Post Office, so I could take the little vial to mask my scent, and then hit the hospital. Except the employees couldn't find my box in the thirty minutes I'd waited.

I'd debated heading to my doctor's appointment without having the vials first. I knew it was stupid, but if it wasn't urgent, I wouldn't have gone. Everything was fine at first. The doctor completed my check-up. I was in and out. It was all going as planned until I returned to the Post Office.

And now someone was following me.

My heart thundered against my rib cage. My guys would be so freaking mad, but I had no idea I'd catch myself a stalker.

I slammed on my gas and took a sharp turn into a lonely street and then took the first turn left. It guided me down a winding road. Leaves fluttered in the wind as raindrops hit them. The headlights were gone from my mirror.

I frowned . . . had I lost him?

Inching the car over a hill, I scanned the barren countryside.

I gagged. Here it came again. I careened to the side of the road and rammed the vehicle into park and shoved the door wide to vomit. My breakfast spread onto the pavement. I needed to get a move on back to my mates.

My hand shook as I tore at the slim box Evie had sent me. I needed to take the damn concoction, that was what put me in this predicament. Okay, realistically, I put myself in this position, but I had to know if my illness was what I thought without my mates hovering over me like psychos.

I tipped the vial into my mouth. Fortunately, the concoction was safe to ingest in my state. Groaning, I pressed my forehead into the steering wheel. This was not how I wanted to be running around after finding out I was pregnant.

I pulled the results document from my hoodie pocket and licked my lips as I read over it again. Nope, wasn't my imagination.

A thump dragged my attention up and my wolf went wild inside me. I lunged to shut the door, but the man blocked it.

I prepared to shift to fight him off, but met the gaze of a concerned . . . human?

His brows were furrowed as he studied me.

"Are you all right, Miss?"

I blinked up at him, adrenaline working through my body.

"Apologies, I live up the road. I didn't mean to startle you, but do you need an ambulance?"

I shook my head quickly, lifting my hands, document and all, and waving them out. Exiting the van, I put my thumb up.

I'd overreacted. The man wasn't stalking me.

"If you're sure . . ."

I nodded and shooed him toward his car. He reluctantly did as I motioned. It was in time for a wave of heat to flush through the mating bites.

Shit.

The small car puttered off and I exhaled with relief. I'd already left without their knowledge, but if they'd found me talking to someone, it was over for the human.

Multiple thumps thudded toward me and three wolves corralled me back a step.

Kit and Camden shifted, standing before me naked.

Camden turned his glare to me, while Kit strode to the door I'd left wide open.

"*Listen,*" I signed, clearing my throat as I took a step back and bumped into Rowan. The paper in my hands fluttered to the ground.

My eyes widened and I dipped to pluck it back up, but Rowan's maw beat me to it. Camden took it from him and I huffed, crossing my arms. They were already pissed . . .

I best get prepared for their reaction.

They would be livid.

My stomach roiled and bitterness crawled up my throat. *Not again.*

Bending over, I vomited. Rowan whined and pushed his head against my thigh. I buried my fingers into his fur, clutching it tightly. Vomiting sucked.

I blinked tears away to Camden standing in front of me. Wasn't he cold with the lack of clothing? Rowan was fine since his fur covered him, but they were always careful to not needlessly pull out their monster form unless we were in our home.

"Will . . ."

His eyes were wide as they flicked from the paper to my face. I audibly swallowed, grimacing.

Camden ripped the bottom of my shirt and lifted it to wipe my lips, his movements almost mechanic.

"Will, are you . . .?"

I nodded tersely and the cloth at my lips trembled from his hand. I didn't know *what* I expected, considering I had used zero contraceptives. It just slipped my mind since it was pretty difficult for werewolves to get pregnant. Nola never told me we had super ovaries.

A grin spread across his face and I puffed out my cheeks. Camden's lips lowered and I quickly turned away before he kissed me. I scowled and kept my face averted. I'd *just* vomited. He dipped, pulling me into his arms, and my feet dangled.

"Fuck, are you all right, honey? Is our little one okay?" Camden gingerly lowered me and his hands hovered over me.

Great.

So commenced the porcelain treatment.

The thump of the driver's side door slamming shut resonated and Kit stormed over, eyebrows lowered. Moody werewolves.

I sighed and pinched my nose. Camden was a bad influence on him.

"You went to the doctor . . . suspecting this?" Kit snapped, fire practically spitting from his gaze.

That speck on his shoulder looked especially enthralling . . .

"Willow," Camden warned, narrowing his eyes. Kit gently tugged me to face him.

I pursed my lips.

"Stop being so obstinate," Kit snapped. Rowan's ears

flicked and I gawked up at Kit. The rain had become the faintest mist.

A palm fell over my shoulder and Camden's chest pushed into my spine.

This banding-together thing . . . I exhaled steadily.

"Whose child is it?"

I twisted to scowl at Camden.

"It doesn't matter whose DNA it is," Kit responded, narrowing his eyelids.

"You can say that because you're twins. I want a child that looks like me and the woman I love."

Kit's jaw twitched. Rowan pressed against my side; his heat radiated through my jeans. It was all that plush fur of his.

"Touché."

I rolled my eyes. Of course, this was how it went.

"Either way, we're pregnant . . . and we can have more until we have all our DNA mixed with her."

They were one hundred percent going to want to continue to fill me until we had a fucking litter. Camden's fingers flexed on my shoulders and Kit raked his hair back with shaking fingers. My shoulders lowered. I shouldn't have taken off.

Guilt twisted my gut. It was a worst-case scenario. I didn't mean to scare them this badly.

"Promise never to leave without one of us."

I pressed my lips together, focused on Kit's chin and nodded. He grunted and collected me into his arms.

*How did you guys know?*

"Rowan saw you leave and contacted us."

"We caught up to you when you left the Post Office."

Pulling away from Kit, I narrowed my eyes at Camden. "No shit, we put trackers on everything, Willow."

I shouldn't have been surprised, but it really fucking came in handy. It wasn't like I would leave again. Lesson learned.

Camden's nose grazed my head. "I really hate that I can't smell you when you take that shit."

"It's what allows her some free—"

"I know, Kit," Camden grumbled, pulling the back seat of the vehicle open.

Kit shuffled me to the seat and fastened the seatbelt around me. Rowan jumped in next to me and I sank my fingers into his fur.

The vehicle swayed as Kit guided it back onto the road.

"Fuck, if she has girls, they'll be Omegas. We're going to have to up security." I whipped my head toward Camden settling in the passenger seat. I hadn't considered that. I licked my lips, my heart rate spiking.

Rowan's side pressed harder into mine and he licked my cheek, a purr starting up in his chest. The thick ball in my throat stopped growing.

"We should be fine as long as we stay off the radar. We could always return to Hector's pack . . ."

I tuned them out as they strategized and threw ideas around. Life was uncertain but my safety was never in question. Trusting them was the smartest decision I had ever made and the most difficult. It required me to release years of crap built up in my head.

I hugged my arms around my torso, closing my eyes. Their presence soothed my wolf and there was no longer anything hollowing my gut, causing me to *miss*. I was complete now that we were all mated.

"Will." Camden stared into my eyes.

"You do nae ever have to worry." Kit added.

Their reassurance melted the stress weighing on my shoulders. There was no reason for me to doubt them. They would do whatever it took to protect me. Of that, I had no doubt.

A smile tipped up the corner of my lips. I'd always feared being discovered as an Omega, but I hadn't had mates to lean on.

There were more of my kind out there and they all successfully remained in hiding—like Evie. I didn't doubt I would remain the same if I took the precautions necessary.

Rowan's purr revved up a notch and I turned into his insistent nudging, cuddling close to my clingy mate.

Camden and Kit continued their conversation, er, or argument. I smirked at the quips they tossed back and forth. They hated each other's existence at the beginning, but they'd become fast friends. Mostly because they liked ganging up on me. I hid my smile in Rowan's fur.

My mates were overbearing oafs, but I loved them to pieces.

I pressed my palm to my belly—and they would love and protect our baby with as much vehemence as was needed.

# Thank You for Reading!

Visit my website for more book information and be sure to join my reader group and follow my social media platforms to keep up with my releases.

# ACKNOWLEDGMENTS

Gina Cortez, Rachel James, Shawna Jimenez, Melissa Tarrington, and Nicole. You guys are truly amazing and I appreciate you guys more than I can express.

I am also incredibly and infinitely grateful to my readers for being so supportive—that includes my amazing ARC team.

Thank you to my sister Claudia, who listens to my book ramblings even though she doesn't *completely* understand my monster obsession.

Aaron—thank you for fueling me with Espressos.

*Y tambien gracias a mi mamá y mi papá.*

# About the Author

Allie obsessively reads books featuring sexy, possessive heroes and headstrong heroines. So, it's no wonder characters just like that bustle to escape her imagination.

When she's not working away at her keyboard, she can be found in bed with a good book or bingeing Netflix.